The Rock of Chickamauga
A Story of the Western Crisis

Joseph A. Altsheler

The Rock of Chickamauga: A Story of the Western Crisis

Copyright © 2020 Bibliotech Press
All rights reserved

The present edition is a reproduction of previous publication of this classic work. Minor typographical errors may have been corrected without note, however, for an authentic reading experience the spelling, punctuation, and capitalization have been retained from the original text.

ISBN: 978-1-61895-741-2

CONTENTS

	FOREWORD	iv
CHAPTER I	AT BELLEVUE	1
CHAPTER II	FORREST	19
CHAPTER III	GRANT MOVES	35
CHAPTER IV	DICK'S MISSION	51
CHAPTER V	HUNTED	62
CHAPTER VI	A BOLD ATTACK	76
CHAPTER VII	THE LITTLE CAPITAL	89
CHAPTER VIII	CHAMPION HILL	101
CHAPTER IX	THE OPEN DOOR	113
CHAPTER X	THE GREAT ASSAULT	127
CHAPTER XI	THE TAKING OF VICKSBURG	140
CHAPTER XII	AN AFFAIR OF THE MOUNTAINS	149
CHAPTER XIII	THE RIVER OF DEATH	158
CHAPTER XIV	THE ROCK OF CHICKAMAUGA	172
CHAPTER XV	BESIDE THE BROOK	187

FOREWORD

"The Rock of Chickamauga," presenting a critical phase of the great struggle in the west, is the sixth volume in the series, dealing with the Civil War, of which its predecessors have been "The Guns of Bull Run," "The Guns of Shiloh," "The Scouts of Stonewall," "The Sword of Antietam" and "The Star of Gettysburg." Dick Mason who fights on the Northern side, is the hero of this romance, and his friends reappear also.

CHAPTER I

AT BELLEVUE

"You have the keenest eyes in the troop. Can you see anything ahead?" asked Colonel Winchester.

"Nothing living, sir," replied Dick Mason, as he swept his powerful glasses in a half-curve. "There are hills on the right and in the center, covered with thick, green forest, and on the left, where the land lies low, the forest is thick and green too, although I think I catch a flash of water in it."

"That should be the little river of which our map tells. And you, Warner, what do your eyes tell you?"

"The same tale they tell to Dick, sir. It looks to me like a wilderness."

"And so it is. It's a low-lying region of vast forests and thickets, of slow deep rivers and creeks, and of lagoons and bayous. If Northern troops want to be ambushed they couldn't come to a finer place for it. Forrest and five thousand of his wild riders might hide within rifle shot of us in this endless mass of vegetation. And so, my lads, it behooves us to be cautious with a very great caution. You will recall how we got cut up by Forrest in the Shiloh time."

"I do, sir," said Dick and he shuddered as he recalled those terrible moments. "This is Mississippi, isn't it?"

Colonel Winchester took a small map from his pocket, and, unfolding it, examined it with minute care.

"If this is right, and I'm sure it is," he replied, "we're far down in Mississippi in the sunken regions that border the sluggish tributaries of the Father of Waters. The vegetation is magnificent, but for a home give me higher ground, Dick."

"Me too, sir," said Warner. "The finest state in this Union is Vermont. I like to live on firm soil, even if it isn't so fertile, and I like to see the clear, pure water running everywhere, brooks and rivers."

"I'll admit that Vermont is a good state for two months in the year," said Dick.

"Why not the other ten?"

"Because then it's frozen up, solid and hard, so I've heard."

The other boys laughed and kept up their chaff, but Colonel Winchester rode soberly ahead. Behind him trailed the Winchester regiment, now reorganized and mounted. Fresh troops had come from Kentucky, and fragments of old regiments practically destroyed at Perryville and Stone River had been joined to it.

It was a splendid body of men, but of those who had gone to Shiloh only about two hundred remained. The great conflicts of the West, and the minor battles had accounted for the others. But it was perhaps one of the reliefs of the Civil War that it gave the lads who fought it little time to think of those who fell. Four years crowded with battles, great and small, sieges and marches absorbed their whole attention.

Now two men, the dreaded Forrest and fierce little Joe Wheeler, occupied the minds of Winchester and his officers. It was impossible to keep track of these wild horsemen here in their own section. They had a habit of appearing two or three hundred miles from the place at which they were expected.

But the young lieutenants while they watched too for their redoubtable foes had an eye also for the country. It was a new kind of region for all of them. The feet of their horses sank deep in the soft black soil, and there was often a sound of many splashings as the regiment rode across a wide, muddy brook.

Dick noted with interest the magnolias and the live oaks, and the great stalks of the sunflower. Here in this Southern state, which bathed its feet in the warm waters of the Gulf, spring was already far along, although snows still lingered in the North.

The vegetation was extravagant in its luxuriance and splendor. The enormous forest was broken by openings like prairies, and in every one of them the grass grew thick and tall, interspersed with sunflowers and blossoming wild plants. Through the woods ran vast networks of vines, and birds of brilliant plumage chattered in the trees. Twice, deer sprang up before them and raced away in the forest. It was the wilderness almost as De Soto had traversed it nearly four centuries before, and it had a majesty which in its wildness was not without its sinister note.

They approached a creek, deeper and wider than usual, flowing in slow, yellow coils, and, as they descended into the marsh that enclosed its waters, there was a sharp crackling sound, followed quickly by another and then by many others. The reports did not cease, and, although blood was shed freely, no man fell from his horse, nor was any wounded mortally. But the assault was vicious and it was pushed home with the utmost courage and tenacity, although many of the assailants fell never to rise again. Cries of pain and anger, and imprecations arose from the stricken regiment.

"Slap! Slap!"

"Bang! Bang!"

"Ouch! He's got his bayonet in my cheek!"

"Heavens, that struck me like a minie ball! And it came, whistling and shrieking, too, just like one!"

"Phew, how they sting! and my neck is bleeding in three places!"

"By thunder, Bill, I hit that fellow, fair and square! He'll never trouble an honest Yankee soldier again!"

The fierce buzzing increased all around them and Colonel Winchester shouted to his trumpeter:

"Blow the charge at once!"

The man, full willing, put the trumpet to his lips and blew loud and long. The whole regiment went across the creek at a gallop—the water flying in yellow showers—and did not stop until, emerging from the marsh, they reached the crest of a low hill a mile beyond. Here, stung, bleeding and completely defeated by the enemy they stopped for repairs. An occasional angry buzz showed that they were not yet safe from the skirmishers, but their attack seemed a light matter after the full assault of the determined foe.

"I suppose we're all wounded," said Dick as he wiped a bleeding cheek. "At least as far as I can see they're hurt. The last fellow who got his bayonet in my face turned his weapon around and around and sang merrily at every revolution."

"We were afraid of being ambushed by Forrest," said Warner, speaking from a swollen countenance. "Instead we struck something worse; we rode straight into an ambush of ten billion high-powered mosquitoes, every one tipped with fire. Have we got enemies like these to fight all the way down here?"

"They sting the rebels, too," said Pennington.

"Yes, but they like newcomers best, the unacclimated. When we rode down into that swamp I could hear them shouting, to one another: 'That fat fellow is mine, I saw him first! I've marked the rosy-cheeked boy for mine. Keep away the rest of you fellows!' I feel as if I'd been through a battle. No more marshes for me."

Some of the provident produced bottles of oil of pennyroyal. Sergeant Daniel Whitley, who rode a giant bay horse, was one of the most foreseeing in this respect, and, after the boys had used his soothing liniment freely, the fiery torment left by the mosquito's sting passed away.

The sergeant seemed to have grown bigger and broader than ever. His shoulders were about to swell through his faded blue coat, and the hand resting easily on the rein had the grip and power of a bear's paw. His rugged face had been tanned by the sun of the far south to the color of an Indian's. He was formidable to a foe, and yet no gentler heart beat than that under his old blue uniform. Secretly he regarded the young lieutenants, his superiors in military rank and education, as brave children, and often he cared for them where his knowledge and skill were greater than theirs or even than that of colonels and generals.

"God bless you, Sergeant," said Dick, "you don't look like an angel, but you are one—that is, of the double-fisted, fighting type."

The sergeant merely smiled and replaced the bottle carefully in his pocket, knowing that they would have good use for it again.

The regiment after salving its wounds resumed its watchful march.

"Do you know where we're going?" Pennington asked Dick.

"I think we're likely if we live long enough to land in the end before Vicksburg, the great Southern fortress, but as I gather it we mean to curve and curl and twist about a lot before then. Grant, they say, intends to close in on Vicksburg, while Rosecrans farther north is watching Bragg at Chattanooga. We're a flying column, gathering up information, and ready for anything."

"It's funny," said Warner thoughtfully, "that we've already got so far south in the western field. We can't be more than two or three hundred miles from the Gulf. Besides, we've already taken New Orleans, the biggest city of the South, and our fleet is coming up the river to meet us. Yet in the East we don't seem to make any progress at all. We lose great battles there and Fredericksburg they say was just a slaughter of our men. How do you make it out, Dick?"

"I've thought of several reasons for it. Our generals in the West are better than our generals in the East, or their generals in the East are better than their generals in the West. And then there are the rivers. In the East they mostly run eastward between the two armies, and they are no help to us, but a hindrance rather. Here in the West the rivers, and they are many and great, mostly run southward, the way we want to go, and they bring our gunboats on their bosoms. Excuse my poetry, but it's what I mean."

"You must be right. I think that all the reasons you give apply together. But our command of the water has surely been a tremendous help. And then we've got to remember, Dick, that there was never a navy like ours. It goes everywhere and it does everything. Why, if Admiral Farragut should tell one of those gunboats to steam across the Mississippi bottoms it would turn its saucy nose, steer right out of the water into the mud, and blow up with all hands aboard before it quit trying."

"You two fellows talk too much," said Pennington. "You won't let President Lincoln and Grant and Halleck manage the war, but you want to run it yourselves."

"I don't want to run anything just now, Frank," rejoined Dick. "What I'm thinking about most is rest and something to eat. I'd like to get rid, too, of about ten pounds of Mississippi mud that I'm carrying."

"Well, I can catch a glint of white pillars through those trees. It means the 'big house' of a plantation, and you'll probably find somewhere back of it the long rows of cabins, inhabited by the dark people, whom we've come to raise to the level of their masters, if not above them. I can see right now the joyous welcome we'll receive from the owners of the big house. They'll be standing on the great piazza, waving Union flags and shouting to us that they have ready cooling drinks and luxurious food for us all."

"It's hardly a joke to me. Whatever the cause of the war, it's the bitterness of death for these people to be overrun. Besides, I remember the words of that old fellow in the blacksmith shop before we fought the battle of Stone River. He said that even if they were beaten they'd still be there holding the land and running things."

"That's true," said Warner. "I've been wondering how this war would end, and now I'm wondering what will happen after it does end. But here we are at the gate. What big grounds! These great planters certainly had space!"

"And what silence!" said Dick. "It's uncanny, George. A place like this must have had a thousand slaves, and I don't see any of them rushing forward to welcome their liberators."

"Probably contraband, gone long ago to Ben Butler at New Orleans. I don't believe there's a soul here."

"Remember that lone house in Tennessee where a slip of a girl brought Forrest down on us and had us cut pretty nearly to pieces."

"I couldn't forget it."

Nor could Colonel Winchester. The house, large and low, stood in grounds covering an area of several acres, enclosed by a paling fence, now sagging in many places. Great stone posts stood on either side of the gateway, but the gate was opened, and it, too, sagged.

The grounds had evidently been magnificent, both with flowers and forest trees. Already many of the flowers were blooming in great luxuriance and brilliancy, but the walks and borders were untrimmed. The house was of wood, painted white with green shutters, and as they drew nearer they appreciated its great size, although it was only two stories in height. A hundred persons could have slept there, and twice as many could have found shade in the wide piazzas which stretched the full length of the four sides.

But all the doors and shutters were closed and no smoke rose from any chimney. They caught a glimpse of the cabins for the slaves, on lower ground some distance behind the great house. The whole regiment reined up as they approached the carriage entrance, and, although they were eight hundred strong, there was plenty of room without putting a single hoof upon a flower.

It was a great place. That leaped to the eye, but it was not marked upon Colonel Winchester's map, nor had he heard of it.

"It's a grand house," he said to his aides, "and it's a pity that it should go to ruin after the slaves are freed, as they certainly will be."

"But it was built upon slave labor," said Warner.

"So it was, and so were many of the most famous buildings in the world. But here, I'm not going to get into an argument about such questions with young men under my command. Besides, I'm fighting to destroy slavery, not to study its history. Sergeant Whitley, you're an experienced trailer: do you see any signs that troops have passed here?"

"None at all, sir. Down near the gate where the drive is out of repair I noticed wheel tracks, but they were several days old. The freshest of them were light, as if made by buggies. I judge, sir, that it was the family, the last to leave."

"And the wagons containing their valuables had gone on ahead?"

"It would seem so, sir."

Colonel Winchester sighed.

"An invader is always feared and hated," he said.

"But we do come as enemies," said Dick, "and this feeling toward us can't be helped."

"That's true. No matter what we do we'll never make any friends here in one of the Gulf states, the very core of Southern feeling. Dick, take a squad of men and enter the house. Pennington, you and Warner go with him."

Dick sprang down instantly, chose Sergeant Whitley first and with the others entered the great portico. The front door was locked but it was easy enough to force it with a gun butt, and they went in, but not before Dick had noticed over the door in large letters the name, "Bellevue." So this was Bellevue, one of the great cotton plantations of Mississippi. He now vaguely remembered that he had once heard his uncle, Colonel Kenton, speak of having stopped a week here. But he could not recall the name of the owner. Strong for the Union as he was Dick was glad that the family had gone before the Northern cavalry came.

The house was on a splendid scale inside also, but all the rugs and curtains were gone. As they entered the great parlor Dick saw a large piece of paper, and he flushed as he read written upon it in tall letters:

TO THE YANKEE RAIDERS:
YOU NEED NOT LOOK FOR THE SILVER.
IT HAS BEEN TAKEN TO VICKSBURG.

"Look at that!" he said indignantly to Warner. "See how they taunt us!"

But Warner laughed.

"Maybe some of our men at New Orleans have laid us open to such a stab," he said. Then he added whimsically:

"We'll go to Vicksburg with Grant, Dick, and get that silver yet."

"The writing's fresh," said Sergeant Whitley, who also looked at the notification. "The paper hasn't begun to twist and curl yet. It's not been posted up there many hours."

Colonel Winchester entered at that moment and the notice was handed to him. He, too, flushed a little when he read it, but the next instant he laughed. Dick then called his attention to the apparent fact that it had been put there recently.

"May I speak a word, Colonel," said Warner, who had been thinking so hard that there was a line the full length of his forehead.

"Yes, George, a dozen if you like. Go ahead. What is it?"

"The sergeant, who has had much experience as a trailer, told us that the tracks made by the buggy wheels were several days old. The slaves probably had been sent southward before that time. Now someone who saw our advance has come back, and, whoever it was, he was thoroughly familiar with the house. He couldn't have been a servant. Servants don't leave taunts of that kind. It must have been somebody who felt our coming deeply, and if it had been an elderly man he would have waited for action, he wouldn't have used saucy words. So, sir, I think it must have been a boy. Just like Pennington there, for instance."

"Good, George, go on with your reasonings."

"As surely, sir, as z plus y equals the total of the two, the one who put up the placard was a son of the owner. He alone would feel deeply enough to take so great a risk. The conditions absolutely demand that the owner has such a son and that he has done it."

"Very good, George. I think you're right, and this youth in giving way to a natural burst of anger, although he did not mean to do so, has posted up for us a warning. A lad of his spirit would go in search of Forrest, and we cannot forget our experience with that general in Tennessee. Now, boys, we'll make ready for the night, which is not far away."

The house was built for a Southern climate, although Dick had learned that it could be cold enough in Central Mississippi in midwinter. But it was spring now and they opened all the doors and windows, letting the pleasant air rush through the musty house.

"It may rain," said Colonel Winchester, "and the officers will sleep inside. The men will spread their blankets on the piazzas, and the horses will be tethered in the grounds. I hate to see the flowers and grass trodden down, but nature will restore them."

Some of the soldiers gathered wood from heaps nearby and fires were kindled in the kitchen, and also on the hearths in the slave quarters. Colonel Winchester had been truly called the father of his regiment. He was invariably particular about its health and comfort, and, as he always led it in person in battle, there was no finer body of men in the Union service.

Now he meant for his men to have coffee, and warm food after this long and trying ride and soon savory odors arose, although the cooking was not begun until after dark, lest the smoke carry a signal to a lurking enemy. The cavalrymen cut the thick grass which grew everywhere, and fed it to their horses, eight hundred massive jaws munching in content. The beasts stirred but little after their long ride and now and then one uttered a satisfied groan.

The officers drank their coffee and ate their food on the eastern piazza, which overlooked a sharp dip toward a creek three or four hundred yards away. The night had rushed down suddenly after the fashion of the far South, and from the creek they heard faintly the hoarse frogs calling. Beyond the grounds a close ring of sentinels watched, because Colonel Winchester had no mind to be surprised again by Forrest or by Fighting Joe Wheeler or anybody else.

The night was thick and dark and moist with clouds. Dick, despite the peace that seemed to hang over everything, was oppressed. The desolate house, even more than the sight of the field after the battle was over, brought home to him the meaning of war.

It was not alone the death of men but the uprooting of a country for their children and their children's children as well. Then his mind traveled back to his uncle, Colonel Kenton, and suddenly he smote his knee.

"What is it, Dick," asked Colonel Winchester, who sat only two or three yards away.

"Now I remember, sir. When I was only seven or eight years old I heard my uncle tell of stopping, as I told you, at a great plantation in Mississippi called Bellevue, but I couldn't recall the name of its owner. I know him now."

"What is the name, Dick?"

"Woodville, John Woodville. He was a member of the Mississippi Senate, and he was probably the richest man in the State."

"I think I have heard the name. He is a Confederate colonel now, with Pemberton's army. No doubt we'll have to fight him later on."

"Meanwhile, we're using his house."

"Fortune of war. But all war is in a sense unfair, because it's usually a question of the greater force. At any rate, Dick, we won't harm Colonel Woodville's home."

"Yet in the end, sir, a lot of these great old country places will go, and what will take their place? You and I, coming from a border state, know that the colored race is not made up of Uncle Toms."

"Well, Dick, we haven't won yet, and until we do we won't bother ourselves about the aftermath of war. I'm glad we found so large a place as this. At the last moment I sent part of the men to the cabins, but at least three or four hundred must lie here on the piazzas. And most of them are already asleep. It's lucky they have roofs. Look how the clouds are gathering!"

As much more room had been made upon the piazzas by the assignment of men to the cabins, Colonel Winchester and some of his officers also rested there. Dick, lying between the two blankets which he always carried in a roll tied to his saddle, was very comfortable now, with his head on his knapsack. The night had turned cooler, and, save when faint and far lightning quivered, it was heavy and dark with clouds. But the young lieutenants, hardened by two years of war and life in the open, felt snug and cosy on the broad, sheltered piazza. It was not often they found such good quarters, and Dick, like Colonel Winchester, was truly thankful that they had reached Bellevue before the coming storm.

It was evident now that the night was going to be wild. The

lightning grew brighter and came nearer, cutting fiercely across the southern sky. The ominous rumble of thunder, which reminded Dick so much of the mutter of distant battle, came from the horizon on which the lightning was flashing.

Colonel Winchester, Pennington and Warner had gone to sleep, but Dick was wakeful. He had again that feeling of pity for the people who had been compelled to flee from such a house, and who might lose it forever. It seemed to him that all the men, save himself and the sentinels, were asleep, sleeping with the soundness and indifference to surroundings shown by men who took their sleep when they could.

The horses stamped and moved uneasily beneath the threat of the advancing storm, but the men slept heavily on.

Dick knew that the sentinels were awake and watchful. They had a wholesome dread of Forrest and Wheeler, those wild riders of the South. Some of them had been present at that terrible surprise in Tennessee, and they were not likely to be careless when they were sure that Forrest might be near, but he remained uneasy nevertheless, and, although he closed his eyes and sought a soft place for his head on the saddle, sleep did not come.

He was sure that his apprehension did not come from any fear of an attack by Forrest or Wheeler. It was deeper-seated. The inherited sense that belonged to his great grandfather, who had lived his life in the wilderness, was warning him. It was not superstition. It seemed to Dick merely the palpable result of an inheritance that had gone into the blood. His famous great-grandfather, Paul Cotter, and his famous friend, Henry Ware, had lived so much and so long among dangers that the very air indicated to them when they were at hand.

Dick looked down the long piazza, so long that the men at either end of it were hidden by darkness. The tall trees in the grounds were nodding before the wind, and the lightning flashed incessantly in the southwest. The thunder was not loud, but it kept up a continuous muttering and rumbling. The rain was coming in fitful gusts, but he knew that it would soon drive hard and for a long time.

Everybody within Dick's area of vision was sound asleep, except himself. Colonel Winchester lay with his head on his arm and his slumber was so deep that he was like one dead. Warner had not stirred a particle in the last half-hour. Dick was angry at himself because he could not sleep. Let the storm burst! It might drive on the wide roof of the piazza and the steady beating sound would make his sleep all the sounder and sweeter. He recalled, as millions of American lads have done, the days when he lay in his bed just under the roof and heard hail and sleet drive against it, merely to make him feel all the snugger in the bed with his covers drawn around him.

The fitful gusts of rain ceased, and then it came with a steady pour and roar, driving directly down, thus leaving the men on the outer edges of the piazzas untouched and dry. Still, Dick did not sleep, and at last he arose and walked softly into the house. Here the sense of danger grew stronger. He was reminded again of his early boyhood, when some one blindfolded was told to find a given object, and the others called "hot" when he was near or "cold" when he was away. He was feeling hot now. That inherited sense, the magnetic feeling out of the past, was warning him.

Dick felt sure that some one not of their regiment was in the building. He neither saw nor heard the least sign of a presence, but he was absolutely certain that he was not alone within Bellevue. Since the lightning had ceased it was pitchy dark inside. There was a wide hall running through the building, with windows above the exits, but he saw nothing through them save the driving rain and the dim outline of the threshing trees.

He turned into one of the side rooms, and then he paused and pushed himself against the wall. He was sure now that he heard a soft footstep. The darkness was so intense that it could be felt like a mist. He waited but he did not hear it again, and then he began to make his way around the wall, stepping as lightly as he could.

He had gone through most of the rooms at their arrival and he still retained a clear idea of the interior of the house. He knew that there was another door on the far side of the chamber in which he stood, and he meant to follow the wall until he reached it. Some one had been in the room with him and Dick believed that he was leaving by the far door.

While he heard no further footsteps he felt a sudden light draught on his face and he knew that the door had been opened and shut. He might go to Colonel Winchester and tell him that a lurking spy or somebody of that character was in the house, but what good would it do? A spy at such a time and in such a place could not harm them, and the whole regiment would be disturbed for nothing. He would follow the chase alone.

He found the door and passed into the next room. Its windows opened upon the southern piazza and two or three shutters were thrown back. A faint light entered and Dick saw that no one was there but himself. He could discern the dim figures of the soldiers sleeping on the piazza and beyond a cluster of the small pines grown on lawns.

Dick felt that he had lost the trail for the time, but he did not intend to give it up. Doubtless the intruder was some one who knew the house and who was also aware of his presence inside. He also felt that he would not be fired upon, because the stranger himself would not wish to bring the soldiers down upon him. So, with a hand upon his pistol butt, he opened the side door and followed once more into the darkness.

The ghostly chase went on for a full half-hour, Dick having nothing to serve him save an occasional light footfall. There was one period of more than half an hour when he lost the fugitive entirely. He wandered up to the second floor and then back again. There, in a room that had been the library, he caught a glimpse of the man. But the figure was so shadowy that he could tell nothing about him.

"Halt!" cried Dick, snatching out his pistol. But when he leveled it there was nothing to aim at. The figure had melted away, or rather it had flitted through another door. Dick followed, chagrined. The stranger seemed to be playing with him. Obviously, it was some one thoroughly acquainted with the house, and that brought to Dick's mind the thought that he himself, instead of the other man, was the stranger there.

He came at last to a passage which led to the kitchen, a great room, because many people were often guests at Bellevue, and here he stopped short, while his heart suddenly beat hard. A distinct odor coming from different points suddenly assailed his nostrils. He had smelled it too often in the last two years to be mistaken. It was smoke, and Bellevue had been set on fire in several places.

He inhaled it once or twice and then he saw again the shadowy figure flitting down to the passage and to a small door that, unnoticed by the soldiers, opened on the kitchen garden in the rear of the house.

Dick never acted more promptly. Instantly he fired his pistol into the ceiling, the report roaring in the confined spaces of the house, and then shouting with all his might: "Fire! Fire! Fire!" as he dashed down the passage he ran through the little door, which the intruder had left open, and pursued him in the darkness and rain into the garden. There was a flash ahead of him and a bullet whistled past his ear, but he merely increased his speed and raced in the direction of the flash. As he ran he heard behind him a tremendous uproar, the voices and tread of hundreds of soldiers, awakened suddenly, and he knew that they would rush through Bellevue in search of the fires.

But it was Dick's impulse to capture the daring intruder who would destroy the house over their heads. Built of wood, it would burn so fast, once the torches were set, that the rain would have little effect upon the leaping flames, unless measures were taken at once, which he knew that the regiment would do, under such a capable man as Colonel Winchester. Meanwhile he was hot in pursuit.

The trail which was not that of footsteps, but of a shadowy figure, ran between tall and close rows of grapevines so high on wooden framework that they hid any one who passed. The suspicion that Dick had held at first was confirmed. This was no stranger, no intruder. He knew every inch of both house and grounds, and, after having set the house on fire, he had selected the only line of retreat, but a safe one, through the thick and lofty vegetation of the garden, which ran down to the edge of the ravine in the rear, where he could slip quietly under the fence, drop through the thick grass into the ravine unseen by the pickets, and escape at his leisure in the darkness.

Dick was so sure of his theory that he strained every effort to overtake the figure which was flitting before him like a ghost. In his eagerness he had forgotten to shout any alarm about the pickets, but it would have been of no avail, as most of them, under the impulse of alarm, had rushed forward to help extinguish the fires.

He saw the fugitive reach the end of the garden, drop almost flat, and then slip under a broken place in the palings. At an ordinary time he would have stopped there, but all the instincts of the hunter were aroused. It was still raining, and he was already soaked. Wet branches and leaves struck him in the face as he passed, but his energy and eagerness were undimmed.

He, too, dropped at the hole under the broken palings and slid forward face foremost. The wet grass was as slippery as ice, and after he passed through the hole Dick kept going. Moreover, his speed increased. He had not realized that the garden went to the very edge of the ravine, and he was shooting down a steep slope to the depth of thirty feet. He grasped instinctively at weeds and grass as he made his downward plunge and fetched up easily at the bottom.

He sprang to his feet and saw the shadowy fugitive running down the ravine. In an instant he followed headlong, tripped once or twice on the wet grass, but was up every time like lightning, and once more in swift pursuit. The fugitive turned once, raised his pistol and pulled the trigger again, evidently forgetful that it was empty. When the hammer snapped on the trigger he uttered a low cry of anger and hurled the useless weapon into the grass. Then he whirled around and faced Dick, who was coming on, eager and panting.

Dick's own pistol was empty and he did not carry his small sword. He stopped abruptly when the other turned, and, in the dim light and rain, he saw that his opponent was a young man or rather youth of about his own size and age. When he saw the lad cast the pistol aside Dick, moved by some chivalrous impulse, dropped his own in the grass.

Then the two stared at each other. They were far beyond the line of the pickets, and as they stood in the deep ravine there was no chance that any one would either see or hear them. As Dick gazed intently, the face and figure of his antagonist shaped themselves more distinctly in the dim light. He beheld before him a tall youth, extremely well built, fair of face, his brown hair slightly long. He wore rain-soaked civilian's garb.

He saw that the youth was panting like himself, but it was not wholly the result of flight. His face expressed savage anger and indignation.

"You dirty Yankee!" he said.

Dick started. No one had ever before addressed him with such venom.

"If by Yankee you mean loyalty to the Union then I'm one," he said, "and I'm proud of it. What's more I'm willing to tell who I am. My name is Richard Mason. I'm from Kentucky, and I'm a lieutenant in the regiment of Colonel Arthur Winchester, which occupies the building behind us."

"From Kentucky and consorting with Yankees! A lot of you are doing it, and you ought to be on our side! We hate you for it more than we do the real Yankees!"

"It's our right to choose, and we've chosen. And now, since you're talking so much about right and wrong, who may you be, Mr. Firebug?"

Even in the dark Dick saw his opponent's face flush, and his eyes flash with deadly hostility.

"My name is Victor Woodville," he replied, "and my father is Colonel John Woodville, C.S.A. He is the owner of the house in which your infamous Yankee regiment is encamped."

"And which you have tried to burn?"

"I'd rather see it burn than shelter Yankees. You'd burn it anyway later on. Grant's troops have already begun to use the torch."

"At any rate you'll go before our colonel. He'll want to ask you a lot of questions."

"I'm not going before your colonel."

"Oh, yes, you are."

"Who's going to take me?"

"I am."

"Then come on and do it."

Dick advanced warily. Both had regained their breath and strength now. Dick with two years of active service in the army had the size and muscles of a man. But so had his opponent. Each measured the other, and they were formidable antagonists, well matched.

Dick had learned boxing at the Pendleton Academy, and, as he approached slowly, looking straight into the eyes of his enemy, he suddenly shot his right straight for Woodville's chin. The Mississippian, as light on his feet as a leopard, leaped away and countered with his left, a blow so quick and hard that Dick, although he threw his head to one side, caught a part of its force just above his ear. But, guarding himself, he sprang back, while Woodville faced him, laughing lightly.

Dick shook his head a little and the singing departed. Just above his ear he felt a great soreness, but he was cool now. Moreover, he was losing his anger.

"First blow for you," he said. "I see that you know how to use your fists."

"I hope to prove it."

Woodville, stepping lightly on his toes and feinting with his left, caught Dick on his cheek bone with his right. Then he sought to spring away, but Dick, although staggered, swung heavily and struck Woodville on the forehead. The Mississippian went down full length on the slippery grass but jumped to his feet in an instant. Blood was flowing from his forehead, whence it ran down his nose and fell to the earth, drop by drop. Dick himself was bleeding from the cut on his cheek bone.

The two faced each other, cool, smiling, but resolute enemies.

"First knockdown for you," said Woodville, "but I mean that the second shall be mine."

"Go in and try."

But Woodville drew back a little, and as Dick followed,

looking for an opening he was caught again a heavy clip on the side of the head. He saw stars and was not able to return the blow, but he sprang back and protected himself once more with his full guard, while he regained his balance and strength.

"Am I a firebug?" asked Woodville tauntingly.

Dick considered. This youth interested him. There was no denying that Woodville had great cause for anger, when he found his father's house occupied by a regiment of the enemy. He considered it defilement. The right or wrong of the war had nothing to do with it. It was to him a matter of emotion.

"I'll take back the epithet 'firebug,'" he said, "but I must stick to my purpose of carrying you to Colonel Winchester."

"Always provided you can: Look out for yourself."

The Mississippian, who was wonderfully agile, suddenly danced in—on his toes it seemed to Dick—and landed savagely on his opponent's left ear. Then he was away so quickly and lightly that Dick's return merely cut the air.

The Kentuckian felt the blood dripping from another point. His ear, moreover, was very sore and began to swell rapidly. One less enduring would have given up, but he had a splendid frame, toughened by incessant hardship. And, above all, enclosed within that frame was a lion heart. He shook his head slightly, because a buzzing was going on there, but in a moment or two it stopped.

"Are you satisfied?" asked young Woodville.

"You remember what Paul Jones said: 'I've just begun to fight.'"

"Was it Paul Jones? Well, I suppose it was. Anyhow, if you feel that way about it, so do I. Then come on again, Mr. Richard Mason."

Dick's blood was up. The half-minute or so of talk had enabled him to regain his breath. Although he felt that incessant pain and swelling in his left ear, his resolution to win was unshaken. Pride was now added to his other motives.

He took a step forward, feinted, parried skillfully, and then stepped back. Woodville, always agile as a panther, followed him and swung for the chin, but Dick, swerving slightly to one side, landed with great force on Woodville's jaw. The young Mississippian fell, but, while Dick stood looking at him, he sprang to his feet and faced his foe defiantly. The blood was running down his cheek and dyeing the whole side of his face. But Dick saw the spirit in his eye and knew that he was far from conquered.

Woodville smiled and threw back his long hair from his face.

"A good one for you. You shook me up," he admitted, "but I

don't see any sign of your ability to carry me to that Yankee colonel, as you boasted you would do."

"But I'm going to do it."

The rain increased and washed the blood from both their faces. It was dark within the ravine, but they had been face to face so long that they could read the eyes of each other. Those of Woodville like those of Dick ceased to express great anger. In the mind of each was growing a respect for his antagonist. The will to conquer remained, but not the desire to hate.

"If you're going to do it, then why don't you?" said Woodville.

Dick moved slowly forward, still watching the eyes of the Mississippian. He believed now that Woodville, agile and alert though he might be, had not fully recovered his strength. There was terrific steam in that last punch and the head of the man who had received it might well be buzzing yet.

Dick then moved in with confidence, but a lightning blow crashed through his guard, caught him on the chin and sent him to earth. He rose, though still half-stunned, and saw that the confident, taunting look had returned to Woodville's face. Fortunate now for Dick that the pure blood of great woods rangers flowed in his veins, and that he had inherited from them too an iron frame. His chin was cut and he had seen a thousand stars. But his eyes cleared and steadily he faced his foe.

"Do I go with you to your colonel?" asked Woodville, ironically.

"You do," replied Dick firmly.

He looked his enemy steadily in the eye again, and he felt a great sense of triumph. After such severe punishment he was stronger than ever and he knew it.

Therefore he must win. He struck heavily, straight for the angle of Woodville's chin. The Mississippian evaded the blow and flashed in with his left. But Dick, who was learning to be very wary, dodged it and came back so swiftly that Woodville was caught and beaten to his knees.

But the son of the house of Bellevue was still so agile that he was able to recover his feet and spring away. Dick saw, however, that he was panting heavily. The blow had taken a considerable part of his remaining strength. He also saw that his antagonist was regarding him with a curious eye.

"You fight well, Yank," said Woodville, "although I ought not to call you Yank, but rather a traitor, as you're a Kentuckian. Still, I've put my marks on you. You're bleeding a lot and you'd be a sight if it weren't for this cleansing rain."

"I've been putting the map of Kentucky on your own face. You don't look as much like Mississippi as you did. You'll take notice too that you didn't burn the house. If you'll glance up the side of this ravine you'll see just a little dying smoke. Eight hundred soldiers put it out in short order."

Woodville's face flushed, and his eyes for the first time since the beginning of the encounter shone with an angry gleam. But the wrathful fire quickly died.

"On the whole, I'm not sorry," he said. "It was an impulse that made me do it. Our army will come and drive you away, and our house will be our own again."

"That's putting it fairly. What's the use of burning such a fine place as Bellevue? Still, we want you. Our colonel has many questions to ask you."

"You can't take me."

Dick judged that the crucial moment had now come. Woodville was breathing much more heavily than he was, and seemed to be near exhaustion. Dick darted boldly in, received a swinging right and left on either jaw that cut his cheeks and made the blood flow. But he sent his right to Woodville's chin and the young Mississippian without a sound dropped to the ground, lying relaxed and flat upon his back, his white face, streaked with red, upturned to the rain.

He was so still that Dick was seized with fear lest he had killed him. He liked this boy who had fought him so well and, grasping him by both shoulders, he shook him hard. But when he loosed him Woodville fell back flat and inert.

Dick heard the waters of a brook trickling down the ravine, and, snatching off his cap, he ran to it. He filled the cap and returned just in time to see Woodville leap lightly to his feet and disappear with the speed of a deer among the bushes.

CHAPTER II

FORREST

Dick dashed after the fugitive, but he had disappeared utterly, and the dense bushes impeded the pursuer. He was hot and angry that he had been deluded so cleverly, but then came the consolation that, after all, he had won in the fistic encounter with an antagonist worthy of anybody. And after this came a second thought that caused him to halt abruptly.

He and Woodville had fought it out fairly. Their fists had printed upon the faces of each other the stamp of a mutual liking. Why should he strive to take young Woodville before Colonel Winchester? Nothing was to be gained by it, and, as the Mississippian was in civilian's garb, he might incur the punishment of a spy. He realized in a flash that, since he had vindicated his own prowess, he was glad of Woodville's escape.

He turned and walked thoughtfully back up the ravine. Very little noise came from the house and the thin spires of smoke had disappeared. He knew now that the fires had been put out with ease, thanks to his quick warning. Before starting he had recovered both his own pistol and Woodville's, and he was particularly glad to find the latter because it would be proof of his story, if proof were needed. The rain had not ceased nor had the heavy darkness lifted, but the looming shadow of the big house was sufficient guide. He found the place where he had slipped down the bank and the torn bushes and grass showed that he had made a fine trail. He pulled himself back up by the bushes and reentered the garden, where he was halted at once by two watchful sentries.

"Lieutenant Richard Mason of Colonel Winchester's staff," he said, "returning from the pursuit of a fugitive."

The men knew him and they said promptly:

"Pass Lieutenant Mason."

But despite the dark they stared at him very curiously, and when he walked on toward the piazza one of them muttered to the other:

"I guess he must have overtook that fugitive he was chasin'."

Dick walked up the steps upon the piazza, where some one had lighted a small lamp, near which stood Colonel Winchester and his staff.

"Here's Dick!" exclaimed Warner in a tone of great relief.

"And we thought we had lost him," said Colonel Winchester,

gladness showing in his voice. Then he added: "My God, Dick, what have you been doing to yourself?"

"Yes, what kind of a transformation is this?" added a major. "You've certainly come back with a face very different from the one with which you left us!"

Dick turned fiery red. He suddenly became conscious that he had a left ear of enormous size, purple and swollen, that his left eye was closing fast, that the blood was dripping from cuts on either cheek, that the blood had flowed down the middle of his forehead and had formed a little stalactite on the end of his nose, that his chin had been gashed in five places by a strong fist, and that he had contributed his share to the bloodshed of the war.

"If I didn't know these were modern times," said Warner, "I'd say that he had just emerged from a sanguinary encounter barehanded in the Roman arena with a leopard."

Dick glared at him.

"It was you who gave the alarm of fire, was it not?" asked Colonel Winchester.

"Yes, sir. I saw the man who set the fires and I pursued him through the garden and into the ravine that runs behind it."

"Your appearance indicates that you overtook him."

Dick flushed again.

"I did, sir," he replied. "I know I'm no beauty at present, but neither is he."

"It looks as if it had been a matter of fists?"

"It was, sir. Both of us fired our pistols, but missed. Then we threw our weapons to one side and clashed. It was a hard and long fight, sir. He hit like a pile driver, and he was as active as a deer. But I was lucky enough to knock him out at last."

"Then why does your face look like a huge piece of pickled beef?" asked the incorrigible Warner mischievously.

"You wait and I'll make yours look the same!" retorted Dick.

"Shut up," said Colonel Winchester. "If I catch you two fighting I may have you both shot as an example."

Dick and Warner grinned good-naturedly at each other. They knew that Colonel Winchester did not dream of carrying out such a threat, and they knew also that they had no intention of fighting.

"And after you knocked him out what happened?" asked the colonel.

Dick looked sheepish.

"He lay so still I was afraid he was dead," he replied. "I ran down to a brook, filled my cap with water, and returned with it in the hope of reviving him. I got there just in time to see him vanishing in the bushes. Pursuit was hopeless."

"He was clever," said the Colonel. "Have you any idea who he was?"

"He told me. He was Victor Woodville, the son of Colonel John Woodville, C.S.A., the owner of this house."

"Ah!" said Colonel Winchester, and then after a moment's thought he added: "It's just as well he escaped. I should not have known what to do with him. But we have you, Dick, to thank for giving the alarm. Now, go inside and change to some dry clothes, if you have any in your baggage, and if not dry yourself before a fire they're going to build in the kitchen."

"Will you pardon me for speaking of something, sir?"

"Certainly. Go ahead."

"I think the appearance of young Woodville here indicates the nearness of Forrest or some other strong cavalry force."

"You're right, Dick, my officers and I are agreed upon it. I have doubled the watch, but now get yourself to that fire and then to sleep."

Dick obeyed gladly enough. The night had turned raw and chill, and the cold water dripped from his clothes as he walked. But first he produced Woodville's pistol and handed it to Colonel Winchester.

"There's my antagonist's pistol, sir," he said. "You'll see his initials on it."

"Yes, here they are," said Colonel Winchester: "'V.W., C.S.A.' It's a fine weapon, but it's yours, Dick, as you captured it."

Dick took it and went to the kitchen, where the big fire had just begun to blaze. He was lucky enough to be the possessor of an extra uniform, and before he changed into it—they slept with their clothes on—he roasted himself before those glorious coals. Then, as he was putting on the fresh uniform, Warner and Pennington appeared.

"What would you recommend as best for the patient, Doctor," said Warner gravely to Pennington.

"I think such a distinguished surgeon as you will agree with me that his wounds should first be washed and bathed thoroughly in cold water."

"And after that a plentiful application of soothing liniment."

"Yes, Doctor. That is the best we can do with the simple medicines we have, but it especially behooves us to reduce the size of that left ear, or some of the boys will say that we have a case of elephantiasis on our hands."

"While you're reducing the size of it you might also reduce the pain in it," said Dick.

"We will," said Pennington; "we've got some fine horse

liniment here. I brought it all the way from Nebraska with me, and if it's good for horses it ought to be good for prize fighters, too. That was surely a hefty chap who fought you. If you didn't have his pistol as proof I'd say that he gave you a durned good licking. Isn't this a pretty cut down the right cheek bone, George?"

"Undoubtedly, but nothing can take away the glory of that left ear. Why, if Dick could only work his ears he could fan himself with it beautifully. When I meet that Woodville boy I'm going to congratulate him. He was certainly handy with his fists."

"Go on, fellows," said Dick, good-naturedly. "In a week I won't have a wound or a sign of a scar. Then I'll remember what you've said to me and I'll lick you both, one after the other."

"Patient is growing delirious, don't you think so, Doctor?" said Warner to Pennington.

"Beyond a doubt. Violent talk is always proof of it. Better put him to bed. Spread his two blankets before the fire, and he can sleep there, while every particle of cold and stiffness is being roasted out of him."

"You boys are very good to me," said Dick gratefully.

"It's done merely in the hope that your gratitude will keep you from giving us the licking you promised," said Pennington.

Then they left him and Dick slept soundly until he was awakened the next day by Warner. The fire was out, the rain had ceased long since and the sun was shining brilliantly.

"Hop up, Dick," said Warner briskly. "Breakfast's ready. Owing to your wound we let you sleep until the last moment. Come now, take the foaming coffee and the luscious bacon, and we'll be off, leaving Bellevue again to its masters, if they will come and claim it."

"Has anything happened in the night?"

"Nothing since you ran your face against a pile driver, but Sergeant Daniel Whitley, who reads the signs of earth and air and wood and water, thinks that something is going to happen."

"Is it Forrest?"

"Don't know, but it's somebody or something. As soon as we can eat our luxurious breakfasts we mean to mount and ride hard toward Grant. We're scouts, but according to Whitley the scouts are scouted, and this is a bad country to be trapped in."

Dick was so strong and his blood was so pure that he felt his wounds but little now. The cuts and bruises were healing fast and he ate with a keen appetite. He heard then of the signs that Whitley had seen. He had found two broad trails, one three miles from the house, and the other about four miles. Each indicated the passage of several hundred men, but he had no way of knowing whether they belonged to the same force. They were bound to be Confederate cavalry as Colonel Winchester's regiment was known to be the only Union force in that section.

Dick knew their position to be dangerous. Colonel Winchester had done his duty in discovering that Forrest and Wheeler were raiding through Mississippi, and that a heavy force was gathering in the rear of Grant, who intended the siege of Vicksburg. It behooved him now to reach Grant as soon as he could with his news.

Refreshed and watchful, the regiment rode away from Bellevue. Dick looked back at the broad roof and the great piazzas, and then he thought of young Woodville with a certain sympathy. They had fought a good fight against each other, and he hoped they would meet after the war and be friends.

It was about an hour after sunrise, and the day was bright and warm. The beads of water that stood on every leaf and blade of grass were drying fast, and the air, despite its warmth, was pure and bracing. Dick, as he looked at the eight hundred men, tanned, experienced and thoroughly armed, under capable leaders, felt that they were a match for any roving Southern force.

"Just let Forrest come on," he said. "I know that the Colonel is aching to get back at him for that surprise in Tennessee, and I believe we could whip him."

"You're showing great spirit for a man who was beaten up in the prize ring as you were last night. I thought you'd want to rest for a few days."

"Drop it, George. I did get some pretty severe cuts and bruises, but I was lucky enough to have the services of two very skillful and devoted young physicians. Their treatment was so fine that I'm all right to-day."

"Unless I miss my guess, we'll need the services of doctors again before night comes. No mountains are here, but this is a great country for ambush. It's mostly in forest, and even in the open the grass is already very tall. Besides, there are so many streams, bayous, and ponds. Notice how far out on the flanks the skirmishers and scouts are riding, and others ride just as far ahead."

Two miles from Bellevue and they came to a small hill, covered with forest, from the protection of which the officers examined the country long and minutely, while their men remained hidden among the deep foliaged trees. Dick had glasses of his own which he put to his eyes, bringing nearer the wilderness, broken here and there by open spaces that indicated cotton fields. Yet the forest was so dense and there was so much of it that a great force might easily be hidden within its depths only a mile away.

"Have we any information at all about Forrest's strength?" whispered Pennington to Dick.

"His full force isn't down here. It is believed he has not more than a thousand or twelve hundred men. But he and his officers know the country thoroughly, and of course the inhabitants, being in full sympathy with them, will give them all the information they need. The news of every movement of ours has been carried straight to the rebel general."

"And yet the country seems to have no people at all. We come to but few houses, and those few are deserted."

"So they are. What was that? Did you see it, Frank?"

"What was what?"

"I forgot that you are not using glasses. I caught a momentary glitter in the woods. I think it was a sunbeam passing through the leaves and striking upon the polished barrel of a rifle. Ah! there it is again! And Colonel Winchester has seen it too."

The colonel and his senior officers were now gazing intently at the point in the wood where Dick had twice seen the gleam, and, keener-eyed than they, he continued to search the leafy screen through his own glasses. Soon he saw bayonets, rifles, horses and men advancing swiftly, and then came two of their own scouts galloping.

"The enemy is advancing!" they cried. "It's Forrest!"

A thrill shot through Dick. The name of Forrest was redoubtable, but he knew that every man in the regiment was glad to meet him again. He glanced at Colonel Winchester and saw that his face had flushed. He knew that the colonel was more than gratified at this chance.

"We'll make our stand here," said Colonel Winchester. "The hill runs to the right, and, as you see over there, it is covered with forest without undergrowth. Thus we can secure protection, and at the same time be able to maneuver, mounted."

The regiment was posted rapidly in two long lines, the second to fire between the intervals of the first. They carried carbines and heavy cavalry sabers, and they were the best mounted regiment in the Northern service.

Yet these men, brave and skillful as they were, were bound to feel trepidation, although they did not show it. They were far in the Southern forest, cut off from their army, and Forrest, in addition to his own cavalry, might have brought with him fresh reserves of the enemy.

Dick, Warner, and Pennington, as usual, remained close to their colonel, and Sergeant Daniel Whitley was not far away. But Colonel Winchester presently rode along the double line of his veterans, and he spoke to them quietly but with emphasis and conviction:

"My lads," he said, "you see Forrest's men coming through the woods to attack us. Forrest is the greatest cavalry leader the South has, west of the Alleghanies. Some of you were with me when we were surprised and cut up by him in Tennessee. But you will not be surprised by him now, nor will you be cut up by him. All of you have become great riders, a match for Forrest's own, and as I look upon your faces here I know that there is no fear in a single heart. You have served under Grant, and you have served under Thomas. They are two generals who always set their faces toward the front and never turn them toward the rear. You will this day prove yourselves worthy of Grant and Thomas."

They were about to cheer, but he checked it with the simple gesture of a raised hand. Then they did a thing that only a beloved leader could inspire. Every man in the regiment, resting his carbine across the pommel of his saddle, drew his heavy cavalry saber and made it whirl in coils of glittering light about his head.

The great pulse in Dick's throat leaped as he saw. The long double line seemed to give back a double flash of flame. Not a word was said, and then eight hundred sabers rattled together as they were dropped back into their scabbards. Colonel Winchester's face flushed deeply at the splendid salute, but he did not speak either. He took off his cap and swept it in a wide curve to all his men. Then he turned his face toward the enemy.

The Southern trumpet was singing in the forest, and the force of Forrest, about twelve hundred strong, was emerging into view. Dick, through his glasses, saw and recognized the famous leader, a powerful, bearded man, riding a great bay horse. He had heard many descriptions of him and he knew him instinctively. He also recognized the fact that the Winchester regiment had before it the most desperate work any men could do, if it beat off Forrest when he came in his own country with superior numbers.

Neither side had artillery, not even the light guns that could be carried horse- or muleback. It must be left to carbine and saber. Colonel Winchester carefully watched his formidable foe, trying to divine every trick and expedient that he might use. He had a memory to avenge. He had news to carry to Grant, and Forrest must not keep him from carrying it. Moreover, his regiment and he would gain great prestige if they could beat off Forrest. There would be glory for the whole Union cavalry if they drove back the Southern attack. Dick saw the glitter of his colonel's eye and the sharp compression of his lips.

But the men of Forrest, although nearly within rifle shot, did not charge. Their bugle sang again, but Dick did not know what the tune meant. Then they melted away into the deep forest on their flank, and some of the troop thought they had gone, daunted by the firm front of their foe.

But Dick knew better. Forrest would never retreat before an inferior force, and he was full of wiles and stratagems. Dick felt like a primitive man who knew that he was being stalked by a saber-toothed tiger through the dense forest.

Colonel Winchester beckoned to Sergeant Whitley. "Pick a half-dozen sharp-eyed men," he said, "and ride into those woods. You're experienced in this kind of war, Whitley, and before you go tell me what you think."

"General Forrest, sir, besides fighting as a white man fights, fights like an Indian, too; that is, he uses an Indian's cunning, which is always meant for ambush and surprise. He isn't dreaming of going away. They're coming back through the thick woods."

"So I think. But let me know as soon as you can."

Ten minutes after the sergeant had ridden forward with his comrades they heard the sound of rapid rifle shots, and then they saw the little band galloping back.

"They're coming, sir," reported the sergeant. "Forrest has dismounted several hundred of his men, and they are creeping forward from tree to tree with their rifles, while the others hold their horses in the rear."

"Then it's an Indian fight for the present," said Colonel Winchester. "We'll do the same."

He rapidly changed his lines of battle. The entire front rank was dismounted, while those behind held their horses. The four hundred in front, spreading out in as long a line as possible in order to protect their flanks, took shelter behind the trees and awaited the onset.

The attack was not long in coming. The Southern sharpshooters, creeping from tree to tree, began to fire. Scores of rifles cracked and Dick, from a convenient place behind a tree, saw the spouts of flame appearing along a line of four or five hundred yards. Bullets whizzed about him, and, knowing that he would not be needed at present for any message, he hugged the friendly bark more tightly.

"It's lucky we have plenty of trees," said a voice from the shelter of the tree next to him. "We have at least one for every officer and man."

It was Warner who spoke and he was quite cheerful. Like Colonel Winchester, he seemed to look forward to the combat with a certain joy, and he added:

"You'll take notice, Dick, old man, that we've not been surprised. Forrest hasn't galloped over us as he did before. He's taking the trouble to make the approach with protected riflemen. Now what is the sergeant up to?"

Sergeant Whitley, after whispering a little with Colonel Winchester, had stolen off toward the right with fifty picked riflemen. When they reached the verge of the open space that lay between the two sides they threw themselves down in the thick, tall grass. Neither Dick nor Warner could see them now. They beheld only the stems of the grass waving as if under a gentle wind. But Dick knew that the rippling movement marked the passage of the riflemen.

Meanwhile the attack in their front was growing hotter. At least six or seven hundred sharpshooters were sending a fire which would have annihilated them if it had not been for the trees. As it was, fragments of bark, twigs, and leaves showered about them. The whistling of the bullets and their chugging as they struck the trees made a continuous sinister note.

The Union men were not silent under this fire. Their own rifles were replying fast, but Colonel Winchester continually urged them to take aim, and, while death and wounds were inflicted on the Union ranks, the Southern were suffering in the same manner.

Dick turned his eyes toward the right flank, where the fifty picked riflemen, Sergeant Whitley at their head, were crawling through the tall grass. He knew that they were making toward a little corner of the forest, thrust farther forward than the rest, and presently when the rippling in the grass ceased he was sure that they had reached it. Then the fifty rifles cracked together and the Southern flank was swept by fifty well-aimed bullets. Lying in their covert, Whitley's men reloaded their breech-loading rifles and again sent in a deadly fire.

The main Northern force redoubled its efforts at the same time. The men in blue sent in swarms of whistling bullets and Dick saw the front line of the South retreating.

"We're rousing the wolves from their lairs," explained Pennington exultantly as he sprang from his tree, just in time for a bullet to send his hat flying from his head. Fortunately, it clipped only a lock of hair, but he received in a good spirit Warner's admonishing words:

"Don't go wild, Frank. We've merely repelled the present attack. You don't think that Forrest with superior forces is going to let us alone, do you?"

"No, I don't," replied Pennington, "and don't you get behind that tree. It's mine, and I'm coming back to it. I've earned it. I held it against all kinds of bullets. Look at the scars made on each side of it by rebel lead."

The firing now died. Whitley's flank movement had proved wholly successful, and Colonel Winchester reinforced him in the little forest peninsula with fifty more picked men, where they lay well hidden, a formidable force for any assailant.

The silence now became complete, save for the stamping of the impatient horses and the drone of insects in the woods and grass. Dick, lying on his stomach and using his glasses, could see nothing in the forest before them. It was to him in all its aspects an Indian battle, and he believed in spite of what Warner had said that the enemy had retired permanently.

Colonel Winchester and all the officers rose to their feet presently and walked among the trees. No bullets came to tell them that they were rash and then the senior officers held a conference, while all the men remounted, save a dozen or so who would ride no more. But the colonel did not abate one whit of his craft or caution.

They resumed the march toward Grant, but they avoided every field or open space. They would make curves and lose time in order to keep in the dense wood, but, as Dick knew, Colonel Winchester still suspected that Forrest was hovering somewhere on his flank, covered by the great forest and awaiting a favorable opportunity to attack.

They approached one of the deep and narrow streams that ultimately find their way to the Mississippi. It had only one ford, and the scouts galloping back informed them that the farther shore was held by a powerful force of cavalry.

"It's Forrest," said Colonel Winchester with quiet conviction. "Knowing every path of the woods, they've gone ahead of us, and they mean to cut us off from Grant. Nevertheless we'll make a way."

He spoke firmly, but the junior officers of the staff did not exactly see how they were going to force a ford defended by a larger number of cavalry under the redoubtable Forrest.

"I didn't think Forrest would let us alone, and he hasn't," said Pennington.

"No, he hasn't," said Warner, "and it seems that he's checkmated us, too. Why, that river is swollen by the rains so much that it's a hard job to cross it if no enemy were on the other side. But you'll note, also, that the enemy, having got to the other side, can't come back again in our face to attack us."

"But we want to go on and they don't," said Dick. "They're satisfied with the enforced status quo, and we're not. Am I right, Professor?"

"You certainly are," replied Warner. "Now, our colonel is

puzzled, as you can tell by his looks, and so would I be, despite my great natural military talents."

The Winchester regiment fell back into the woods, leaving the two forces out of rifle shot of each other. Sentinels were posted by both commanders not far from the river and the rest, dismounting, took their ease, save the officers, who again went into close conference.

Afterward they sat among the trees and waited. It was low ground, with the earth yet soaked from the heavy rain of the night before, and the heat grew heavy and intense. The insects began to drone again, and once more mosquitoes made life miserable. But the soldiers did not complain. It was noon now, and they ate food from their knapsacks. Two springs of clear water were found a little distance from the river and all drank there. Then they went back to their weary waiting.

On the other side of the river they could see the dismounted troopers, playing cards, sleeping or currying their horses. They seemed to be in no hurry at all. Colonel Winchester sent divisions of scouts up and down the stream, and, both returning after a while, reported that the river was not fordable anywhere.

Colonel Winchester sat down under a tree and smoked his pipe. The longer he smoked the more corrugated his brow became. He looked angrily at the ford, but it would be folly to attempt a passage there, and, containing himself as best he could, he waited while the long afternoon waned. His men at least would get a good rest.

Dick and his comrades, selecting the dryest place they could find, spread their blankets and lay down. Protecting their faces from the mosquitoes with green leaves, they sank into a deep quiet. Dick even drowsed for a while. He could not think of a way out of the trap, and he was glad it was the duty of older men like Colonel Winchester and the majors and captains to save them.

The heat of the day increased with the coming of afternoon, and Dick's eyelids grew heavier. He had become so thoroughly hardened to march and battle that the presence of the enemy on the other side of a river did not disturb him. What was the use of bothering about the rebels as long as they did not wish to fire upon one?

His eyes closed for a few minutes, and then his dreaming mind traversed space with incredible rapidity. He was back in Pendleton, sitting on the portico with his mother, watching the flowers on the lawn nod in the gentle wind. His cousin Harry Kenton saluted him with a halloo and came bounding toward the porch, and the halloo caused Dick to awake and sit up. He rubbed his eyes violently and looked around a little bit ashamed. But two captains older than himself were sound asleep with their backs against trees.

Dick stood up and shook himself violently. Whatever others might do he must not allow himself to relax so much. He saw that the sun was slowly descending and that the full heat of the afternoon was passing. Colonel Winchester had withdrawn somewhat among the trees and he beckoned to him. Sergeant Whitley was standing beside the colonel.

"Dick," said Colonel Winchester, "colored men have brought us news that Colonel Grierson of our army, with a strong raiding force of nearly two thousand cavalry is less than a day's march away and on the same side of this river that we are. We have received the news from three separate sources and it must be true. Probably Forrest's men know it, too, but expect Grierson to pass on, wholly ignorant that we're here. I have chosen you and Sergeant Whitley to bring Grierson to our relief. The horses are ready. Now go, and God speed you. The sergeant will tell you what we know as you ride."

Dick sprang at once into the saddle, and with a brief good-bye he and the sergeant were soon in the forest riding toward the southeast. Dick was alive and energetic again. All that laziness of mind and body was gone. He rode on a great ride and every sense was alert.

"Tell me," he said, "just about what the news is."

"Three men," replied the sergeant, "came in at different times with tales, but the three tales agree. Grierson has made a great raid, even further down than we have gone. He has more than double our numbers, and if we can unite with him it's likely that we can turn Forrest into the pursued instead of the pursuer. They say we can hit his trail about twenty-five miles from here, and if that's so we'll bring him up to the ford by noon to-morrow. Doesn't it look promising to you, Lieutenant Mason?"

"It does look promising, Sergeant Whitley, if we don't happen to be taken by the Johnnies who infest this region. Besides, you'll have to guide through the dark to-night. You're trained to that sort of thing."

"You can see pretty well in the dark yourself, sir; and since our way lies almost wholly through forest I see no reason why we should be captured."

"That's so, sergeant. I'm just as much of an optimist as you are. You keep the course, and I'm with you to the finish."

They rode rather fast at first as the sun had not yet set, picking their way through the woods, and soon left their comrades out of sight. The twilight now came fast, adding a mournful and somber red to the vast expanse of wilderness. The simile of an Indian fight returned to Dick with increased force. This was not like any battle with white men in the open fields. It was a combat of raiders who advanced secretly under cover of the vast wilderness.

The twilight died with the rapidity of the South, and the darkness, thick at the early hours, passed over the curve of the earth. For a time Dick and the sergeant could not see many yards in front and they rode very slowly. After a while, as the sky lightened somewhat and their eyes also grew keen, they made better speed. Then they struck a path through the woods leading in the right direction, and they broke into a trot.

The earth was so soft that their horses' feet gave back but little sound, and both were confident they would not meet any enemy in the night at least.

"Straight southeast," said the sergeant, "and we're bound to strike Grierson's tracks. After that we'd be blind if we couldn't follow the trail made by nearly two thousand horsemen."

The path still led in the direction they wished and they rode on silently for hours. Once they saw a farmhouse set back in the woods, and they were in fear lest dogs come out and bark alarm, but there was no sound and they soon left it far behind.

They passed many streams, some of which were up to their saddle girths, and then they entered a road which was often so deep in mud that they were compelled to turn into the woods on the side. But no human being had interfered with their journey, and their hopes rose to the zenith.

They came, finally, into an open region of cotton fields, and the sergeant now began to watch closely for the great trail they hoped to find. A force as large as Grierson's would not attempt a passage through the woods, but would seek some broad road and Sergeant Whitley expected to find it long before morning.

It was now an hour after midnight and they reckoned that they had come about the right distance. There was a good moon and plenty of stars and the sergeant gave himself only a half-hour to find the trail.

"There's bound to be a wide road somewhere among these fields, the kind we call a county road."

"It's over there beyond that rail fence," said Dick. They urged their horses into a trot, and soon found that Dick was right. A road of red clay soft from the rains stretched before them.

"A man doesn't have to look twice here for a trail. See," said the sergeant.

The road from side to side was plowed deep with the hoofs of horses, every footprint pointing northward.

"Grierson's cavalry," said Dick.

"I take it that it can't be anything else. There is certainly in these parts no rebel force of cavalry large enough to make this trail."

"How old would you say these tracks are?"

"Hard to tell, but they can't have been made many hours ago. We'll press forward, lieutenant, and we can save time going through the fields on the edge of the road."

Although they had to take down fences they made good speed and just as the sun was rising they saw the light of a low campfire among some trees, lining either bank of a small creek. They approached warily, until they saw the faded blue uniforms. Then they galloped forward, shouting that they were friends, and in a few minutes were in the presence of Grierson himself.

He had been making a great raid, but he was eager now for the opportunity to strike at Forrest. He must give his horses a short rest, and then Dick and the sergeant should guide him at speed to the ford where the opposing forces stood.

"It's twenty-five miles, you tell me?" said Grierson to Dick.

"As nearly as I can calculate, sir. It's through swampy country, but I think we ought to be there in three or four hours."

"Then lead the way," said Grierson. "Like your colonel, I'll be glad to have a try at Forrest."

Sergeant Whitley rode in advance. A lumberman first and then a soldier of the plains, he had noted even in the darkness every landmark and he could lead the way back infallibly. But he warned Grierson that such a man as Forrest would be likely to have out scouts, even if they had to swim the river. It was likely that they could not get nearer by three or four miles to Colonel Winchester without being seen.

"Then," said Grierson, who had the spirit of a Stuart or a Forrest, "we'll ride straight on, brushing these watchers out of our way, and if by any chance their whole force should cross, we'll just meet and fight it."

"The little river is falling fast," said the sergeant. "It's likely that it'll be fordable almost anywhere by noon."

"Then," said Grierson, "it'll be all the easier for us to get at the enemy."

Dick, just behind Grierson, heard these words and he liked them. Here was a spirit like Colonel Winchester's own, or like that of the great Southern cavalry leaders. The Southerners were born on horseback, but the Northern men were acquiring the same trick of hard riding. Dick glanced back at the long column. Armed with carbine and saber the men were riding their trained horses like Comanches. Eager and resolute it was a formidable force, and his heart swelled with pride and anticipation. He believed that they were going to give Forrest all he wanted and maybe a little more.

Up rose the sun. Hot beams poured over forest and field, but the cavalrymen still rode fast, the scent of battle in their nostrils. Dick knew that these Southern streams, flooded by torrents of rain, rose fast and also fell fast.

"How much further now, sergeant?" asked Grierson, as they turned from a path into the deep woods.

"Not more than three miles, sir."

"And they know we're coming. Listen to that!"

Several rifles cracked among the trees and bullets whizzed by them. Forrest's skirmishers and scouts were on the south side of the stream. As they had foreseen, the river had sunk so much that it was fordable now at many points. Dick was devoutly grateful that they had found Grierson. Otherwise the Winchester regiment would have been flanked, and its destruction would have followed.

Skirmishers were detached from Grierson's command and drove off the Southern riflemen. Dick heard the rattling fire of their rifles in the deep wood, but he seldom saw a figure. Then he heard another fire, heavy and continuous, in their front, coming quite clearly on a breeze that blew toward them.

"Your whole regiment is engaged," exclaimed Grierson. "Forrest must have forded the river elsewhere!"

He turned and shook aloft his saber.

"Forward, lads!" he shouted. "Gallant men of our own army will be overwhelmed unless we get up in time!"

The whole force broke into a gallop through the woods, the fire in their front rapidly growing heavier. In ten minutes they would be there, but rifles suddenly blazed from the forest on their flank and many saddles were emptied. Nothing upsets like surprise, and for a few moments the whole command was in disorder. It was evident that Forrest was attacking Winchester with only a part of his force, while he formed an ambush for Grierson.

But the Northern cavalrymen had not learned in vain through disaster and experience. Grierson quickly restored order and drew his men back into the forest. As the enemy followed the Northern carbines began to flash fast. The troopers in gray were unable to flank them or drive them back. Grierson, sure of his superior numbers, pushed on toward Winchester, while fighting off the foe at the same time.

Dick and the sergeant kept in the van, and presently they came within sight of Colonel Winchester's men, who, dismounted, were holding off as best they could the overwhelming attack of Forrest. The Southern leader, after sending the majority of his men to a new crossing lower down had forced the ford before the Winchester regiment, and would have crushed it if it had not been for the opportune arrival of Grierson.

But a tremendous cheer arose as the Northern cavalry leader, who was already proving his greatness, charged into the battle with his grim troopers. The men in blue were now more numerous, and, fighting with the resolve to win or die, they gradually forced back Forrest. Dick began to foresee a victory won over the great Southern cavalryman.

But the astute Forrest, seeing that the odds were now heavily against him, ordered a retreat. The trumpets sang the recall and suddenly the Southern horsemen, carrying their dead with them, vanished in the forest, where the Northern cavalry, fearful of ambushes and new forces, did not dare to pursue.

But Winchester and Grierson were shaking hands, and Winchester thanked the other in brief but emphatic words.

"Say no more, colonel," exclaimed Grierson. "We're all trying to serve our common country. You'd help me just the same if we had the chance, and I think you'll find the road clear to Grant. While the siege of Vicksburg was determined on long ago, as you know, I believe that he is now moving toward Grand Gulf. You know he has to deal with the armies of Johnston and Pemberton."

"We'll find him," said Winchester.

A quarter of an hour later his regiment was galloping toward Grant, while Grierson's command rode eastward to deal with other forces of the Confederacy.

CHAPTER III

GRANT MOVES

The Winchester regiment had not suffered greatly. A dozen men who had fallen were given speedy burial, and all the wounded were taken away on horseback by their friends. Dick rejoiced greatly at their escape from Forrest, and the daring and skill of Grierson. He felt anew that he was in stronger hands in the West than he had been in the East. In the East things seemed to go wrong nearly always, and the West they seemed to go right nearly always. It could not be chance continued so long. He believed in his soul that it was Grant, the heroic Thomas, and the great fighting powers of the western men, used to all the roughness of life out-of-doors and on the border.

They turned their course toward the Mississippi and that afternoon they met a Union scout who told them that Grant, now in the very heart of the far South, was gathering his forces for a daring attack upon Grand Gulf, a Confederate fortress on the Mississippi. In the North and at Washington his venture was regarded with alarm. There was a telegram to him to stop, but it was sent too late. He had disappeared in the Southern wilderness.

But Dick understood. He had both knowledge and intuition. Colonel Winchester on his long and daring scout had learned that the Confederate forces in the South were scattered and their leaders in doubt. Grant, taking a daring offensive and hiding his movements, had put them on the defensive, and there were so many points to defend that they did not know which to choose. Joe Johnston, just recovered from his wound at Fair Oaks the year before, and a general of the first rank, was coming, but he was not yet here.

Meanwhile Pemberton held the chief command, but he seemed to lack energy and decision. There were forces under other generals scattered along the river, including eight thousand commanded by Bowen, who held Grand Gulf, but concert of action did not exist among them.

This knowledge was not Dick's alone. It extended to every man in the regiment, and when the colonel urged them to greater speed they responded gladly.

"If we don't ride faster," he said, "we won't be up in time for the taking of Grand Gulf."

No greater spur was needed and the Winchester regiment went forward as fast as horses could carry them.

"I take it that Grant means to scoop in the Johnnies in detail," said Warner.

"It seems so," said Pennington. "This is a big country down here, and we can fight one Confederate army while another is mired up a hundred miles away.

"That's General Grant's plan. He doesn't look like any hero of romance, but he acts like one. He plunges into the middle of the enemy, and if he gets licked he's up and at 'em again right away."

Night closed in, and they stopped at an abandoned plantation—it seemed to Dick that the houses were abandoned everywhere—where they spent the night. The troopers would have willingly pushed on through the darkness, but the horses were so near exhaustion that another hour or two would have broken them down permanently. Moreover, Colonel Winchester did not feel much apprehension of an attack now. Forrest had certainly turned in another direction, and they were too close to the Union lines to be attacked by any other foe.

The house on this plantation was not by any means so large and fine as Bellevue, but, like the other, it had broad piazzas all about it, and Dick, in view of his strenuous experience, was allowed to take his saddle as a pillow and his blankets and go to sleep soon after dark in a comfortable place against the wall.

Never was slumber quicker or sweeter. There was not an unhealthy tissue in his body, and most of his nerves had disappeared in a life amid battles, scoutings, and marchings. He slept heavily all through the night, inhaling new strength and vitality with every breath of the crisp, fresh air. There was no interruption this time, and early in the morning the regiment was up and away.

They descended now into lower grounds near the Mississippi. All around them was a vast and luxuriant vegetation, cut by sluggish streams and bayous. But the same desolation reigned everywhere. The people had fled before the advance of the armies. Late in the afternoon they saw pickets in blue, then the Mississippi, and a little later they rode into a Union camp.

"Dick," said Colonel Winchester, "I shall want you to go with the senior officers and myself to report to General Grant on the other side of the Mississippi. You rode on that mission to Grierson and he may want to ask you questions."

Dick was glad to go with them. He was eager to see once more the man who had taken Henry and Donelson and who had hung on at Shiloh until Buell came. The general's tent was in a grove on a bit of high ground, and he was sitting before it on a little camp stool, smoking a short cigar, and gazing reflectively in the direction of Grand Gulf.

He greeted the three officers quietly but with warmth and then he listened to Colonel Winchester's detailed account of what he had seen and learned in his raid toward Jackson. It was a long narrative, showing how the Southern forces were scattered, and, as he listened, Grant's face began to show satisfaction.

But he seldom interrupted.

"And you think they have no large force at Jackson?" he said.

"I'm quite sure of it," replied Colonel Winchester.

Grant chewed his cigar a little while and then said:

"Grierson is doing well. It was an achievement for you and him to beat off Forrest. It will raise the prestige of our cavalry, which needs it. I believe it was you, Lieutenant Mason, who brought Grierson."

"It was chiefly, sir, a sergeant named Whitley. I rode with him and outranked him, but he is a veteran of the plains, and it was he who did the real work."

The general's stern features were lightened by a smile.

"I'm glad you give the sergeant credit," he said. "Not many officers would do it."

He listened a while longer and then the three were permitted to withdraw to their regiment, which was posted back of Grand Gulf, and which had quickly become a part of an army flushed with victory and eager for further action.

Before sunset Dick, Warner, and Pennington looked at Grand Gulf, a little village standing on high cliffs overlooking the Mississippi, just below the point where the dark stream known as the Big Black River empties into the Father of Waters. Around the crown of the heights was a ring of batteries and lower down, enclosing the town, was another ring.

Far off on the Mississippi the three saw puffing black smoke marking the presence of a Union fleet, which never for one instant in the whole course of the war relaxed its grip of steel upon the Confederacy. Dick's heart thrilled at the sight of the brave ships. He felt then, as most of us have felt since, that whatever happened the American navy would never fail.

"I hear the ships are going to bombard," said Warner.

"I heard so, too," said Pennington, "and I heard also that they will have to do it under the most difficult circumstances. The water in front of Grand Gulf is so deep that the ships can't anchor. It has a swift current, too, making at that point more than six knots an hour. There are powerful eddies, too, and the batteries crowning the cliffs are so high that the cannon of the gunboats will have trouble in reaching them."

"Still, Mr. Pessimist," said Dick, "remember what the gunboats did at Fort Henry. You'll find the same kind of men here."

"I wasn't trying to discourage you. I was merely telling the worst first. We're going to win. We nearly always win here in the West, but it seems to me the country is against us now. This doesn't look much like the plains, Dick, with its big, deep rivers, its high bluffs along the banks, and its miles and miles of swamp or wet lowlands. How wide would you say the Mississippi is here?"

"Somewhere between a mile and a mile and a half."

"And they say it's two or three hundred feet deep. Look at the steamers, boys. How many are there?"

"I count seven pyramids of smoke," said Warner, "four in one group and three in another. All the pyramids are becoming a little faint as the twilight is advancing. Dick, you call me a cold mathematical person, but this vast river flowing in its deep channel, the dark bluffs up there, and the vast forests would make me feel mighty lonely if you fellows were not here. It's a long way to Vermont."

"Fifteen hundred or maybe two thousand miles," said Dick, "but look how fast the dark is coming. I was wrong in saying it's coming. It just drops down. The smoke of the steamers has melted into the night, and you don't see them any more. The surface of the river has turned black as ink, the bluffs of Grand Gulf have gone, and we've turned back three or four hundred years."

"What do you mean by going back three or four hundred years?" asked Warner, looking curiously at Dick.

"Why, don't you see them out there?"

"See them out there? See what?"

"Why, the queer little ships with the high sides and prows! On my soul, George, they're the caravels of Spain! Look, they're stopping! Now they lower something in black over the side of the first caravel. I see a man in a black robe like a priest, holding a cross in his hand and standing at the ship's edge saying something. I think he's praying, boys. Now sailors cut the ropes that hold the dark object. It falls into the river and disappears. It's the burial of De Soto in the Father of Waters which he discovered!"

"Dick, you're dreaming," exclaimed Pennington.

"Yes, I know, but once there was a Chinaman who dreamed that he was a lily. When he woke up he didn't know whether he was a Chinaman who had dreamed he was a lily or a lily now dreaming he was a Chinaman."

"I like that story, Dick, but you've got too much imagination.

The tale of the death and burial of De Soto has always been so vivid to you that you just stood there and re-created the scene for yourself."

"Of course that's it," said Pennington, "but why can't a fellow create things with his mind, when things that don't exist jump right up before his eyes? I've often seen the mirage, generally about dark, far out on the western plains. I've seen a beautiful lake and green gardens where there was nothing but the brown swells rolling on."

"I concede all you say," said Dick readily. "I have flashes sometimes, and so does Harry Kenton and others I know."

"Flashes! What do you mean?" asked Warner.

"Why, a sort of lightning stroke out of the past. Something that lasts only a second, but in which you have a share. Boys, one day I saw myself a Carthaginian soldier following Hannibal over the Alps."

"Maybe," said Pennington, "we have lived other lives on this earth, and sometimes a faint glimpse of them comes to us. It's just a guess."

"That's so," said Warner, "and we'd better be getting back to the regiment. Grand Gulf defended by Bowen and eight thousand good men is really enough for us. I think we're going to see some lively fighting here."

The heavy boom of a cannon from the upper circle of batteries swept over the vast sheet of water flowing so swiftly toward the Gulf. The sound came back in dying echoes, and then there was complete silence among besieged and besiegers.

The Winchesters had found a good solid place, a little hill among the marshes, and they were encamped there with their horses. Dick had no messages to carry, but he remained awake, while his comrades slept soundly. He had slept so much the night before that he had no desire for sleep now.

From his position he could see the Confederate bluffs and a few lights moving there, but otherwise the two armies were under a blanket of darkness. He again felt deeply the sense of isolation and loneliness, not for himself alone, but for the whole army. Grant had certainly shown supreme daring in pushing far into the South, and the government at Washington had cause for alarm lest he be reckless. If there were any strong hand to draw together the forces of the Confederacy they could surely crush him. But he had already learned in this war that those who struck swift and hard were sure to win. That was Stonewall Jackson's way, and it seemed to be Grant's way, too.

Still unable to sleep, he walked to a better position, where he could see the shimmering dark of the river and the misty heights with their two circles of cannon. A tall figure standing there turned at his tread and he recognized Colonel Winchester.

"Uneasy at our position, Dick?" said the colonel, fathoming his mind at once.

"A little, sir, but I think General Grant will pull us through."

"He will, Dick, and he'll take this fort, too. Grant's the hammer we've been looking for. Look at his record. He's had backsets, but in the end he's succeeded in everything he's tried. The Confederate government and leaders have made a mess of their affairs in the West and Southwest, and General Grant is taking full advantage of it."

"Do we attack in the morning, sir?"

"We do, Dick, though not by land. Porter, with his seven gunboats, is going to open on the fort, but it will be a hazardous undertaking."

"Because of the nature of the river, sir?"

"That's it. They can't anchor, and with full steam up, caught in all the violent eddies that the river makes rounding the point, they'll have to fire as best they can."

"But the gunboats did great work at Fort Henry, sir."

"So they did, Dick, and we've come a long way South since then, which means that we're making progress and a lot of it here in the West. Well, we'll see to-morrow."

They walked back to their own camp and sleep came to Dick at last. But he awoke early and found that the thrill of expectation was running through the whole army. Their position did not yet enable them to attack on land, but far out on the river they saw the gunboats moving. Porter, the commander, divided them into two groups. Four of the gunboats were to attack the lower circle of batteries and three were to pour their fire upon the upper ring.

Dick by day even more than by night recognized the difficulty of the task. Before them flowed the vast swift current of the Mississippi, gleaming now in the sunshine, and beyond were the frowning bluffs, crested and ringed with cannon. Grant had with him twenty thousand men and his seven gunboats, and Bowen, eight thousand troops. But if the affair lasted long other Southern armies would surely come.

Dick and his comrades had little to do but watch and thousands watched with them. When the sun was fully risen the seven boats steamed out in two groups, four farther down the river in order to attack the lower batteries, while the other three up the stream would launch their fire against those on the summit.

He watched the crest of the cliffs. He saw plainly through his glasses the muzzles of cannon and men moving about the batteries.

Then there was a sudden blaze of fire and column of smoke and a shell struck in the water near one of the gunboats. The boat replied and its comrades also sent shot and shell toward the frowning summit. Then the batteries, both lower and upper, replied with full vigor and all the cliffs were wrapped in fire and smoke.

The boats steamed in closer and closer, pouring an incessant fire from their heavy guns, and both rings of batteries on the cliffs responded. The water of the river spouted up in innumerable little geysers and now and then a boat was struck. Over both cliffs and river a great cloud of smoke lowered. It grew so dense that Dick and his comrades, watching with eagerness, were unable to tell much of what was happening.

Yet as the smoke lifted or was shot through with the blaze of cannon fire they saw that their prophecies were coming true. The boats in water too deep for anchorage were caught in the powerful eddies and their captains had to show their best seamanship while they steamed back and forth.

The battle between ship and shore went on for a long time. It seemed at last to the watching Union soldiers that the fire from the lower line of batteries was diminishing.

"We're making some way," said Warner.

"It looks like it," said Dick. "Their lower batteries are not so well protected as the upper."

"If we were only over there, helping with our own guns."

"But there's a big river in between, and we've got to leave it to the boats for to-day, anyhow."

"Look again at those lower batteries. Their fire is certainly decreasing. I can see it die down."

"Yes, and now it's stopped entirely. The boats have done good work!"

A tremendous cheer burst from the troops on the west shore as they saw how much their gallant little gunboats had achieved. Every gun in the lower batteries was silent now, but the top of the cliffs was still alive with flame. The batteries there were far from silent. Instead their fire was increasing in volume and power.

The four gunboats that had silenced the lower batteries now moved up to the aid of their comrades, and the seven made a united effort, steaming forward in a sort of half-moon, and raining shot and shell upon the summits. But the guns there, well-sheltered and having every advantage over rocking steamers, maintained an accurate and deadly fire. The decks of the gunboats were swept more than once. Many men were killed or wounded. Heavy shot crashed through their sides, and Dick expected every instant to see some one of them sunk by a huge exploding shell.

"They can't win! They can't win!" he exclaimed. "They'd better draw off before they're sunk!"

"So they had," said Warner sadly. "Boats are at a disadvantage fighting batteries. The old darky was right when he preferred a train wreck to a boat wreck, 'ef the train's smashed, thar you are on the solid ground, but ef the boat blows up, whar is you?' That's sense. The boats are retiring! It's sad, but it's sense. A boat that steams away will live to fight another day."

Dick was dejected. He fancied he could hear the cheering of their foes at what looked like a Union defeat, but he recalled that Grant, the bulldog, led them. He would never think of retiring, and he was sure to be ready with some new attempt.

The gunboats drew off to the far western shore and lay there, puffing smoke defiantly. Their fight with the batteries had lasted five hours and they had suffered severely. It seemed strange to Dick that none of them had been sunk, and in fact it was strange. All had been hit many times, and one had been pierced by nearly fifty shot or shell. Their killed or wounded were numerous, but their commanders and crews were still resolute, and ready to go into action whenever General Grant wished.

"Spunky little fellows," said Pennington. "We don't have many boats out where I live, but I must hand a bunch of laurel to the navy every time."

"And you can bind wreaths around the hair of those navy fellows, too," said Warner, "and sing songs in their honor whether they win or lose."

"Now I wonder what's next," said Dick.

To their surprise the gunboats opened fire again just before sundown, and the batteries replied fiercely. Rolling clouds of smoke mingled with the advancing twilight, and the great guns from either side flashed through the coming darkness. Then from a stray word or two dropped by Colonel Winchester Dick surmised the reason of this new and rather distant cannonade.

He knew that General Grant had transports up the river above Grand Gulf, and he believed that they were now coming down the stream under cover of the bombardment and the darkness. He confided his belief to Warner, who agreed with him. Presently they saw new coils of smoke in the darkness and knew they were right. The transports, steaming swiftly, were soon beyond the range of the batteries, and then the gun boats, drawing off, dropped down the river with them.

Long before the boats reached a point level with Grant's camp the army was being formed in line for embarkation on the gunboats and transports. The horses were to be placed on one or two of the transports and the men filled all the other vessels.

"You can't down Grant," said Pennington. "A failure with him merely means that he's going to try again."

"But don't forget the navy and the Father of Waters," said Dick, as their transports swung from the shore upon the dark surface of the river. "The mighty rivers help us. Look how we went up the Cumberland and the Tennessee and now we've harnessed a flowing ocean for our service."

"Getting poetical, Dick," said Warner.

"I feel it and so do you. You can't see the bluffs any more. There's nothing in sight, but the lights of the steamers and the transports. We must be somewhere near the middle of the stream, because I can't make out either shore."

There were two regiments aboard the transport, the Winchester and one from Ohio, which had fought by their side at both Perryville and Stone River. Usually these boys chattered much, but now they were silent, permeated by the same feelings that had overwhelmed Dick. In the darkness—all lights were concealed as much as possible—with both banks of the vast river hidden from them, they felt that they were in very truth afloat upon a flowing ocean.

They knew little about their journey, except that they were destined for the eastern shore, the same upon which Grand Gulf stood, but they did not worry about this lack of knowledge. They were willing to trust to Grant, and most of them were already asleep, upon the decks, in the cabins, or in any place in which a human body could secure a position.

Dick did not sleep. The feeling of mystery and might made by the tremendous river remained longer in his sensitive and imaginative nature. His mind, too, looked backward. He knew that the great grandfathers of Harry Kenton and himself, the famous Henry Ware and the famous Paul Cotter, had passed up and down this monarch of streams. He knew of their adventures. How often had he and his cousin, who now, alas! was on the other side, listened to the stories of those mighty days as they were handed from father to son! Those lads had floated in little boats and he was on a steamer, but it seemed to him that the river with its mighty depths took no account of either, steamer or canoe being all the same to its vast volume of water.

He was standing by the rail looking over, when happening to glance back he saw by the ship's lantern what he thought was a familiar face. A second glance and he was sure. He remembered that fair-haired Ohio lad, and, smiling, he said:

"You're one of those Ohio boys who, marching southward from its mouth in the Ohio, drank the tributary river dry clear to its source, the mightiest achievement in quenching thirst the world has ever known. You're the boy, too, who told about it."

The youth moved forward, gazed at him and said:

"Now I remember you, too. You're Dick Mason of the Winchester regiment. I heard the Winchesters were on board, but I haven't had time to look around. It was hot when we drank up the river, but it was hotter that afternoon at Perryville. God! what a battle! And again at Stone River, when the Johnnies surprised us and took us in flank. It was you Kentuckians then who saved us."

"Just as you would have saved us, if it had been the other way."

"I hope so. But, Mason, we left a lot of the boys behind. A big crowd stopped forever at Perryville, and a bigger at Stone River."

"And we left many of ours, too. I suppose we'll land soon, won't we, and then take these Grand Gulf forts with troops."

"Yes, that's the ticket, but I hear, Mason, it's hard to find a landing on the east side. The banks are low there and the river spreads out to a vast distance. After the boats go as far as they can we'll have to get off in water up to our waists and wade through treacherous floods."

The question of landing was worrying Grant at that time and worrying him terribly. The water spread far out over the sunken lands and he might have to drop down the river many miles before he could find a landing on solid ground, a fact which would scatter his army along a long line, and expose it to defeat by the Southern land forces. But his anxieties were relieved early in the morning when a colored man taken aboard from a canoe told him of a bayou not five miles below Grand Gulf up which his gunboats and transports could go and find a landing for the troops on solid ground.

Dick was asleep when the boats entered the bayou, but he was soon awakened by the noise of landing. It was then that most of the Winchester and of the Ohio regiment discovered that they were comrades, thrown together again by the chances of war, and there was a mighty welcome and shaking of hands. But it did not interfere with the rapidity of the landing. The Winchester regiment was promptly ordered forward and, advancing on solid ground, took a little village without firing a shot.

All that day troops came up and Grant's army, after having gone away from Grand Gulf in darkness, was coming back to it in daylight.

"They say that Pemberton at Vicksburg could gather together

fifty thousand men and strike us, while we've only twenty thousand here," said Pennington.

"But he isn't going to do it," said Warner. "How do I know? No, I'm not a prophet nor the son of a prophet. There's nothing mysterious about it. This man Grant who leads us knows the value of time. He makes up his mind fast and he acts fast. The Confederate commander doesn't do either. So Grant is bound to win. Let z equal resolution and y equal speed and we have z plus y which equals resolution and speed, that is victory."

"I hope it will work out that way," said Dick, "but war isn't altogether mathematics."

"Not altogether, but that beautiful study plays a great part in every campaign. People are apt to abuse mathematics, when they don't know what they're talking about. The science of mathematics is the very basis of music, divine melody, heaven's harmony."

"You needn't tell me," said Pennington, "that a plus b and z minus y lie at the basis of 'Home, Sweet Home' and the 'Star Spangled Banner.' I accept a lot of your tales because you come from an old state like Vermont, but there's a limit, George."

Warner looked at him pityingly.

"Frank," he said, "I'm not arguing with you. I'm telling you. Haven't you known me long enough to accept whatever I say as a fact, and to accept it at once and without question? Not to do so is an insult to me and to the truth. Now say over slowly with me: 'The basis of music is mathematics.'"

They said slowly together:

"The basis of music is mathematics."

"Now I accept your apologies," said Warner loftily.

Pennington laughed.

"You're a queer fellow, George," he said. "When this war is over and I receive my general's uniform I'm coming up into the Vermont mountains and look your people over. Will it be safe?"

"Of course, if you learn to read and write by then, and don't come wearing your buffalo robe. We're strong on education and manners."

"Why, George," said Pennington in the same light tone, "I could read when I was two years old, and, as for writing, I wrote a lot of text-books for the Vermont schools before I came to the war."

"Shut up, you two," said Dick. "Don't you know that this is a war and not a talking match?"

"It's not a war just now, or at least there are a few moments between battles," retorted Warner, "and the best way I can use them is in instructing our ignorant young friend from Nebraska."

Their conversation was interrupted by Colonel Winchester,

who ordered the regiment to move to a new point. General Grant had decided to attack a little town called Port Gibson, which commanded the various approaches to Grand Gulf. If he could take that he might shut up Bowen and his force in Grand Gulf. On the other hand, if he failed he might be shut in himself by Confederate armies gathering from Jackson, Vicksburg, and elsewhere. The region, moreover, was complicated for both armies by the mighty Mississippi and the Big Black River, itself a large stream, and there were deep and often unfordable bayous.

But Grant showed great qualities, and Dick, who was experienced enough now to see and know, admired him more than ever. He pushed forward with the utmost resolution and courage. His vanguard, led by McClernand, and including the Winchester regiment, seized solid ground near Port Gibson, but found themselves confronted by a formidable Southern force. Bowen, who commanded in Grand Gulf, was brave and able. Seeing the Union army marching toward his rear, and knowing that if Grant took it he would be surrounded, both on land and water, by a force outnumbering his nearly three to one, he marched out at once and took station two miles in front of Port Gibson.

Dick was by the side of Colonel Winchester as he rode forward. The faint echo of shots from the skirmishers far in front showed that they had roused up an enemy. Glasses were put in use at once.

"The Confederates are before us," said Colonel Winchester.

"So they are, and we're going to have hard fighting," said a major. "Look what a position!"

Dick said nothing, but he was using his glasses, too. He saw before him rough ground, thickly sown with underbrush. There was also a deep ravine or rather marsh choked with vines, bushes, reeds, and trees that like a watery soil. The narrow road divided and went around either end of the long work, where the two divisions united again on a ridge, on which Bowen had placed his fine troops and artillery.

"I don't see their men yet, except a few skirmishers," said Dick.

"No, but we'll find them in some good place beyond it," replied Colonel Winchester, divining Bowen's plan.

It was night when the army in two divisions, one turning to the right and the other to the left, began the circuit of the great marshy ravine. Dick noticed that the troops who had struggled so long in mud and water were eager. Here, west of the Alleghanies, the men in blue were always expecting to win.

The sky was sown with stars, casting a filmy light over the

marching columns. Dick was with the troops passing to the right, and he observed again their springy and eager tread.

Nor was the night without a lively note. Skirmishers, eager riflemen prowling among the bushes, fired often at one another, and now and then a Union cannon sent a shell screaming into some thick clump of forest, lest a foe be lurking there for ambush.

The reports of the rifles and cannon kept every one alert and watchful. Early in the night while it was yet clear Dick often saw the flashes from the firing, but, as the morning hours approached, heavy mists began to rise from that region of damp earth and great waters. He shivered more than once, and on the advice of Sergeant Whitley wrapped his cavalry cloak about him.

"Chills and fever," said the sergeant sententiously. "So much water and marsh it's hard to escape it. The sooner we fight the better."

"Well, that's what General Grant thinks already," said Dick; "so I suppose he doesn't need chills and fever to drive him on. All the same, Sergeant, I'll wrap up as you say."

All the men in the Winchester regiment were soon doing the same. The mists of the Mississippi, the Big Black and the bayous were raw and cold, although it would be hot later on. But the period of coldness did not last long. Soon the low sun showed in the east and the warm daylight came. In the new light they saw the Confederate forces strongly posted on the ridge where the halves of the road rejoined. As the Union column came into view a cannon boomed and a shell burst in the road so near that dirt was thrown upon them as it exploded and one man was wounded. At the same time the column on the left under Osterhaus appeared, having performed its semicircle about the marsh, and the whole Union army, weary of body but eager of soul, pressed forward. The Winchester regiment and the Ohio regiment beside it charged hotly, but were received with a fire of great volume and accuracy that swept them from the road. Another battery on their far left also raked them with a cross fire, and so terrible was their reception that they were compelled to abandon some of their own cannon and seek shelter.

The Winchester regiment, except the officers, were not mounted in this march, as Grant would not wait for their horses, which were on another transport. The very fact saved from death many who would have made a more shining target. Dick's own horse was killed at the first fire, and as he leaped clear to escape he went down to his waist in a marsh, another fact which saved his life a second time as the new volleys swept over his head. The horses of other officers also were killed, and the remainder, finding themselves such conspicuous targets, sprang to the ground. The frightened animals, tearing the reins from their hands, raced through the thickets or fell into the marsh.

All the time Dick heard the shells and bullets shrieking and whining over his head. But, regaining his courage and presence of mind, he slowly pulled himself out of the marsh, taking shelter behind a huge cypress that grew at its very edge. As he dashed the mud out of his eyes he heard a voice saying:

"Don't push! There's room enough here for the three of us. In fact, there's room enough behind the big trees for all the officers."

It was Warner who was speaking with such grim irony, and Pennington by his side was hugging the tree. Shells and shot shrieked over their heads and countless bullets hummed about them. The soldiers also had taken shelter behind the trees, and Warner's jest about the officers was a jest only. Nevertheless the Southern fire was great in volume and accuracy. Bowen was an able commander with excellent men, and from his position that covered the meeting of the roads he swept both Union columns with a continuous hail of death.

"We must get out of this somehow," said Dick. "If we're held here in these swamps and thickets any longer the Johnnies can shoot us down at their leisure."

"But we won't be held!" exclaimed Pennington. "Look! One of our brigades is through, and it's charging the enemy on the right!"

It was Hovey who had forced his way through a thicket, supposed to be impenetrable, and who now, with a full brigade behind him, was rushing upon Bowen's flank. Then, while the Southern defense was diverted to this new attack, the Winchester and the Ohio regiment attacked in front, shouting with triumph.

Hovey's rush was overpowering. He drove in the Southern flank, taking four cannon and hundreds of prisoners, but the dauntless Confederate commander, withdrawing his men in perfect order, retreated to a second ridge, where he took up a stronger position than the first.

Resolute and dangerous, the men in gray turned their faces anew to the enemy and sent back a withering fire that burned away the front ranks of the Union army. Osterhaus, in spite of every effort, was driven back, and the Winchesters and their Ohio friends were compelled to give ground too. It seemed that the utmost of human effort and defiance of death could not force the narrow passage.

But a new man, a host in himself, came upon the field. Grant, who had been on foot for two days, endeavoring to get his army through the thickets and morasses, heard the booming of the cannon and he knew that the vanguards had clashed. He borrowed a cavalry horse and, galloping toward the sound of the guns, reached the field at mid-morning. Grant was not impressive in either figure or manner, but the soldiers had learned to believe in him as they always believe in one who leads them to victory.

A tremendous shout greeted his coming and the men, snatching off their hats and caps, waved them aloft. Grant took no notice but rapidly disposed his troops for a new and heavier battle. Dick felt the strong and sure hand over them. The Union fire grew in might and rapidity. McPherson arrived with two brigades to help Osterhaus, and the strengthened division was able to send a brigade across a ravine, where it passed further around Bowen's flank and assailed him with fury.

Dick felt that their own division under McClernand was also making progress. Although many men were falling they pressed slowly forward, and Grant brought up help for them too. For a long time the struggle was carried on. It was one of the little battles of the war, but its results were important and few were fought with more courage and resolution. Bowen, with only eight thousand against twenty thousand, held fast throughout all the long hot hours of the afternoon. Grant, owing to the nature of the field, was unable to get all his numbers into battle at once.

But when the twilight began to show Dick believed that victory was at hand. They had not yet driven Bowen out, but they were pressing him so close and hard, and Grant was securing so many new positions of advantage, that the Southern leader could not make another such fight against superior numbers in the morning.

Twilight turned into night and Bowen and his men, who had shown so much heroism, retreated in the dark, leaving six guns and many prisoners as trophies of the victors.

It was night when the battle ceased. Cannon and rifles flashed at fitful intervals, warning skirmishers to keep away, but after a while they too ceased and the Union army, exhausted by the long march of the night before and the battle of the day, threw itself panting upon the ground. The officers posted the sentinels in triple force, but let the remainder of the men rest.

As Dick lay down in the long grass two or three bullets dropped from his clothes and he became conscious, too, that a bullet had grazed his shoulder. But these trifles did not disturb him. It was so sweet to rest! Nothing could be more heavenly than merely to lie there in the long, soft grass and gaze up at the luminous sky, into which the stars now stole to twinkle down at him peacefully.

"Don't go to sleep, Dick," said a voice near him. "I admit the temptation is strong. I feel it myself, but General Grant may have to send you and me forward to-night to win another battle."

"George, I'm glad to hear your preachy voice over there. Hurt any?"

"No. A million cannon balls brushed my right cheek and another million brushed my left cheek, but they didn't touch me. They scared me to death, but in the last few minutes I've begun to come back to life. In a quarter of an hour I'll be just as much alive as I ever was."

"Do you know anything of Pennington?"

"Yes. The rascal is lying about six feet beyond me, sound asleep. In spite of all I could do he wouldn't stay awake. I've punched him all over to see if he was wounded, but as he didn't groan at a single punch, he's all right."

"That being the case, I'm going to follow Pennington's example. You may lecture me as much as you please, George, but you'll lecture only the night, because I'll be far away from here in a land of sweet dreams."

"All right, if you're going to do it, I will too. You'll hear my snore before I hear yours."

Both sank in a few minutes into a deep slumber, and when they awoke the next morning they found that Bowen had abandoned Port Gibson and had retreated into Grand Gulf again. There was great elation among the lads and Dick began to feel that the position of the Union army in the far South was strengthened immeasurably. He heard that Sherman, who had stood so staunchly at Shiloh, was on his way to join Grant. Their united forces would press the siege of Grand Gulf and would also turn to strike at any foe who might approach from the rear.

Never since the war began had Dick felt so elated as he did that morning. When he saw the short, thick-set figure of Grant riding by he believed that the Union, in the West at least, had found its man at last.

CHAPTER IV

DICK'S MISSION

The night came down warm and heavy. Spring was far advanced in that Southern region, and foliage and grass were already rich and heavy. Dick, from his dozing position beside a camp fire, saw a great mass of tall grass and green bushes beyond which lay the deep waters of a still creek or bayou. The air, although thick and close, conduced to rest and the peace that reigned after the battle was soothing to his soul.

His friends, the two lads, who were knitted to him by so many hardships and dangers shared, were sound asleep, and he could see their tanned faces when the light of the flickering fires fell upon them. Good old Warner! Good old Pennington! The comradeship of war knitted youth together with ties that never could be broken.

He moved into an easier position. He lay upon the soft turf and he had doubled his blanket under his head as a pillow. At first the droning noises of camp or preparation had come from afar, but soon they ceased and now the frogs down by the sluggish waters began to croak.

It was a musical sound, one that he had heard often in his native state, and, singularly enough, the lad drew encouragement from it. "Be of good cheer! Be of good cheer! Trust in the future! Trust in the future!" said all those voices down among the swamps and reeds. And then Dick said to himself: "I will trust and I will have hope!" He remembered his last glimpse of Grant's short, strong figure and the confidence that this man inspired in him. He, with tens of thousands of others, Abraham Lincoln at their head, had been looking for a man, they had looked long and in vain for such a man, but Dick was beginning to believe that they had found him at last.

It would take much of a man to stand before the genius of Lee, but it might be Grant. Dick's faith in the star of his country, shattered so often for the moment, began to rise that night and never sank again.

He fell asleep to the homely music of the frogs among the reeds, and slept without stir until nearly dawn.

Just as the first strip of gray showed in the east Colonel Winchester walked toward the spot where Dick and his comrades lay. The colonel had not slept that night. His fine face was worn and thin, but the blue eyes were alight with strength and energy. He had just left a conference of high officers, and he came upon a mission. He reached the three lads, and looked down at them with a sort of pity. He knew that it was his duty to awake them at once and send them upon a perilous errand, but they were so young, and they had already been through so much that he hesitated.

He put his hand upon Dick's shoulder and shook him. But it took more than one shake to awaken the lad, and it was fully a minute before he opened his eyes and sat up. Dick conscious but partly and rubbing his sleepy eyes, asked:

"What is it? Are we to go into battle again? Yes, sir! Yes, sir! I'm ready!"

"Not that, Dick, but I've orders for you."

Dick now awoke completely and saw that it was Colonel Winchester. He sprang to his feet and saluted.

"We'll wake up Warner and Pennington next," said the colonel, "because they go also on the kind of duty to which you're assigned."

"I'm glad of that," said Dick warmly.

Warner and Pennington were aroused with difficulty, but, as soon as they realized that Colonel Winchester was before them and that they were selected for a grave duty, they became at once keen and alert.

"Lads," said the colonel briefly, "you've all felt that we're now led by a great commander. But energy and daring on the part of a leader demand energy and daring on the part of his men. General Grant is about to undertake a great enterprise, one that demands the concentration of his troops. I want you, Warner, to go to General Sherman with this dispatch, and here is one for you, Pennington, to take to General Banks."

He paused a moment and Dick asked:

"Am I to be left out?"

Colonel Winchester smiled.

He liked this eagerness on the part of his boys, and yet there was sadness in his smile, too. Young lieutenants who rode forth on errands often failed to come back.

"You're included, Dick," he said, "and I think that yours is the most perilous mission of them all. Pennington, you and Warner can be making ready and I'll tell Dick what he's to do."

The Vermonter and the Nebraskan hurried away and Colonel Winchester, taking Dick by the arm, walked with him beyond the circle of firelight.

"Dick," he said gently, "they asked me to choose the one in my command whom I thought most fit for this duty to be done, and I've selected you, although I'm sending you into a great peril."

Dick flushed with pride at the trust. Youth blinded him at present to its perils.

"Thank you, sir," he said simply.

"You will recall Major Hertford, who was with us in Kentucky before the Shiloh days?"

"I could not forget him, sir. One of our most gallant officers."

"You speak truly. He is one of our bravest, and also one of our ablest. I speak of him as Major Hertford, but he has lately been promoted to the rank of colonel, and he is operating toward the East with a large body of cavalry, partly in conjunction with Grierson, who saved us at the ford."

"And you want me to reach him, sir!"

"You've divined it. He is near Jackson, the capital of this state, and, incidentally, you're to discover as much as you can about Jackson and the Confederate dispositions in that direction. We wish Hertford to join General Grant's advance, which will presently move toward Jackson, and we rely upon you to find him."

"I'll do it, if he's to be found at all," said Dick fervently.

"I knew it, but, Dick, you're to go in your uniform. I'll not have you executed as a spy in case you're taken. Nor are you to carry any written message to Colonel Hertford. He knows you well, and he'll accept your word at once as truth. Now, this is a ride that will call for woodcraft as well as soldiership."

"I start at once, do I not, sir?"

"You do. Warner and Pennington are ready now, and your own horse is waiting for you. Here is a small map which I have reason to believe is accurate, at least fairly so, although few of our men know much of this country. But use it, lad, as best you can."

It was a sheet of thick fibrous paper about six inches square and, after a hasty glance at it, Dick folded it up carefully and put it in his pocket. Warner and Pennington appeared then, mounted and armed and ready to tell him good-bye. He and Colonel Winchester watched them a moment or two as they rode away, and then an orderly appeared with Dick's own horse, a fine bay, saddled, bridled, saddlebags filled with food, pistols in holsters, and a breech-loading rifle strapped to the saddle.

"I've made your equipment the best I could," said Colonel Winchester, "and after you start, lad, you must use your own judgment."

He wrung the hand of the boy, for whom his affection was genuine and deep, and Dick sprang into the saddle.

"Good-bye, colonel," he said, "I thank you for this trust, and I won't fail."

It was not a boast. It was courage speaking from the heart of youth and, as Dick rode out of the camp on his good horse, he considered himself equal to any task. He felt an enormous pride because he was chosen for such an important and perilous mission, and he summoned every faculty to meet its hardships and dangers.

He had the password, and the sentinels wished him good luck. So did the men who were gathering firewood. One, a small, weazened fellow, gave him an envious look.

"Wish I was going riding with you," he said. "It's fine in the woods now."

Dick laughed through sheer exuberance of spirits.

"Maybe it is and maybe it isn't," he said. "Perhaps the forest is filled with rebel sharpshooters."

"If you ride toward Jackson you're likely to strike Confederate bands."

"I didn't say where I'm going, but you may be certain I'll keep a watch for those bands wherever I may be."

The little man was uncommonly strong nevertheless, as he carried on his shoulder a heavy log which he threw down by one of the fires, but Dick, absorbed in his journey, forgot the desire of the soldier to be riding through the forest too.

He soon left the camp behind. He looked back at it only once, and beheld the luminous glow of the campfires. Then the forest shut it out and he rode on through a region almost abandoned by its people owing to the converging armies. He did not yet look at his map, because he knew that he would soon come into the main road to Jackson. It would be sufficient to determine his course then.

Dick was not familiar with the farther South, which was a very different region from his own Kentucky. His home was a region of firm land, hills and clear streams, but here the ground lay low, the soil was soft and the waters dark and sluggish. But his instincts as a woodsman were fortified by much youthful training, and he felt that he could find the way.

It gave him now great joy to leave the army and ride away through the deep woods. He was tired of battle and the sight of wounds and death. The noises of the camp were painful to his ear, and in the forest he found peace.

He was absolutely alone in his world, and glad of it. The woods were in all the depth and richness of a Southern spring. Vast masses of green foliage billowed away to right and left. Great festoons of moss hung from the oaks, and trailing vines wrapped many of the trees almost to their tops. Wild flowers, pink, yellow and blue, unknown by name to Dick, bloomed in the open spaces.

The air of early morning was crisp with the breath of life. He had come upon a low ridge of hard ground, away from the vast current and low, sodden shores of the Mississippi. Here was a clean atmosphere, and the forest, the forest everywhere. A mockingbird, perched on a bough almost over his head, began to pour forth his liquid song, and from another far away came the same song like an echo. Dick looked up but he could not see the bird among the branches. Nevertheless he waved his hand toward the place from which the melody came and gave a little trill in reply. Then he said aloud:

"It's a happy omen that you give me. I march away to the sound of innocent music."

Then he increased his speed a little and rode without stopping until he came to the main road to Jackson. There he examined his map upon which were marked many rivers, creeks, lagoons and bayous, with extensive shaded areas meaning forests. In the southeastern corner of the map was Jackson, close to which he meant to go.

He rode on at a fair pace, keeping an extremely careful watch ahead and on either side of the road. He meant to turn aside soon into the woods, but for the present he thought himself safe in the road—it was not likely that Southern raiders would come so near to the Union camp.

His feeling of peace deepened. He was so far away now that no warlike sound could reach him. Instead the song of the mockingbird pursued him. Dick, full of youth and life, began to whistle the tune with the songster, and his horse perhaps soothed too by the rhythm broke into the gentle pace which is so easy for the rider.

It was early dawn, and the west was not yet wholly light. The east was full of gold, but the silver lingered on the opposite horizon, and the hot sun of Mississippi did not yet shed its rays over the earth. Instead, a cool breeze blew on Dick's face, and the quick blood was still leaping in his veins. The road dipped down and he came to a brook, which was clear despite its proximity to the mighty yellow trench of the Mississippi.

He let his horse drink freely, and, while he drank, he surveyed the country as well as he could. On his left he saw through a fringe of woods a field of young corn and showing dimly beyond it a small house. Unbroken forest stretched away on his right, but in field as well as forest there was no sign of a human being.

He studied his map again, noting the great number of water courses, which in the spring season were likely to be at the flood, and, for the first time, he realized the extreme difficulty of his mission. Mississippi was in the very heart of the Confederacy. He could not expect any sympathetic farmers to help him or show him the way. More likely as he advanced toward Jackson he would find the country swarming with the friends of the Confederacy, and to pass through them would demand the last resource of skill and courage. Perhaps it would have been wiser had he put on citizens clothes and taken his chances as a spy! He did not know that Colonel Winchester would have ordered the disguise had the one who rode on this most perilous mission been any other than he.

The realization brought with it extreme caution. Growing up in a country which was still mainly in forest, not differing much from its primitive condition, save for the absence of Indians and big game, he had learned to be at home in the woods, and now he turned from the path, riding among the trees.

He kept a course some distance from the road, where he was sheltered by the deep foliage and could yet see what was passing along the main artery of travel. The ground at times was spongy, making traveling hard, and twice his horse swam deep creeks. He would have turned into the road at these points but the bridges were broken down and he had no other choice.

The morning waned, and the coolness departed. The sun hung overhead, blazing hot, and the air in the forest grew dense and heavy. He would have been glad to turn back into the road, in the hope of finding a breeze in the open space, but caution still kept him in the forest. He soon saw two men in brown jeans riding mules, farmers perhaps, but carrying rifles on their shoulders, and, drawing his horse behind a big tree, he waited until they passed.

They rode on unseeing and he resumed his journey, to stop an hour later and eat cold food, while he permitted his horse to graze in an opening. He had seen only three houses, one a large colonial mansion, with the smoke rising from several chimneys, and the others small log structures inhabited by poor farmers, but nobody was at work in the fields.

When he resumed the journey he was thankful that he had kept to the woods as a body of Confederate cavalry, coming out of a path from the north, turned into the main road and advanced at a good pace toward Jackson. They seemed to be in good spirits, as he could hear them talking and laughing, but he was glad when they were out of sight as these Southerners had keen eyes and a pair of them might have discerned him in the brush.

He went deeper into the woods and made another long study of his map. It seemed to him now that he knew every hill and lagoon and road and path, and he resolved to ride a straight course through the forest. There was a point, distinctly marked north of Jackson, where he was to find Hertford if he arrived in time, or to wait for him if he got there ahead of time, and he believed that with the aid of the map he could reach it through the woods.

He rode now by the sun and he saw neither path nor fields. He was in the deep wilderness once more. The mockingbirds sang around him again and through the rifts in the leaves he saw the sailing hawks seeking their prey. Three huge owls sitting in a row on a bough slept undisturbed while he passed. He took it as an omen that the wilderness was deserted, and his confidence was strong.

But the firm ground ceased and he rode through a region of swamps. The hoofs of his horse splashed through mud and water. Now and then a snake drew away its slimy length and Dick shuddered. He could not help it. Snakes, even the harmless, always gave him shivers.

The wilderness now had an evil beauty. The vegetation was almost tropical in its luxuriance, but Dick liked better the tender green of his more northern state. Great beds of sunflowers nodded in the light breeze. Vast masses of vines and creepers pulled down the trees, and on many of the vines deep red roses were blooming. Then came areas of solemn live oaks and gloomy cypresses, where no mockingbirds were singing.

He rode for half a mile along a deep lagoon or bayou, he did not know which, and saw hawks swoop down and draw fish from its dark surface. The whole scene was ugly and cruel, and he was glad when he left it and entered the woods again. Once he thought he heard the mellow voice of a negro singing, but that was the only sound, save the flitting of small wild animals through the undergrowth.

He came, mid-afternoon, to a river, which he made his horse swim boldly and then entered forest that seemed more dense than ever. But the ground here was firmer and he was glad of a chance to rest both himself and his mount. He dismounted, tethered the horse and stretched his own limbs, weary from riding.

It was a pretty little glade, surrounded by high forest, fitted for rest and peace, but his horse reared suddenly and tried to break loose. There was a heavy crashing in the undergrowth and a deer, wild with alarm, darting within a dozen feet of Dick, disappeared in the forest, running madly.

He knew there were many deer in the Mississippi woods, but he was observant and the flight aroused his attention. His first thought that he and his horse had scared the deer could not be true, because it had come from a point directly behind and had rushed past them. Then its alarm must have been caused by some other human being near by in the forest or by a panther. His theory inclined to the human being.

Dick was troubled. The more he thought of the incident the less he liked it. He made no effort to hide from himself the dangers that surrounded him in the land of the enemy, and remounting he rode briskly forward. As the ground was firm and the forest was free enough from undergrowth to permit of speed he finally broke into a gallop which he maintained for a half-hour.

He struck marsh again and was a long time in passing through it. But when he was a half-mile on the other side he drew into a dense cluster of bushes and waited. He could not get the flight of the deer out of his mind, and knowing that it was well in the wilderness to obey premonitions he watched more closely.

Dick sat on his horse behind the bush a full five minutes, and presently he became conscious that his heart was pounding heavily. He exerted his will and called himself foolish, but in vain. The flight of the deer persisted in his mind. It was a warning that somebody else was in the woods not far behind him, and, while he waited, he saw a shadow among the trees.

It was only a shadow, but it was like the figure of a man. A single glimpse and he was gone. The stranger, whoever he was, had darted back in the undergrowth. Dick waited another five minutes, but the shadow did not reappear. He felt a measure of relief because all doubts were gone now. He was sure that he was followed, but by whom?

He knew that his danger had increased manifold. Some Southern scout or skirmisher had discovered his presence and, in such a quest, the trailer had the advantage of the trailed. Yet he did not hesitate. He knew his general direction and, shifting the pistols from the saddle-holsters to his belt he again urged his horse forward.

When they came to good ground he walked, leading his mount, as the animal was much exhausted by the effort the marshes needed. But whenever the undergrowth grew dense he stopped to look and listen. He did not see the shadow and he heard nothing save the ordinary sounds of the woods, but either instinct or imagination told him that the stranger still followed.

The sun was far down the westward slope, but it was still very hot in the woods. There was no breeze. Not a leaf, nor a blade of grass stirred. Dick heard his heart still pounding. The unseen pursuit—he had no doubt it was there—was becoming a terrible strain upon his nerves. The perspiration ran down his face, and he sought with angry eyes for a sight of the fellow who presumed to hang upon his tracks.

He began to wonder what he would do when the night came. There would be no rest, no sleep for him, even in the darkness.

Twice he curved from his course and hid in the undergrowth to see his pursuer come up, but there was nothing. Then he reasoned with himself. He had not really seen the flitting figure of a man. It was merely the effect of an alarmed imagination, and he told himself to ride straight on, looking ahead, not back. But reason again yielded to instinct and he curved once more into the deep forest, where the tangle of vines and undergrowth also was so thick that it would take a keen eye to find him.

Dick looked back along the path which he had come and he was confident that he saw some of the tall bushes shake a little. It could not be wind, because the air was absolutely still, and soon he was convinced that his instinct had been right all the time. Fancy had played him no trick and the shadow that he had seen was a human figure.

He felt with all the force of conviction that he was in great danger, but he did not know what to do. So he did nothing, but sat quietly on his horse among the bushes. The heat was intense there and innumerable flies, gnats, and mosquitoes assailed him. The mosquitoes were so fierce that they drew blood from his face a half-dozen times.

Alone in the heat of the deep marshy wilderness he felt fear more than in battle. Danger threatened here in a mysterious, invisible fashion and he could only wait.

He saw a bush move again, but much nearer, and then came the crack of a rifle. If his horse, alarmed perhaps, had not thrown up his head suddenly, and received the bullet himself the lad's career would have ended there.

The horse made a convulsive leap, then staggered for a few seconds, giving his rider time to spring clear, and fell among the bushes. Dick dropped down behind him and quickly unstrapped the rifle from the saddle, meaning to use the animal's body as a breastwork against renewed attack.

His fear, the kind of fear that the bravest feel, had been driven away by rage. The killing of his innocent horse, although the bullet was intended for him, angered him as much as if he had received a wound himself. The spirit of his ancestor, the shrewd and wary Indian fighter, descended upon him again, and, lying upon his stomach behind the horse, with the rifle ready he was anxious for the attack to come.

Dick was firmly convinced that he had but a single enemy. Otherwise he would have been attacked in force earlier, and more than one shot would have been fired. But the report of the rifle was succeeded by deep silence. The forest was absolutely still, not a breath of wind stirring. His enemy remained invisible, but the besieged youth was confident that he was lying quiet, awaiting another chance. Dick, still hot with anger, would wait too.

But other enemies were far more reckless than the hidden marksman. The swarm of gnats, flies, and mosquitoes assailed him again and he could have cried out in pain. His only consolation lay in the fact that the other man might be suffering just as much.

He was aware that his enemy might try a circling movement in order to reach him on the flank or from behind, but he believed that his ear would be keen enough to detect him if he came near. Moreover he lay in a slight dip with the body of the horse in front of him, and it would require an uncommon sharpshooter to reach him with a bullet. If he could only stand those terrible mosquitoes an hour he felt that he might get away, because then the night would be at hand.

He saw with immense relief that the sun was already very low. The heat, gathered in the woods, was at its worst, and over his head the mosquitoes buzzed and buzzed incessantly. It seemed to him a horrible sort of irony that he might presently be forced from his shelter by mosquitoes and be killed in flight to another refuge.

But he was endowed with great patience and tenacity and he clung to his shelter, relying rather upon ear than eye to note the approach of an enemy. Meanwhile the sun sank down to the rim of the wood, and the twilight thickened rapidly in the east. Then a shot was fired from the point from which the first had come. Dick heard the bullet singing over his head, but it gave him satisfaction because he was able to locate his enemy.

He sought no return fire, but lay in the dip, wary and patient. The sun sank beyond the rim, the western sky flamed blood red for a few moments, and then the Southern night swept down so suddenly that it seemed to come with violence. Dick believed that his escape was now at hand, but he still showed an infinite patience.

He did not stir from his place until the night was almost black, and then, carrying his weapons and the saddlebag of provisions, he crept among the thickets.

When he stood up he found himself stiff from lying long in a cramped position. His face burned from the bites of the mosquitoes, which still hung in swarms about him, and he felt dizzy.

But Dick remembered his mission, and his resolve to perform it was not shaken a particle. He had lost his horse, but he could walk. Perhaps his chance of success would be greater on foot in such a dangerous country.

He advanced now with extreme caution, feeling the way carefully and testing the ground before he put his foot down solidly. Still trusting to his ears he stopped now and then, and listened for some sound from his enemy in pursuit. But nothing came, and soon he became quite sure that he had shaken him off. He was merely a dot in the wilderness in the dark, and, feeling secure now, he pressed forward with more speed.

He was hoping to get to a piece of firm, high ground, where he might secure a measure of protection from those terrible mosquitoes which still buzzed angrily about his head. In an hour chance favored him, as he reached a low ridge much rockier than usual in that region. He would have built a little smudge fire to protect himself from the mosquitoes, but it would be sure to draw the lurking sharpshooter, and instead he found a nook in the ridge, under the low boughs of a great oak. Then he took a light blanket which he carried tied to his saddlebags, and wrapped it around his neck and face, covering everything but his mouth and eyes.

He sank into the nook with his back against the turf, and the reclining position was wonderfully easy. The mosquitoes, apparently finding the points of exposure too small, left him alone and went away. His face still burned from numerous stings, but he forgot it in present comfort. There was food in the saddlebags, and he ate enough for his needs. Then he laid the saddlebags beside him and the rifle across his knees and stared out into the darkness.

He felt a great relief after his extreme danger and long exertions. It was both physical and mental, and sitting there alone in a sunken wilderness he was nevertheless happy. Believing that the mosquitoes would not come back, he wrapped the blanket about his whole body by and by, and pulled his cap down over his eyes.

Dick had no plans for the night. He did not know whether he intended to remain there long or not, but nature settled doubts for him. His head drooped, and soon he slept as easily and peacefully as if he had been at home at Pendleton in his own bed.

Then the wilderness blotted him out for the time. The little wild animals scurried through the grass or ran up trees. In the far distance an owl hooted solemnly at nothing, and he slept the mighty sleep of exhaustion.

CHAPTER V

HUNTED

Dick slept the whole night through, which was a very good thing for him, because he needed it, and because he could have made no progress in the thick darkness through the marshy wilderness. No human beings saw him, but the wild animals took more than one look. Not all were little. One big clumsy brute, wagging his head in a curious, comic way, shuffled up from the edge of the swamp, sniffed the strange human odor, and, still wagging his comic head, came rather close to the sleeping boy. Then the black bear decided to be afraid, and lumbered back into the bushes.

An owl perched on a bough almost over Dick's head, but this was game far too large for Mr. Owl's beak and talons, and he soon flew away in search of something nearer his size. A raccoon on a bough stared with glowing eyes and then slid out of sight.

Man, although he had just come, became king of this swamp, king for the night. The prowling beasts and birds of prey, after their first look, gave Dick all the berth he needed, and he did not awake until a bright sun was well above the edge of the earth. Then he rose, shook himself, much like an animal coming from its lair, and bathed his face in a little stream which ran down the hill into the swamp. It was swollen and painful from the mosquito bites, but he resolved not to think of them, and ate breakfast from the saddlebags, after which he studied his map a little.

Baggage and rifle on shoulder, he pursued a course south by east. There was a strong breeze which gave him a rest from the dreaded insects, and he pushed on with vigorous footsteps. The country remained thoroughly wild, and he soon had proof of it. Another deer, this time obviously started up by himself, sprang from the canebrake and darted away in the woods. He noted tracks of bear and resolved some day when the war was over to come there hunting.

His course led him again from firm ground into a region of marshes and lagoons, which he crossed with difficulty, arriving about an hour before noon at a considerable river, one that would require swimming unless he found a ford somewhere near. He was very weary from the journey through the marsh and, sitting on a log, he scraped from his clothes a portion of the mud they had accumulated on the way.

He was a good swimmer, but he had his arms and

ammunition to keep dry, and he did not wish to trust himself afloat on the deep current. Wading would be far better, and, when his strength was restored, he walked up the bank in search of a shallower place.

He came soon to a point, where the cliff was rather high, although it was clothed in dense forest here as elsewhere, and when he reached the crest he heard a sound like the swishing of waters. Alert and suspicious he sank down among the trees and peered over the bank. Two men in a canoe were paddling in a leisurely manner along the stream.

The men were in faded and worn Confederate uniforms, and Dick saw their rifles lying in the bottom of the boat. He also saw that they had strong, resolute faces. They were almost opposite him and they were closely scanning the forest on his side of the river. He was glad that he had not tried to swim the stream, and he was glad too that he had kept so well under cover. The men in the canoe were surely keen of eye, and they must be a patrol.

He sank closer to the earth and did not stir. One of the watchers drew in his paddle and took up his rifle, while the other propelled the canoe very slowly. It seemed that they expected something or somebody, and it suddenly occurred to him that it might be he. He felt a little shiver of apprehension. How could they know he was coming? It was mysterious and alarming.

He waited for them to pass down the river and out of sight, but at the curve they turned and came back against the stream, the man with the rifle in his hand still keenly watching the western shore, where Dick lay hidden. Neither of them spoke, and the only sound was the swishing of the paddle. The hoot of an owl came from the depths of the forest behind him and he knew that it was a signal. The hair of his head lifted.

He felt the touch of the supernatural. The invisible pursuer was behind him again, and the silent soldiers held the crossing. The hoot of the owl came again, a little nearer now. He was tempted to rise and run, but his will held him back from such folly. His unknown enemy could pursue, because his boots left a deep trail in the soft earth. That was why he had been able to follow again in the morning.

He crept back some distance from the river and then, rising, retreated cautiously up the stream. He caught glimpses of the water twice through the bushes, and each time the canoe was moving up the river also, one man paddling and the other, rifle on his arm, watching the western shore.

Dick had a feeling that he was trapped. Colonel Winchester had been wise to make him wear his uniform, because it was now certain that he was going to be taken, and death had always been the punishment of a captured spy. He put down the thought resolutely, and began to run through the forest parallel with the river. If it were only the firm hard ground of the North he could hide his trail from the man behind him, but here the soil was so soft that every footstep left a deep mark. Yet he might find fallen trees thrown down by hurricanes, and in a few minutes he came to a mass of them. He ran deftly from trunk to trunk, and then continued his flight among the bushes. It broke his trail less than a rod, but it might take his pursuer ten minutes to recover it, and now ten minutes were precious.

The soil grew harder and he made better speed, but when he looked through the foliage he saw the canoe still opposite him. It was easy for them, on the smooth surface of the river, to keep pace with him, if such was their object. Furious anger took hold of him. He knew that he must soon become exhausted, while the men in the canoe would scarcely feel weariness. Then came the idea.

The canoe was light and thin almost like the birch bark Indian canoe of the north, and he was a good marksman. It was a last chance, but raising his rifle he fired the heavy bullet directly at the bottom of the canoe. As the echo of the first shot was dying he slipped in a cartridge and sent a second at the same target. He did not seek to kill the men, his object was the canoe, and as he ran rapidly away he saw it fill with water and sink, the two soldiers in the stream swimming toward the western shore.

Dick laughed to himself. He had won a triumph, although he did not yet know that it would amount to anything. At any rate the men could no longer glide up and down the river at their leisure looking for him to come forth from the forest.

He knew that the shots would bring the single pursuer at full speed, and, as he had saved some ounces of strength, he now ran at his utmost speed. The river curved again and just beyond the curve it seemed shallow to him. He plunged in at once, and waded rapidly, holding his rifle, pistols and saddlebags above his head. He was in dread lest he receive a bullet in his back, but he made the farther shore, ran into the dense undergrowth and sank down dripping and panting.

He had made the crossing but he did not forget to be ready. He rapidly reloaded his rifle, and fastened the pistols at his belt. Then he looked through the bushes at the river. The two canoemen, water running from them in streams, were on the other bank, though a little farther down the stream. He believed that they were no longer silent. He fondly imagined that they were cursing hard, if not loud.

His relief was so great that, forgetting his own bedraggled condition, he laughed. Then he looked again to see what they were going to do. A small man, his face shaded by the broad brim of a hat, emerged from the woods and joined them. Dick was too far away to see his face, even had it been uncovered, but his figure looked familiar. Nevertheless, although he tried hard, he could not recall where he had seen him before. But, as he carried a long-barreled rifle, Dick was sure that this was his unknown pursuer. There had certainly been collusion also between him and the men in the boat, as the three began to talk earnestly, and to point toward the woods on the other side.

Dick felt that he had avenged himself upon the boatmen, but his rage rose high against the little man under the broad-brimmed hat. It was he who had followed him so long, and who had tried ruthlessly to kill him. The lad's rifle was of the most improved make and a bullet would reach. He was tempted to try it, but prudence came to his rescue. Still lying close he watched them. He felt sure that they would soon be hunting for his footprints, but he resolved to stay in his covert, until they began the crossing of the river, to which his trail would lead when they found it.

He saw them cease talking and begin searching among the woods. It might be at least a half-hour before they found the trail and his strength would be restored fully then. His sinking of the canoe had been in reality a triumph, and so he remained at ease, watching the ford.

He was quite sure that when his trail was found the little man would be the one to find it, and sure enough at the end of a half-hour the weazened figure led down to the ford. Dick might have shot one of them in the water, but he had no desire to take life. It would serve no purpose, and, refreshed and strengthened, he set out through the forest toward Jackson.

He came to a brook soon, and, remembering the old device of Indian times, he waded in it at least a half-mile. When he left it he passed through a stretch of wood, crossed an old cotton field and entered the woods again. Then he sat down and ate from his store, feeling that he had shaken off his pursuers. Another examination of his map followed. He had kept fixed in his mind the point at which he was to find Hertford, and, being a good judge of direction, he felt sure that he could yet reach it.

The sun, now high and warm, had dried his clothing, and, after the food, he was ready for another long march. He struck into a path and walked along it, coming soon to a house which stood back a little distance from a road into which the path merged. A man and two women standing on the porch stared at him curiously, but he pretended to take no notice. After long exposure to weather, blue uniforms did not differ much from gray, and his own was now covered with mud. He could readily pass as a soldier of the Confederacy unless they chose to ask too many questions.

"From General Pemberton's army?" called the man, when he was opposite the house.

Dick nodded and stepped a little faster.

"Won't you stop for a bite and fresh water with friends of the cause?"

"Thanks, but important dispatches. Must hurry." They repeated the invitation. He shook his head, and went on. He did not look back, but he was sure that they stared at him as long as he was in sight. Then, for safety's sake, he left the road and entered the wood once more.

He had now come to country comparatively free from swamp and marsh, and pursued his way through a great forest, beautiful with live oaks and magnolias. In the afternoon he took a long rest by the side of a clear spring, where he drew further upon the store of food in his saddlebags, which he calculated held enough for another day. After that he would have to forage upon the country.

He would sleep the second night in the forest, his blanket being sufficient protection, unless rain came, which he would have to endure as best he could. Another look at his map and he believed that on the following afternoon he could reach Hertford.

He took the remaining food from his saddlebags, wrapped it in his blanket, and strapped the pack on his back. Then, in order to lighten his burden, he hung the saddlebags on the bough of a tree and abandoned them, after which he pressed forward through the woods with renewed speed.

He came at times to the edge of the forest and saw houses in the fields, but he always turned back among the trees. He could find only enemies here, and he knew that it was his plan to avoid all human beings. Precept and example are of great power and he recalled again much that he had heard of his famous ancestor, Paul Cotter. He had been compelled to fight often for his life and again to flee for it from an enemy who reserved torture and death for the captured. Dick felt that he must do as well, and the feeling increased his vigor and courage.

A little later he heard a note, low, faint and musical. It was behind him, but he was sure at first that it was made by negroes singing. It was a pleasing sound. The negro had a great capacity for happiness, and Dick as a young lad had played with and liked the young colored lads of his age.

But as he walked on he heard the low, musical note once more and, as before, directly behind him. It seemed a little nearer. He paused and listened. It came again, always nearer and nearer, and now it did not seem as musical as before. There was a sinister thread in that flowing note, and suddenly Dick remembered.

He was a daring horseman and with his uncle and cousin and others at Pendleton he had often ridden after the fox. It was the note of the hounds, but of bloodhounds, and this time they were following him. From the first he had not the slightest doubt of it. Somebody, some traitor in the Union camp, knew the nature of his errand, and was hanging on to the pursuit like death.

Dick knew it was the little man whom he had seen by the river, and perhaps the canoemen were with him—he would certainly have comrades, or his own danger would be too great—and they had probably obtained the bloodhounds at a farmhouse. Nearly everybody in Mississippi kept hounds.

The long whining note came again and much nearer. Now all music was gone from it for Dick. It was ferocious, like the howl of the wolf seeking prey, and he could not restrain a shudder. His danger had returned with twofold force, because the hounds would unerringly lead his pursuers through the forest as fast as they could follow.

He did not yet despair. A new resolution was drawn from the depths of his courage. He did not forget that he was a good marksman and he had both rifle and pistols. He tried to calculate from that whining, ferocious note how many hounds were pursuing, and he believed they were not many. Now he prepared for battle, and, as he ran, he kept his eye on the ground in order that he might choose his own field.

He saw it presently, a mass of fallen timber thrown together by a great storm, and he took his place on the highest log, out of reach of a leaping hound. Then, lying almost flat on the log and with his rifle ready, he waited, his heart beating hard with anger that he should be pursued thus like an animal.

The howling of the hounds grew more ferocious, and it was tinged with joy. The trail had suddenly grown very hot, and they knew that the quarry was just before them. Dick caught a good view of a long, lean, racing figure bounding among the trees, and he fired straight at a spot between the blazing eyes. The hound fell without a sound, and with equal ease he slew the second. The third and last drew back, although the lad heard the distant halloo of men seeking to drive him on.

Dick sprang from his log and ran through the forest again. He knew that the lone hound after his first recoil would follow, but he had his reloaded rifle and he had proved that he knew how to shoot. It would please him for the hound to come within range.

When he took to renewed flight the hound again whined ferociously and Dick glanced back now and then seeking a shot. Once he caught a glimpse of two or three dusky figures some distance behind the hound, urging him on, and his heart throbbed with increased rage. If they presented an equal target he would fire at them rather than the hound.

He could run no longer, and his gait sank to a walk. His very exhaustion brought him his opportunity, as the animal came rapidly within range, and Dick finished him with a single lucky shot. Then, making an extreme effort, he fled on a long time, and, while he was fleeing, he saw the sun set and the night come.

The strain upon him had been so great that his nerves and brain were unsteady. Although the forest was black with night he saw it through a blood-red mist. Something in him was about to burst, and when he saw a human figure rising up before him it broke and he fell.

Dick was unconscious a long time. But when he awoke he found himself wrapped in a blanket, while another was doubled under his head. It was pitchy dark, but he beheld the outline of a human figure, sitting by his side. He strove to rise, but a powerful hand on his shoulder pushed him back, though gently, and a low voice said:

"Stay still, Mr. Mason. We mustn't make any sound now!"

Dick recognized in dim wonder the voice of Sergeant Daniel Whitley. How he had come there at such a time, and what he was doing now was past all guessing, but Sergeant Whitley was a most competent man. He knew more than most generals, and he was filled with the lore of the woods. He would trust him. He let his head sink back on the folded blanket, and his heavy eyes closed again.

When Dick roused from his stupor the sergeant was still by his side, and, as his eyes grew used to the darkness, he noticed that Whitley was really kneeling rather than sitting, crouched to meet danger, his finger on the trigger of a rifle. Dick's brain cleared and he sat up.

"What is it, Sergeant?" he whispered.

"I see you're all right now, Mr. Mason," the sergeant whispered back, "but be sure you don't stir."

"Is it the Johnnies?"

"Lean over a little and look down into that dip."

Dick did so, and saw four men hunting among the trees, and the one who seemed to be their leader was the little weazened fellow, with the great, flap-brimmed hat.

"They're looking for your trail," whispered the sergeant, "but they won't find it. It's too dark, even for a Sioux Indian, and I've seen them do some wonderful things in trailing."

"I seem to have met you in time, Sergeant."

"So you did, sir, but more of that later. Perhaps you'd better lie down again, as you're weak yet. I'll tell you all they do."

"I'll take your advice, Sergeant, but am I sound and whole? I felt something in me break, and then the earth rose up and hit me in the face."

"I reckon it was just the last ounce of breath going out of you with a pop. They're hunting hard, Mr. Mason, but they can't pick up the trace of a footstep. Slade must be mad clean through."

"Slade! Slade! Who's Slade?"

"Slade is a spy partly, and an outlaw mostly, 'cause he often works on his own hook. He's the weazened little fellow with so much hat-brim, and he's about twenty different kinds of a demon. You've plenty of reason to fear him, and it's lucky we've met."

"It's more than luck for me, Sergeant. It's salvation. I believe it wouldn't have been half as hard on me if somebody had been with me, and you're the first whom I would have chosen. Are they still in the dip, Sergeant?"

"No, they've passed to the slope on the right, and I think they'll go over the hill. We're safe here so long as we remain quiet; that is, safe for the time. Slade will hang on as long as there's a possible chance to find us."

"Sergeant, if they do happen to stumble upon us in the dark I hope you'll promise to do one thing for me."

"I'll do anything I can, Mr. Mason."

"Kill Slade first. That little villain gives me the horrors. I believe the soul of the last bloodhound I shot has been reincarnated in him."

"All right, Mr. Mason," returned the sergeant, placidly, "if we have to fight I'll make sure of Slade at once. Is there anybody else you'd like specially to have killed?"

"No thank you, Sergeant. I don't hate any of the others, and I suppose they'd have dropped the chase long ago if it hadn't been for this fellow whom you call Slade. Now, I think I'll lie quiet, while you watch."

"Very good, sir. I'll tell you everything I can see. They're passing over the hill out of sight, and if they return I won't fail to let you know."

Sergeant Whitley, a man of vast physical powers, hardened by the long service of forest and plain, was not weary at all, and, in the dusk, he looked down with sympathy and pity at the lad who had closed his eyes. He divined the nature of the ordeal through which he had gone. Dick's face, still badly swollen from the bites of the mosquitoes, showed all the signs of utter exhaustion. The sergeant could see, despite the darkness, that it was almost the face of the dead, and he knew that happy chance had brought him in the moment of Dick's greatest need.

He ceased to whisper, because Dick, without intending it, had gone to sleep again. Then the wary veteran scouted in a circle about their refuge, but did not discover the presence of an enemy.

He sat down near the sleeping lad, with his rifle between his knees, and watched the moon come out. Owing to his wilderness experience he had been chosen also to go on a scout toward Jackson, though he preferred to make his on foot, and the sound of Dick's shots at the hounds had drawn him to an observation which finally turned into a rescue.

After midnight the sergeant slept a little while, but he never awakened Dick until it was almost morning. Then he told him that he would go with him on the mission to Hertford, and Dick was very glad.

"What's become of Slade and his men?" asked Dick.

"I don't know," replied the sergeant, "but as they lost the trail in the night, it's pretty likely they're far from here. At any rate they're not bothering us just now. How're you feeling, Mr. Mason?"

"Fine, except that my face still burns."

"We'll have to hold up a Confederate house somewhere and get oil of pennyroyal. That'll cure you, but I guess you've learned now, Mr. Mason, that mosquitoes in a southern swamp are just about as deadly as bullets."

"So they are, Sergeant, and this is not my first experience. Luck has been terribly against me this trip, but it turned when I met you last night."

"Yes, Mr. Mason. In this case two rifles are better than one. We're prowling right through the heart of the Confederacy, but I'm thinking we'll make it. We've got a great general now, and we mustn't fail to bring up Colonel Hertford and his cavalry. I've an idea in my head that General Grant is going to carry through big plans."

"Then I think it's time we were starting."

"So do I, Mr. Mason, and now will you take these crackers and smoked ham? I've plenty in my knapsack. I learned on the plains never to travel without a food supply. If a soldier starves to death what use is he to his army? And I reckon you need something to eat. You were about tired out when I met you last night."

"I surely was, Sergeant, but I'm a new man this morning. You and I together can't fail."

Dick, in truth, felt an enormous relief. He and his young comrades had learned to trust Sergeant Whitley implicitly, with his experience of forest and plain and his infinite resource.

"Where do you figure we are, Sergeant?" he asked.

"In the deep woods, Mr. Mason, but we haven't turned much from the line leading you to the place where you were to meet Colonel Hertford. You haven't really lost time, and we'll start again straight ahead, but we've got to look out for this fellow Slade, who's as tricky and merciless as they ever make 'em."

"Tell me more about Slade, Sergeant."

"I don't know a lot, but I heard of him from some of our scouts. He was an overseer of a big plantation before the war. From somewhere up North, I think, but now he's more of a rebel than the rebels themselves. Often happens that way. But you've got to reckon with him."

"Glad I know that much. He reminds me of a man I've seen, though I can't recall where or when. It's enough, though, to watch out for Slade. Come on, Sergeant, I'm feeling so fine now that with your help I'm able to fight a whole army."

The two striding through the forest, started toward the meeting place with Hertford. Now that he had the powerful comradeship of Sergeant Whitley, the wilderness became beautiful instead of gloomy for Dick. The live oaks and magnolias were magnificent, and there was a wild luxuriance of vegetation. Birds of brilliant plumage darted among the foliage, and squirrels chattered on the boughs. He saw bear tracks again, and called the sergeant's attention to them.

"It would be nice to be hunting them, instead of men," said Whitley. "You can find nice, black fellows down here, good to eat, and it's a deal safer to hunt them than it is the grizzlies and silver-tips of the Rockies."

They saw now much cleared land, mostly cotton fields, and now and then a white man or a negro working, but there was always enough forest for cover. They waded the numerous brooks and creeks, allowing their clothing to dry in the warm sun, as they marched, and about two hours before sunrise the sergeant, wary and always suspicious, suggested that they stop a while.

"I've an idea," he said, "that Slade and his men are still following us. Oh, he's an ugly fellow, full of sin, and if they're not far behind us we ought to know it."

"Just as you say," said Dick, glad enough to shift the

responsibility upon such capable shoulders. "How would this clump of bushes serve for a hiding place while we wait?"

"Good enough. Indians pursued, often ambush the pursuer, and as we've two good men with two good rifles, Mr. Mason, we'll just see what this Slade is about."

"When I last saw him," said Dick, "he had the two canoemen with him, and perhaps they've picked up the owner of the hounds."

"That's sure, and they're likely to be four. We're only two, but we've got the advantage of the ambush, and that's a big one. If you agree with me, Mr. Mason, we'll wait here for 'em. We were sent out to take messages, not to fight, but since these fellows hang on our trail we may get to Colonel Hertford all the quicker because we do fight."

"Your opinion's mine too, Sergeant. I'm not in love with battle, but I wouldn't mind taking a shot or two at these men. They've given me a lot of trouble."

The sergeant smiled.

"That's the way it goes," he said. "You don't get mad at anybody in particular in a big battle, but if two or three fellows lay around in the woods popping away at you you soon get so you lose any objections to killing, and you draw a bead on 'em as soon as a chance comes."

"That's the way I feel, Sergeant. It isn't Christian, but I suppose it has some sort of excuse."

"Of course it has. Drop a little lower, Mr. Mason. I see the bushes out there shaking."

"And that's the sign that Slade and his men have come. Well, I'm not sorry."

Both Dick and the sergeant lay almost flat with their heads raised a little, and their rifles pushed forward. The bushes ceased to shake, but Dick had no doubt their pursuers were before them. They had probably divined, too, that the quarry was at bay and was dangerous. Evidently the sergeant had been correct when he said Slade was full of craft and cunning.

While they waited the spirit of Dick's famous ancestor descended upon him in a yet greater measure. Their pursuers were not Indians, but this was the deep wilderness and they were merely on a skirt of the great war. Many of the border conditions were reproduced, and they were to fight as borderers fought.

"What do you think they're doing?" Dick whispered.

"Feeling around for us. Slade won't take any more risk than he has to. Did you see those two birds fly away from that bough, sudden-like? I think one of the men has just crept under it. But the fellow who exposes himself first won't be Slade."

Dick's inherited instinct was strong, and he watched not only in front, but to right and left also. He knew that cunning men would seek to flank and surprise them, and he noticed that the sergeant also watched in a wide circle. He still drew tremendous comfort from the presence of the skillful veteran, feeling that his aid would make the repulse of Slade a certainty.

A rifle cracked suddenly in the bushes to their right, and then another by his side cracked so suddenly that only a second came between. Dick heard a bullet whistle over their heads, but he believed that the one from his comrade's rifle had struck true.

"I've no way of telling just now," said the sergeant, calmly, "but I don't believe that fellow will bother any more. If we can wing another they're likely to let us alone and we can go on. They must know by the trail that we're now two instead of one, and that their danger has doubled."

Dick had felt that the danger to their pursuers had more than doubled. He had an immense admiration for the sergeant, who was surely showing himself a host. The man, trained so long in border war, was thoroughly in his element. His thick, powerful figure was drawn up in the fashion of a panther about to spring. Bulky as he was he showed ease and grace, and wary eyes, capable of reading every sign, continually scanned the thickets.

"They know just where we are, of course," whispered the sergeant, "but if we stay close they'll never get a good shot at us."

Dick caught sight of a head among some bushes and fired. The head dropped back so quickly that he could not tell whether or not his bullet sped true. After a long wait the sergeant suggested that they creep away.

"I think they've had enough," he said. "They've certainly lost one man, and maybe two. Slade won't care to risk much more."

Dick was glad to go and, following the sergeant's lead, he crawled four or five hundred yards, a most painful but necessary operation. Then they stood up, and made good time through the forest. Both would have been willing to stay and fight it out with Slade and what force he had left, but their mission was calling them, and forward they went.

"Do you think they'll follow us?" asked Dick.

"I reckon they've had enough. They may try to curve ahead of us and give warning, but the salute from the muzzles of our rifles has been too warm for any more direct pursuit. Besides, we're going to have a summer storm soon, and like as not they'll be hunting shelter."

Dick, in the excitement of battle and flight, had not noticed the darkening skies and the rising wind. Clouds, heavy and menacing, already shrouded the whole west. Low thunder was heard far in the distance.

"It's going to be a whopper," said the sergeant, "something like those big storms they have out on the plains. We must find shelter somewhere, Mr. Mason, or it will leave us so bedraggled and worn out that for a long time we won't be able to move on."

Dick agreed with him entirely, but neither yet knew where the shelter was to be found. They hurried on, looking hopefully for a place. Meanwhile the storm, its van a continual blaze of lightning and roar of thunder, rolled up fast from the southwest. Then the lightning ceased for a while and the skies were almost dark. Dick knew that the rain would come soon, and, as he looked eagerly for shelter, he saw a clearing in which stood a small building of logs.

"A cornfield, Sergeant," he exclaimed, "and that I take it is a crib."

"A crib that will soon house more than corn," said the sergeant. "Two good Union soldiers are about to stop there. It's likely the farmer's house itself is just beyond that line of trees, but he won't be coming out to this crib to-night."

"Not likely. Too much darkness and rain. Hurry, Sergeant, I can hear already the rush of the rain in the forest."

They ran across the field, burst open the door of the crib, leaped in and banged the door shut again, just as the van of the rain beat upon it with an angry rush.

Save for a crack or two they had no light, but they stood upon a dry floor covered deep with corn shucks, and heard the rain sweep and roar upon the roof. On one side was a heap of husked corn which they quickly piled against the door in order to hold it before the assaults of the wind, and then they sought warm places among the shucks.

It was a small crib, and the rain drove in at the cracks, but it furnished abundant shelter for its two new guests. Dick had never been in a finer hotel. He lay warm and dry in a great heap of shucks, and heard the wind and rain beat vainly upon walls and roof and the thunder rumble as it moved off toward the east. He felt to the full the power of contrast.

"Fine in here, isn't it, Sergeant?" he said.

"Fine as silk," replied the sergeant from his own heap of shucks. "We played in big luck to find this place, 'cause I think it's going to rain hard all night."

"Let it. It can't get me. Sergeant, I've always known that corn is our chief staple, but I never knew before that the shucks, which so neatly enclose the grains and cob, were such articles of luxury. I'm lying upon the most magnificent bed in the United States, and it's composed wholly of shucks."

"It's no finer than mine, Mr. Mason."

"That's so. Yours is just like mine, and, of course, it's an exception. Now, I wish to say, Sergeant, the rain upon the roof is so soothing that I'm likely to go to sleep before I know it."

"Go ahead, Mr. Mason, and it's more'n likely I'll follow. All trails will be destroyed by the storm and nobody will think of looking here for us to-night."

Both soon slept soundly, and all through the night the rain beat upon the roof.

CHAPTER VI

A BOLD ATTACK

Dick was the first to awake. The sergeant had not slept the night before at all, and, despite his enormous endurance, he was overpowered. Having fallen once into slumber he remained there long.

It was not yet morning and the rain was yet falling steadily. Its sweep upon the roof was still so pleasant and soothing that Dick resolved to go to sleep again, after he had looked about a little. He had grown used to dusk and he could see just a little. The sergeant, buried all but his head among the corn shucks, was breathing deeply and peacefully.

He looked out at one of the cracks, but he saw only rain sweeping by in misty sheets. The road that ran by the field was invisible. He gave devout thanks that this tight little corn crib had put itself in their way. Then he returned to his slumbers, and when he awoke again the sergeant was sitting by one of the cracks smoothing his thick hair with a small comb.

"I always try to keep as neat as I can, Mr. Mason," he said, apologizing for such weakness. "It gives you more courage, and if I get killed I want to make a decent body. Here's your breakfast, sir. There's enough left for the two of us, and I've divided it equally."

Cold ham, bacon and crackers were laid out on clean shucks, and they ate until nothing was left. It was now full daylight, and the rain was dying away to a sprinkle. The farmer might come out at any time to his crib, and they felt that they must be up and away.

They bade farewell to their pleasant shelter of a night, and, after pulling through the deep mud of the field, entered again the forest, which was now soaking wet.

"If Colonel Hertford is near where we reckon he is we ought to meet him by nightfall," said Sergeant Whitley.

"We're sure to reach him before then," said Dick joyously.

"Colonel Hertford is a mighty good man, and if he says he's going to be at a certain place at a certain time I reckon he'll be there, Mr. Mason."

"And then we'll bring him back and join General Grant. What do you think of our General, Sergeant?"

Dick spoke with all the freedom then so prevalent in the American armies, where officer and man were often on nearly a common footing, and the sergeant replied with equal freedom.

"General Grant hits and hammers, and I guess that's what war is," he said. "On the plains we had a colonel who didn't know much about tactics. He said the only way to put down hostile Indians was to find 'em, and beat 'em, and I guess that plan will work in any war, big or little."

"I heard before I left the army that Washington was getting scared, afraid that he was taking too big a risk here in the heart of the Confederacy, and that his operations might be checked by orders from the capital."

Sergeant Whitley smiled a wise smile.

"We sergeants learn to know the officers," he said, "and I've had the chance to look at General Grant a lot. He doesn't say much, but I guess he's doing a powerful lot of thinking, while he's chawing on the end of his cigar. You notice, Mr. Mason, that he takes risks."

"He took a big one at Shiloh, and came mighty near being nipped."

"But he wasn't nipped after all, and now, if I can judge by the signs, he's going to take another chance here. I wouldn't be surprised if he turned and marched away from the Mississippi, say toward Jackson."

"But that wouldn't be taking Vicksburg."

"No, but he might whip an army of the Johnnies coming to relieve Vicksburg, and I've a sneaking idea that the General has another daring thought in mind."

"What is it, Sergeant?"

"When he turns eastward he'll be away from the telegraph. Maybe he doesn't want to receive any orders from the capital just now."

"I believe you've hit it, Sergeant. At least I hope so, and anyway we want to reach Colonel Hertford right away."

Still following the map and also consulting their own judgment, they advanced now at a good rate. But as they came into a more thickly populated country they were compelled to be exceedingly wary. Once a farmer insisted on questioning them, but they threatened him with their rifles and then plunged into a wood, lest he bring a force in pursuit.

In the afternoon, lying among some bushes, they saw a large Confederate force, with four cannon, pass on the road toward Jackson.

"Colonel Hertford might do them a lot of damage if he could fall on them with his cavalry," said the sergeant thoughtfully.

"So he could," said Dick, "but I imagine that General Grant wants the colonel to come at once."

They turned northward now and an hour later found numerous hoofprints in a narrow road.

"All these were made by well-shod horses," said the sergeant, after examining the tracks critically. "Now, we've plenty of horseshoes and the Johnnies haven't. That's one sign."

"What's the other?"

"I calculate that about six hundred men have passed here, and that's pretty close to the number Colonel Hertford has, unless he's been in a hot fight."

"Good reasoning, Sergeant, and I'll add a third. Those men are riding directly toward the place where, according to our maps and information, we ought to meet Colonel Hertford."

"All these things make me sure our men have passed here, Mr. Mason. Suppose we follow on as hard as we can?"

Cheered by the belief that they were approaching the end of their quest they advanced at such a rate that the great trail rapidly grew fresher.

"Their horses are tired now," said the sergeant, "and likely we're going as fast as they are. They're our men sure. Look at this old canteen that one of 'em has thrown away. It's the kind they make in the North. He ought to have been punished for leaving such a sign."

"I judge, Sergeant, from the looks of this road, that they can't now be more than a mile away."

"Less than that, Mr. Mason. When we reach the top of the hill yonder I think we'll see 'em."

The sergeant's judgment was vindicated again. From the crest they saw a numerous body of muddy horsemen riding slowly ahead. Only the brilliant sunlight made their uniforms distinguishable, but they were, beyond a doubt, the troops of the Union. Dick uttered a little cry of joy and the sergeant's face glowed.

"We've found 'em," said the sergeant.

"And soon we ride," said Dick.

They hurried forward, shouted and waved their rifles.

The column stopped, and two men, one of whom was Colonel Hertford himself, rode back, looking curiously at the haggard and stained faces of the two who walked forward, still swinging their rifles.

"Colonel Hertford," said Dick joyfully, "we've come with a message for you from General Grant."

"And who may you be?" asked Hertford in surprise.

"Why, Colonel, don't you know me? I'm Lieutenant Richard Mason of Colonel Winchester's regiment, and this is Sergeant Daniel Whitley of the same regiment."

The colonel broke into a hearty laugh, and then extended his hand to Dick.

"I should have known your voice, my boy," he said, "but it's certainly impossible to recognize any one who is as thickly covered with dry Mississippi mud as you are. What's your news, Dick?"

Dick told him and the sergeant repeated the same tale. He knew them both to be absolutely trustworthy, and their coming on such an errand through so many dangers carried its own proof.

"We've several spare horses, bearing provisions and arms," said Colonel Hertford. "Two can be unloaded and be made ready for you and the sergeant. I fancy that you don't care to keep on walking, Dick?"

"I've had enough to last me for years, Colonel."

They were mounted in a few minutes, and rode with the colonel. The world had now changed for Dick. Astride a good horse and in a column of six hundred men he was no longer the hunted. These troopers and he were hunters now.

The column turned presently into another road and advanced with speed in the direction of Grant. Colonel Hertford asked Dick many questions about Slade.

"I've been hearing of him since we were on this raid," he said. "He's more of a guerilla than a regular soldier, but he may be able to gather a considerable force. I wish we could cut him off."

"So do I," said Dick, but his feeling was prompted chiefly by Slade's determined attempts upon his life.

Colonel Hertford now pushed forward his men. He, too, was filled with ambitions. He began to have an idea of Grant's great plans, in which all the Union leaders must cooperate, and he meant that his own little command should be there, whenever the great deed, whatever it might be, was done. He talked about it with Dick, who he knew was a trusted young staff officer, and the two, the lad and the older man, fed the enthusiasm of each other.

This attack deep into the flank of the Confederacy appealed to them with its boldness, and created a certain romantic glow that seemed to clothe the efforts of a general so far from the great line of battle in the East. They talked, too, of the navy which had run past forts on the Mississippi, and which had shown anew all its ancient skill and courage.

As they talked, twilight came, and the road led once more through the deep woods, where the shade turned the twilight into the darkness of night. Then rifles flashed suddenly in the thickets, and a half-dozen horsemen fell. The whole column was thrown for an instant or two into disorder, frightened horses rearing and stamping, and, before their riders could regain control, another volley came, emptying a half-dozen saddles.

Colonel Hertford gave rapid commands. Then, shouting and waving his saber he galloped boldly into the forest, reckless of trees and bushes, and Dick, the sergeant, and the whole troop followed. The lad was nearly swept from his horse by a bough, but he recovered himself in time to see the figures of men on foot fleeing rapidly through the dusk.

Bullets pattered on bark and leaves, and the angry horsemen, after discharging their carbines, swept forward with circling sabers. But the irregulars who had ambushed them, save a few fallen before the bullets, escaped easily in the dense woods, and under cover of the darkness which was now coming down, thick and fast.

A trumpet sounded the recall and the cavalrymen, sore and angry, drew back into the road. They had lost a dozen good men, but Colonel Hertford felt that they could not delay for vengeance. Grant's orders were to come at once; and he intended to obey them.

"I'd wager a year's pay against a Confederate five-dollar note," said Sergeant Whitley to Dick, "that the man who laid that ambush was Slade. He'll keep watch on us all the way to Grant, and he'll tell the Southern leaders everything the general is doing. Oh, he's a good scout and spy."

"He's proved it," said Dick, "and I'd like to get a fair shot at him."

They rode nearly all night and most of the next day, and, in the afternoon, they met other men in blue who told them that a heavy Union force was advancing. They had no doubt now that Grant's great plan was already working and in a short time they reached McPherson, advancing with Logan's division. Hertford reported at once to McPherson, who was glad enough to have his cavalry, and who warmly praised Dick and the sergeant for the dangerous service they had done so well. As it would have been unwise for them to attempt to reach Grant then he kept them with him in the march on Jackson.

Dick slept that night under the stars, but thousands of Union men were around him and he felt neither the weight of responsibility, nor the presence of danger. He missed Warner and Pennington, but he and the sergeant were happy. Beyond a doubt now Grant was going to strike hard, and all the men were full of anticipation and hope. His force in different divisions was advancing on Jackson, leaving Vicksburg behind him and the Southern army under Pemberton on one side.

Dick heard, too, that the redoubtable Joe Johnston was

coming to take command of the Southern garrison in Jackson, and a leader less bold than Grant might have shrunk from such a circle of enemies, but Grant's own courage increased the spirit of his men, and they were full of faith.

"I expect they're alarmed in Washington," said the sergeant, as they sat on their blankets. "There ain't any telegraph station nearer than Memphis. They've heard in the capital that the general has begun to move toward Jackson, but they won't know for days what will happen."

"I don't blame the President for being disturbed," said Dick. "After all the army is to serve the nation and fights under the supreme civilian authority. The armies don't govern."

"That's so, but there come times when the general who has to do the fighting can judge best how it ought to be done."

Dick lay down on one blanket and put another over him. It was well into May, which meant hot weather in Mississippi, but, if he could, he always protected himself at night. He was not a vain lad, but he felt proud over his success. Hertford's six hundred horse were a welcome addition to any army.

He lay back soon with a knapsack as a pillow under his head and listened to the noises of the camp, blended now into a rather musical note. Several cooking fires still burned here and there and figures passed before them. Dick observed them sleepily, taking no particular note, until one, small and weazened, came. The figure was about fifty yards away, and there was a Union cap instead of a great flap-brimmed hat on the head, but Dick sprang to his feet at once, snatched a pistol from his belt and rushed toward it.

The evil figure melted away like a shadow, and two astonished soldiers seized the youth, who seemed to be running amuck in the camp, pistol in hand.

"Let go!" exclaimed Dick. "I've seen a man whom I know to be a spy, and a most dangerous one, too."

They could find no trace of Slade. Dick returned crestfallen to his blanket, but he recalled something now definitely and clearly. Slade was the little man whom he had seen carrying the log the morning he left General Grant's camp, on his mission.

The sergeant, who had never stirred from his own blanket, sat up when Dick returned.

"Who was he, Mr. Mason?" he asked.

"Slade himself. He must have seen me jump up, because he vanished like a ghost. But I gained something. I know now that I saw him here in our uniform just before I started to find Colonel Hertford. That was why I was followed."

"The cunning of an Indian. Well, we'll be on the watch for him now, but I imagine he's already on the way to Jackson with the news of our advance and an estimate of our numbers. We can't do anything to head him off."

On the second day after joining the column Dick was ahead with the cavalry, riding beside Colonel Hertford, and listening to occasional shots in their front on the Jackson road. Both believed they would soon be in touch with the enemy. Sergeant Whitley, acting now as a scout, had gone forward through a field and in a few minutes galloped back.

"The enemy is not far away," he said. "They're posted along a creek, with high banks and in a wood. They've got a strong artillery too, and I think they about equal us in numbers."

Dick carried the report to the commander of the column, and soon the trumpets were calling the men to battle. The crackle of rifle shots ahead increased rapidly. The skirmishers were already pulling trigger, and, as Dick galloped back to Hertford he saw many puffs of white smoke down the road and in the fields and woods on either side. The Union men began to cheer. In the West they had suffered no such defeats as their brethren in the East, and every pulse beat with confidence. As the whole line moved forward the Southern cannon began to crash and their shells swept the road.

The cavalry were advancing in a field, but they were yet held back to a slow walk. Dick heard many impatient exclamations, but he knew the restraint was right. He saw the accuracy of the Southern gunners. They were driving the Northern infantry from the road. Their fire was rapid and deadly, and, for a while, the Union army was checked.

Hertford was calmly examining the Southern position through his glasses, while he restrained his eager men. The volume of Southern fire was growing fast. Shells and shrapnel rained death over a wide area, and the air was filled with whistling bullets. It was certain destruction for any force to charge down the road in face of the Southern cannon, and the Northern army began to spread out, wheeling toward either flank.

An aide arrived with an order to Hertford, and then he loosed his eager cavalry. Turning to one side they galloped toward the creek. Some of the Southern gunners, seeing them, sent shells toward them, and a swarm of riflemen in a wood showered them with bullets. But they passed so rapidly that not many saddles were emptied, and the trumpeter blew a mellow note that urged on spirits already willing enough.

The sweep of the cavalry charge exhilarated Dick. The thought of danger passed away for the moment. He saw all around him the eager faces of men, and horses that seemed just as eager. Dust and dirt flew beneath the thudding hoofs, and the dust and floating smoke together made a grimy cloud through which they galloped.

They passed around still further on the flank. They seemed, for a few minutes, to be leaving the battle, which was now at its height, the Southern artillery still holding the road and presenting an unbroken front.

Dick saw a flash of water and then the whole troop thundered into the creek, almost without slackened rein. Up the bank they went, and with a wild shout charged upon the Southern infantry. On the other flank another Northern force which also had crossed the creek attacked with fire and spirit.

But the battle still swayed back and forth. Hertford and his cavalry were thrown off, merely to return anew to the charge. A portion of the Northern force was driven back on the creek. The strong Southern batteries poured forth death. Dick felt that they might yet lose, but they suddenly heard a tremendous cheer, and a fresh force coming up at the double quick enabled them to sweep the field. Before sunset the Southern army retreated toward Jackson, leaving the field to the men in blue.

Dick dismounted and, examining himself carefully, found that he had suffered no wound. Colonel Hertford and the sergeant had also taken no hurt. But the lad and his elder comrade secured but little rest. They were bidden to ride across the country at once to General Sherman with the news of the victory. Sherman was at the head of another column, and Grant was farther away with the main body.

Dick and the sergeant, with the battle smoke still in their eyes, were eager for the service.

"When you're with Grant you don't stay idle, that's certain," said Dick as they rode across the darkening fields.

"No, you don't," said the sergeant, "and I'm thinking that we've just begun. I know from the feel of it that big things are going to happen fast. Sheer away from the woods there, Mr. Mason. We don't want to be picked off by sharpshooters."

They arrived after dark in Sherman's camp and he received them himself. Dick remembered how he had seen this thin, dry man holding fast with his command at Shiloh, and he saluted him with the deepest respect. He knew that here was a bold and tenacious spirit, kin to that of Grant. Sherman had heard already of the battle, but he wished more and definite news.

"You say that our victory was complete?" he asked tersely.

"It was, sir," replied Dick. "The entire force of the enemy retired rapidly toward Jackson, and our men are eager to advance on that city."

"It would be a great stroke to take the capital of Mississippi," said Sherman musingly. Then he added in his crisp manner:

"Are you tired?"

"Not if you wish me to do anything," replied Dick quickly.

Sherman smiled.

"The right spirit," he said. "I wish you and your comrade to ride at once with this news to General Grant. He may hear it from other sources, but I want to send a letter by you."

In ten minutes Dick and the sergeant were riding proudly away on another mission, and, passing through all the dangers of Southern scouts and skirmishers, they reached General Grant, to whom they delivered the letter from Sherman. Grant, who had recently been in doubt owing to the threat of Pemberton on his flank, hesitated no longer when he heard of the victory, and resolved at once upon the capture of Jackson.

Dick, after his battle and two rides, went to sleep in a wagon, while an orderly took his horse. When he awoke unknown hours afterward he found that he was moving. He knew at once that the army was advancing. Before him and behind him he heard all the noises of the march, the beat of horses' hoofs, the grinding of wheels, the clanking of cannon, the cracking of whips and the sounds of many voices.

He was wonderfully comfortable where he lay and he had the satisfaction and pride of much duty done. He felt that he was entitled to rest, and, turning on his side, he went to sleep again. After another unknown time his second awakening came and he remained awake.

He quietly slipped out at the tail of the wagon, and stood for a few moments, dazzled by the blazing sunlight. Then a loud, cheery voice called out:

"Well, if it isn't our own Lucky Dick come back again, safe and well to the people to whom he belongs!"

"If z equals Dick and y equals his presence then we have z plus y, as Dick is certainly present," called out another voice not quite so loud, but equally cheery. "Luck, Frank, is only a minor factor in life. What we usually call luck is the result of foresight, skill and courage. There are facts that I wouldn't have you to forget, even if it is a hot day far down in Mississippi."

Warner and Pennington sprang from their horses and greeted Dick warmly. They had returned a day or two before from their own less perilous errands, but they were in great anxiety about their comrade. They were glad too, when they heard that the sergeant had joined him and that he had come back safe.

"I suppose it means a battle at Jackson," said Warner. "We're surely on the move, and we're going to keep the Johnnies busy for quite a spell."

"Looks like it," said Dick.

Colonel Winchester came soon, and his face showed great relief when he shook hands with Dick.

"It was a dangerous errand, Dick, my lad," he said, "but I felt that you would succeed and you have. It was highly important that we gather all our forces for a great stroke."

Dick resumed at once his old place in the Winchester regiment, with Warner, Pennington and his other comrades around him. Refreshed by abundant sleep and good food he was in the highest of spirits. They were embarked upon a great adventure and he believed that it would be successful. His confidence was shared by all those about him. Meanwhile the army advanced in diverging columns upon the Mississippi capital.

Jackson, on Pearl River, had suddenly assumed a vast importance in Dick's mind, and yet it was but a tiny place, not more than three or four thousand inhabitants. The South was almost wholly agricultural, and cities, great in a political and military sense, were in reality but towns. Richmond, itself the capital of the Confederacy, around which so much centered, had only forty thousand people.

The Winchester regiment was detached that afternoon and sent to join the column under McPherson, which was expected to reach Jackson first. Dick was mounted again, and he rode with Warner and Pennington on either side of him. They speculated much on what they would find when they approached Jackson.

"If Joe Johnston is there," said Warner, "I think we'll have a hard fight. You'll remember that he did great work against us in Virginia, until he was wounded."

"And they'll know, of course, just when to expect us and in what force," said Dick. "Slade will tell them that. He probably has a large body of spies and scouts working under him. But I don't think he'll come inside our camp again."

"Not likely since he's been recognized," said Warner, thoughtfully. "But I don't think General Grant is afraid of anything ahead. That's why he made the separation from our own world so complete, and our men are out cutting down the telegraph lines, so the Johnnies in Jackson can't communicate with their own government either. It's important to us that we take Jackson before Pemberton with his army can come up."

Warner had estimated the plan correctly. Grant, besides cutting himself off from his own superiors at Washington, was also destroying communication between the garrison of Jackson and

Pemberton's army of Vicksburg, which was not far away. The two united might beat him, but he meant to defeat them separately, and then besiege Vicksburg. It was a complicated plan, depending upon quickness, courage and continued success. Yet the mind of Grant, though operating afterward on fields of greater numbers, was never clearer or more vigorous.

They went into camp again after dark, knowing that Jackson was but a short distance away, and they expected to attack early in the morning. Dick carried another dispatch to Sherman, who was only a little more than two miles from them, and on his way back he joined Colonel Winchester, who, with Warner, Pennington and a hundred infantry, had come out for a scout. The dismounted men were chosen because they wished to beat up a difficult piece of wooded country.

They went directly toward Jackson, advancing very cautiously through the forest, the mounted officers riding slowly. The night was hot and dark, moon and stars obscured by drifting clouds. Pennington, who was an expert on weather, announced that another storm was coming.

"I can feel a dampness in the air," he said. "I'm willing to risk my reputation as a prophet and say that the dawn will come with rain."

"I hope it won't be a big rain," said Colonel Winchester, "because if it is it will surely delay our attack. Our supply of cartridges is small, and we can't risk wetting them."

Pennington persisted that a storm was at hand. His father had taught him, he said, always to observe the weather signs on the great Nebraska plains. They were nearly always hoping for rain there, and he had learned to smell it before it came. He could smell it now in the same way here in Mississippi.

His opinion did not waver, when the clouds floated away for a while, disclosing a faint moon and a few stars. They were now on the banks of a brook, flowing through the wood, and Colonel Winchester thought he saw a movement in the forest beyond it. It was altogether likely that so skillful a leader as Joe Johnston would have out bodies of scouts, and he stopped, bidding his men to take cover.

Dick sat on his horse by the colonel's side under the thick boughs of a great tree, and studied the thickets before them. He, too, had noticed a movement, and he was confident that the Southern sharpshooters were there. At the command of the colonel all of the officers dismounted, and orderlies took the horses to the rear. On foot they continued their examination of the thickets, and the colonel sent for Sergeant Whitley, who confirmed his opinion that the enemy was before them. At his suggestion the Union force was spread out, lest it be flanked and annihilated in the thickets.

Just as the movement was completed rifles began to crack in front and on both flanks, and the piercing yell of the South arose.

It was impossible to tell the size of the force that assailed them, but the Winchester men were veterans now, and they were not afraid. Standing among the bushes or sheltered by the trees they held their fire until they saw dusky figures in the thickets.

It had all the aspects of an old Indian battle in the depths of the great forest. Darkness, the ambush and the caution of sharpshooters were there. Dick carried a rifle, but he did not use it. He merely watched the pink beads of flame among the bushes, while he stayed by the side of his colonel and observed the combat.

It soon became apparent to him that it would have no definite result. Each side was merely feeling out its foe that night, and would not force the issue. Yet the Southern line approached and some bullets whistled near him. He moved a little to one side, and watched for an enemy. It was annoying to have bullets come so close, and since they were shooting at him he might as well shoot at them.

While he was absorbed in watching, the colonel moved in the other direction, and Dick stood alone behind a bush. The fire in front had increased somewhat, although at no time was it violent. Occasional shots from his own side replied. The clouds that had drifted away were now drifting back, and he believed that darkness alone would soon end the combat.

Then he saw a bush only a dozen yards in his front move a little, and a face peered through its branches. There was yet enough light for him to see that the face was youthful, eager and handsome. It was familiar, too, and then with a shock he remembered. Woodville, the lad with whom he had fought such a good fight, nature's weapons used, was before him.

Dick raised his rifle. Young Woodville was an easy target. But the motion was only a physical impulse. He knew in his heart that he had no intention of shooting the young Southerner, and he did not feel the slightest tinge of remorse because he evaded this part of a soldier's work.

Yet Woodville, seeing nobody and hearing nothing, would come on. Dick, holding his rifle in the crook of his left arm, drew a pistol and fired it over the lad's head. At the same moment he dropped almost flat upon the ground. The bullet cut the leaves above Woodville and he sprang back, startled. A half-dozen Southern skirmishers fired at the flash of Dick's pistol, but he, too, lying on the ground, heard them cutting leaves over his head.

Dick saw the face of Woodville disappear from the bush, and then he crept away, rejoining Colonel Winchester and his comrades. Five minutes later the skirmish ceased by mutual consent, and each band fell back on its own army, convinced that both were on the watch.

They were to advance at four o'clock in the morning, but Pennington's prediction came true. After midnight, flashes of lightning cut the sky and the thunder rolled heavily. Then the rain came, not any fugitive shower, but hard, cold and steady, promising to last many hours.

It was still pouring when the advance began before dawn, but Grant's plans were complete. He had drawn up his forces on the chessboard, and they were converging closely upon Jackson. They must keep their cartridges dry and advance at all costs.

The Winchesters were in the van in a muddy road. Dick, Warner and Pennington were in the saddle, and they were wet through and through. The rain and dusk were so heavy that they could not see fifty feet, and they shivered with cold. But their souls were eager and high, and they were glad when the army toiled slowly forward to battle.

CHAPTER VII

THE LITTLE CAPITAL

Dick was bent down in his saddle, trying to protect himself a little from the driving rain which beat in his eyes and soaked through his clothing. Warner and Pennington beside him were in the same condition, and he saw just before him the bent back of Colonel Winchester, with his left arm raised as a shield for his face. Hoofs and wheels made a heavy, sticky sound as they sank in the mud, and were then pulled out again.

"Do you see any signs of daylight, Dick?" asked Pennington.

"Not a sign. I see only a part of our regiment, trees on either side of us bending before the wind, and rain, and mud, mud everywhere. I'll be glad when it's over."

"So will I," said Warner. "I wonder what kind of hotels they have in Jackson. I'd like to have a bath, good room and a big breakfast."

"The Johnnies are holding breakfast for you," said Pennington. "Their first course is gunpowder, their second bullets, their third shells and shrapnel, and their fourth bayonets."

"They'll have to serve a lot at every course," said Dick, "because General Grant is advancing with fifty thousand men, and so many need a lot of satisfying."

The storm increased in violence. The rain, falling in a deluge, was driven by a wind like a hurricane. The horses strove to turn their heads from it, and confusion arose among the cavalry. The infantry mixed in the mud swore heavily. Staff officers had the utmost difficulty in keeping the regiments together. It was time for the sun, but it did not appear. Everything was veiled in clouds and driving rain.

Dick looked at his watch, and saw that it was seven o'clock. They had intended to attack at this hour, but further advance was impossible for the time, and, bending their heads, they sought to protect their ammunition. Presently they started again and toiled along slowly and painfully for more than two hours. Then, just as they saw the enemy ahead of them, the storm seemed to reach the very zenith of its fury.

Dick, in the vanguard, beheld earthworks, cannon and troops before Jackson, but the storm still drove so hard that the Union forces could not advance to the assault.

"This is certainly a most unusual situation," said Colonel

Winchester, with an effort at cheerfulness. "Here we are, ready to attack, and the Southerners are ready to defend, but a storm holds us both fast in our tracks. Our duty to protect our cartridges is even greater than our duty to attack the enemy."

"The biggest rain must come to an end," said Dick.

But it was nearly noon before they could advance. Then, as the storm decreased rapidly the trumpets sounded the charge, and horse, foot and artillery, they pressed forward eagerly through the mud.

The sun broke through the clouds, and Dick saw before them a wood, a ravine full of thickets, and the road commanded by strong artillery. The Northern skirmishers were already stealing forward through the wet bushes and grass, and soon their rifles were crackling. But the Southern sharpshooters in the thickets were in stronger force, and their rapid and accurate fire drove back the Northern men. Then their artillery opened and swept the road, while the Northern batteries were making frantic efforts to get up through the deep, sticky mud.

But the trumpets were still calling. The Winchester regiment and others, eager for battle and victory, swept forward. Dick felt once more the fierce thrill of combat, and, waving his revolver high above his head, he shouted with the others as they rushed on. The stream of bullets from the ravine thickened, and the cannon were crashing fast. But the Union masses did not check their rush for an instant. Although many fell they charged into the ravine, driving out the enemy, and pursued him on the other side.

But the Southern cannon, manned by daring gunners, still held the field and, aided by the thick mud which held back charging feet, they repulsed every attack. The Winchester regiment was forced to cover, and then Dick heard the booming of cannon in another direction. He knew that Grant and Sherman were coming up there, and he expected they would rush at once into Jackson, but it was a long time before the distant thunder came any nearer.

Johnston, whose astuteness they feared, was proving himself worthy of their opinion. Knowing that his forces were far too small to defend Jackson, he had sent away the archives of the state and most of the army. Only a small force and seventeen cannon were left to fight and cover his retreat. But so bold and skillful were they that it was far beyond noon before Grant and Sherman found that practically nothing was in front of them.

But where Dick and his comrades rode the fighting was severe for a while. Then everything seemed to melt away before them. The fire of the Southern cannon ceased suddenly, and Colonel Winchester exclaimed that their works had been abandoned. They charged forward, seized the cannon, and now rode without resistance into the capital of the state, from which the President of the Confederacy hailed, though by birth a Kentuckian.

Dick and his comrades were among the first to enter the town, and not until then did they know that Johnston and all but a few hundreds of his army were gone.

"We've got the shell only," Dick said.

"Still we've struck a blow by taking the capital of the state," said Colonel Winchester.

Dick looked with much curiosity at the little city into which they were riding as conquerors. It was too small and new to be imposing. Yet there were some handsome houses, standing back on large lawns, and surrounded by foliage. The doors and shutters of all of them were closed tightly. Dick knew that their owners had gone away or were sitting, hearts full of bitterness, in their sealed houses.

The streets were deep in mud, and at the corners little knots of negroes gathered and looked at them curiously.

"They don't seem to welcome us as deliverers," said Warner.

"They don't yet know what to think of us," said Dick. "There's the Capitol ahead of us, and some of our troops are going into it."

"Others have gone into it already," said Pennington. "Look!"

They saw the flag of the Union break out above its dome, the beautiful stars and stripes, waving gently in the light breeze. A spontaneous cheer burst from the Union soldiers, and the bitter hearts in the sealed houses grew more bitter.

The army was now pouring in by every road and Colonel Winchester and his staff sought quarters. They were on the verge of exhaustion. All their clothing was wet and they were discolored with mud. They felt that they were bound to have rest and cleanliness.

The victorious troops were making their camp, wherever they could find dry ground, and soon they were building the fires for cooking. But many of the officers were assigned to the residences, and Colonel Winchester and his staff were directed by the general to take quarters in a large colonial house, standing on a broad lawn, amid the finest magnolias and live oaks that Dick had ever seen.

Remembering an earlier experience during the Shiloh campaign Colonel Winchester and his young officers approached the house with some reluctance. In ordinary times it must have been brilliant with life. Two little fountains were playing on either side of the graveled walk that led to the front door. After the old fashion, three or four marble statues stood in the shrubbery. Everything indicated wealth. Probably the town house of a great planter, reflected Dick. In Mississippi a man sometimes owned as many as a thousand slaves, and lived like a prince.

The house offered them no welcome. Its doors and windows were closed, but Dick had seen thin smoke rising from a chimney in the rear. He expected that they would have to force the door, but at the first knock it was thrown open by a tall, thin woman of middle years. The look she gave them was full of bitter hatred—Dick sometimes thought that women could hate better than men—but her manner and bearing showed distinction. He, as well as his comrades, took her to be the lady of the house.

"We ask your pardon, madame, for this intrusion," said Colonel Winchester, "but we are compelled to occupy your house a while. We promise you as little trouble as possible."

"We ask no consideration of any kind from men who have come to despoil our country and ruin its people," she said icily.

Colonel Winchester flushed.

"But madame," he protested, "we do not come to destroy."

"I do not care to argue with you about it," she said in the same lofty tone, "and also you need not address me as madame. I am Miss Woodville."

Dick started.

"Does this house belong to Colonel John Woodville?" he asked.

"It does not," she replied crisply, "but it belongs to his elder brother, Charles Woodville, who is also a colonel, and who is my father. What do you know of Colonel John Woodville?"

"I met his son once," replied Dick briefly.

She glanced at him sharply. Dick thought for a moment that he saw alarm in her look, but he concluded that it was only anger.

They stood confronting each other, the little group of officers and the woman, and Colonel Winchester, embarrassed, but knowing that he must do something, went forward and pushed back a door opening into the hall. Dick automatically followed him, and then stepped back, startled.

A roar like that of a lion met them. An old man, with a high, bald and extremely red forehead lay in a huge bed by a window. It was a great head, and eyes, set deep, blazed under thick, white lashes. His body was covered to the chin.

Dick saw that the man's anger was that of the caged wild beast, and there was something splendid and terrible about it.

"You infernal Yankees!" he cried, and his voice again rumbled like that of a lion.

"Colonel Charles Woodville, I presume?" said Colonel Winchester politely.

"Yes, Colonel Charles Woodville," thundered the man, "fastened here in bed by a bullet from one of your cursed vessels in the Mississippi, while you rob and destroy!"

And then he began to curse. He drew one hand from under the cover and shook his clenched fist at them in a kind of rhythmic beat while the oaths poured forth. To Dick it was not common swearing. There was nothing coarse and vulgar about it. It was denunciation, malediction, fulmination, anathema. It had a certain majesty and dignity. Its richness and variety were unequaled, and it was hurled forth by a voice deep, powerful and enduring.

Dick listened with amazement and then admiration. He had never heard its like, nor did he feel any offense. The daughter, too, stood by, pursing her prim lips, and evidently approving. Colonel Winchester was motionless like a statue, while the infuriated man shook his fist at him and launched imprecations. But his face had turned white and Dick saw that he was fiercely angry.

When the old man ceased at last from exhaustion Colonel Winchester said quietly:

"If you had spoken to me in the proper manner we might have gone away and found quarters elsewhere. But we intend to stay here and we will repay your abuse with good manners."

Dick saw the daughter flush, but the old man said:

"Then it will be the first time that good manners were ever brought from the country north of the Mason and Dixon line."

Colonel Winchester flushed in his turn, but made no direct reply.

"If you will assign us rooms, Miss Woodville," he said, "we will go to them, otherwise we'll find them for ourselves, which may be less convenient for you. I repeat that we desire to give you as little trouble as possible."

"Do so, Margaret," interrupted Colonel Woodville, "because then I may get rid of them all the sooner."

Colonel Winchester bowed and turned toward the door. Miss Woodville, obedient to the command of her father, led the way. Dick was the last to go out, and he said to the old lion who lay wounded in the bed:

"Colonel Woodville, I've met your nephew, Victor."

He did not notice that the old man whitened and that the hand now lying upon the cover clenched suddenly.

"You have?" growled Colonel Woodville, "and how does it happen that you and my nephew have anything in common?"

"I could scarcely put it that way," replied Dick, refusing to be angered, "unless you call an encounter with fists something in common. He and I had a great fight at his father's plantation of Bellevue."

"He might have been in a better business, taking part in a common brawl with a common Yankee."

"But, sir, while I may be common, I'm not a Yankee. I was born and grew up south of the Ohio River in Kentucky."

"Then you're a traitor. All you Kentuckians ought to be fighting with us."

"Difference of opinion, but I hope your nephew is well."

The deep eyes under the thick white thatch glared in a manner that Dick considered wholly unnecessary. But Colonel Woodville made no reply, merely turning his face to the wall as if he were weary.

Dick hurried into the hall, closing the door gently behind him. The others, not missing him, were already some yards away, and he quickly rejoined Pennington and Warner. The younger men would have been glad to leave the house, but Colonel Winchester's blood was up, and he was resolved to stay. The little party was eight in number, and they were soon quartered in four rooms on the lower floor. Miss Woodville promptly disappeared, and one of the camp cooks arrived with supplies, which he took to the kitchen.

Dick and Warner were in one of the rooms, and, removing their belts and coats, they made themselves easy. It was a large bedroom with high ceilings and wicker furniture. There were several good paintings on the walls and a bookcase contained Walter Scott's novels and many of the eighteenth century classics.

"I think this must have been a guest chamber," said Dick, "but for us coming from the rain and mud it's a real palace."

"Then it's fulfilling its true function," said Warner, "because it has guests now. What a strange household! Did you ever see such a peppery pair as that swearing old colonel and his acid daughter?"

"I don't know that I blame them. I think, sometimes, George, that you New Englanders are the most selfish of people. You're too truly righteous. You're always denouncing the faults of others, but you never see any of your own. Away back in the Revolution when Boston called, the Southern provinces came to her help, but Boston and New England have spent a large part of their time since then denouncing the South."

"What's struck you, Dick? Are you weakening in the good cause?"

"Not for a moment. But suppose Mississippi troops walked into your own father's house in Vermont, and, as conquerors, demanded food and shelter! Would you rejoice over them, and ask them why they hadn't come sooner?"

"I suppose not, Dick. But, stop it, and come back to your normal temperature. I won't quarrel with you."

"I won't give you a chance, George. I'm through. But remember that while I'm red hot for the Union, I was born south of the Ohio River myself, and I have lots of sympathy for the people against whom I'm fighting."

"For the matter of that, so've I, Dick, and I was born north of the Ohio River. But I'm getting tremendously hungry. I hope that cook will hurry."

They were called soon, and eight officers sat at the table. The cook himself served them. Miss Woodville had vanished, and not a servant was visible about the great house. Despite their hunger and the good quality of the food the group felt constraint. The feeling that they were intruders, in a sense brigands, was forced upon them. Dick was sure that the old man with the great bald head was swearing fiercely and incessantly under his breath.

The dining-room was a large and splendid apartment, and the silver still lay upon the great mahogany sideboard. The little city, now the camp of an overwhelming army, had settled into silence, and the twilight was coming.

With the chill of unwelcome still upon them the officers said little. As the twilight deepened Warner lighted several candles. The silver glittered under the flame. Colonel Winchester presently ordered the cook to take a plate of the most delicate food to Colonel Woodville.

As the cook withdrew on his mission he left open the door of the dining-room and they heard the sound of a voice, uplifted in a thunderous roar. The cook hurried back, the untouched plate in his hand and his face a little pale.

"He cursed me, sir," he said to Colonel Winchester. "I was never cursed so before by anybody. He said he would not touch the food. He was sure that it had been poisoned by the Yankees, and even if it were not he'd rather die than accept anything from their hands."

Colonel Winchester laughed rather awkwardly.

"At any rate, we've tendered our good offices," he said. "I suppose his daughter will attend to his wants, and we'll not expose ourselves to further insults."

But the refusal had affected the spirits of them all, and as soon as their hunger was satisfied they withdrew. The soldier who had acted as cook was directed to put the dining-room back in order and then he might sleep in a room near the kitchen.

Dick and Warner returned to their own apartment. Neither had much to say, and Warner, lying down on the bed, was soon fast asleep. Dick sat by the window. The town was now almost lost in the obscurity. The exhausted army slept, and the occasional glitter from the bayonet of a sentinel was almost the only thing that told of its presence.

Dick was troubled. In spite of will and reason, his conscience hurt him. Theory was beautiful, but it was often shivered by practice. His sympathies were strongly with the old colonel who had cursed him so violently and the grim old maid who had given them only harsh words. Besides, he had pleasant memories of Victor Woodville, and these were his uncle and cousin.

He sat for a long time at the window. The house was absolutely quiet, and he was sure that everybody was asleep. There could be no doubt about Warner, because he slumbered audibly. But Dick was still wide awake. There was some tension of mind or muscle that kept sleep far from him. So he remained at the window, casting up the events of the day and those that might come.

The evening was well advanced when he was quite sure that he heard a light step in the hall. He would have paid little attention to it at an ordinary time, but, in all that silence and desolation, it called him like a drum-beat. Only a light step, and yet it filled him with suspicion and alarm. He was in the heart of a great and victorious Union army, but at the moment he felt that anything could happen in this strange house.

Slipping his pistol from his belt, he opened the door on noiseless hinges and stepped into the hall. A figure was disappearing in its dim space, but, as he saw clearly, it was that of a woman. He was sure that it was Miss Woodville and he stepped forward. He had no intention of following her, but his foot creaked on the floor, and, stopping instantly, she faced about. Then he saw that she carried a tray of food.

"Are we to have our house occupied and to be spied upon also?" she asked.

Dick flushed. Few people had ever spoken to him in such a manner, and it was hard to remember that she was a woman.

"I heard a footstep in the hall, and it was my duty to see who was passing," he said.

"I have prepared food and I am taking it to my father. He would not accept it from Yankee hands."

"Colonel Woodville sups late. I should think a wounded man would be asleep at this hour, if he could."

She gave him a glance full of venom.

"What does it matter?" she said.

Dick refused to be insulted.

"Let me take the tray for you," he said, "at least to the door. Your father need not know that my hands have touched it."

She shrank back and her eyes blazed.

"Let us alone!" she exclaimed. "Go back to your room! Isn't it sufficient that this house shelters you?"

She seemed to Dick to show a heat and hate out of all proportion to the occasion, but he did not repeat the offer.

"I meant well," he said, "but, since you do not care for my help, I'll return to my room and go to sleep. Believe me, I'm sincere when I say I hope your father will recover quickly from his wound."

"He will," she replied briefly.

Dick bowed with politeness and turned toward his own room. Nevertheless his curiosity did not keep him from standing a moment or two in the dark against the wall and looking back at the woman who bore the tray. He drew a long breath of astonishment when he saw her pass Colonel Woodville's door, and hurry forward now with footsteps that made no sound.

The suspicion which had lain deep in his mind sprang at once into life. Keeping close to the wall, he followed swiftly and saw her disappear up a stairway. There he let the pursuit end and returned thoughtfully to his room.

Dick was much troubled. An ethical question had presented itself to him. He believed that he had divined everything. The solution had come to him with such suddenness and force that he was as fully convinced as if he had seen with his own eyes. Military duty demanded that he invade the second floor of the Woodville house. But there were feelings of humanity and mercy, moral issues not less powerful than military duty, and maybe more so.

He was pulled back and forth with great mental violence. He was sorry that he had seen Miss Woodville with the tray. And then he wasn't. Nevertheless, he stayed in his own room, and Warner, waking for a moment, regarded him with wonder as he sat outlined against the window which they had left unshuttered and opened to admit air.

"What's the matter, Dick? Have you got a fever?" he asked. "Why haven't you gone to bed?"

"I'm going to do so right away. Don't bother yourself about me, George. My nerves have been strained pretty hard, and I had to wait until they were quiet until I could go to sleep."

"Don't have nerves," said Warner, as he turned back on his side and returned to slumber.

Dick undressed and got into bed. It was the first time in many nights that he had not slept in his clothes, and beds had been unknown for many weeks. It was a luxury so penetrating and powerful that it affected him like an opiate. Such questions as military and moral duty floated swiftly away, and he slept the sleep of youth and a good heart.

Breakfast was almost a repetition of supper. The army cook prepared and served it, and the Woodvilles remained invisible. Colonel Winchester informed the young officers that they would remain in Jackson two or three days, and then great events might be expected. All felt sure that he was predicting aright. Pemberton must be approaching with the Vicksburg army. The wary and skillful Johnston had another army, and he could not be far away. Moreover, this was the heart of the Confederacy and other unknown forces might be gathering.

They felt the greatness of the hour, Grant's daring stroke, and the possibility that he might yet be surrounded and overwhelmed. Their minds were attuned, too, to other and yet mightier deeds, but they were glad, nevertheless, of a little rest. The Woodville house was a splendid place, and in the morning they did not feel so much the chill of embarrassment that had been created for them the night before.

Dick went straight to the room of Colonel Woodville, opened the door without knocking, and closed it behind him quickly but noiselessly.

The colonel was propped up in his bed and a tray bearing light and delicate food lay on a chair. His daughter stood beside the bed, speechless with anger at this intrusion. Dick lifted his hand, and the look upon his face checked one of the mightiest oaths that had ever welled up from the throat of Colonel Charles Woodville, king of swearers.

"Stop!" said Dick in a voice not loud, but sharp with command.

"Can't we at least have privacy in the room of an old and wounded man?" asked Miss Woodville.

"You can hereafter," replied Dick quietly. "I shall not come again, but I tell you now to get him out of the house to-night, unless he's too badly hurt to be moved."

"Why should my father be taken away?" demanded Miss Woodville.

"I'm not speaking of your father."

"Of whom, then?"

Dick did not answer, but he met her gaze steadily, and her face fell. Then he turned, walked out of the room without a word, and again closed the door behind him. When he went out on the piazza he saw excitement among his comrades. The moment for great action was coming even sooner than Colonel Winchester had expected.

"Johnston is communicating with Pemberton," said Warner, "and he has ordered Pemberton to unite with him. Then they will attack us. He sent the same order by three messengers, but one of them was in reality a spy of ours, and he came straight to General Grant with it. We're forewarned, and the trap can't shut down on us, because General Grant means to go at once for Pemberton."

Dick understood the situation, which was both critical and thrilling. Grant was still in the heart of the Confederacy, and its forces were converging fast upon him. But the grim and silent man, instead of merely trying to escape, intended to strike a blow that would make escape unnecessary. All the young officers saw the plan and their hearts leaped.

Dick, in the excitement of the day, forgot about the Woodville house and its inmates. Troops were already marching out of Jackson to meet the enemy, but the Winchester regiment would not leave until early the next morning. They were to spend a second night, or at least a part of it, in Colonel Woodville's house.

It was the same group that ate supper there and the same army cook served them. They did not go to the bedrooms afterward, but strolled about, belted, expecting to receive the marching call at any moment.

Dick went into the library, where a single candle burned, and while he was there Miss Woodville appeared at the door and beckoned to him. She had abated her severity of manner so much that he was astonished, but he followed without a word.

She saw that the hall was clear and then she led quickly into her father's room. Colonel Woodville was propped up against the pillows, and there was color in his face.

"Young man," he said, "come here. You can afford to obey me, although I'm a prisoner, because I'm so much older than you are. You have a heart and breeding, young sir, and I wish to shake your hand."

He thrust a large hand from the cover, and Dick shook it warmly.

"I wouldn't have shaken it if you had been born north of the Ohio River," said Colonel Woodville.

Dick laughed.

"My chief purpose in having you brought here," said Colonel Woodville, "was to relate to you an incident, of which I heard once. Did I read about it, or was it told to me, Margaret?"

"I think, sir, that some one told you of it."

"Ah, well, it doesn't matter. A few words will tell it. In an old, forgotten war a young soldier quartered in the house of his defeated enemy—but defeated only for the time, remember—saw something which made him believe that a wounded nephew of the house was hid in an upper room. But he was generous and he did not search further. The second night, while the young officer and his comrades were at supper, the nephew, who was not hurt badly, was slipped out of the house and escaped from the city in the darkness. It's not apropos of anything, and I don't know why I'm relating it to you, but I suppose this terrible war we are fighting is responsible for an old man's whim."

"I've found it very interesting, sir," said Dick, "and I think it's relevant, because it shows that even in war men may remain Christian human beings."

"Perhaps you're right, and I trust, young sir, that you will not be killed in this defeat to which you are surely marching."

Dick bowed to both, and left them to their fears and hopes. The glow was still about his heart when he rode forth with the Winchester regiment after midnight. But, owing to the need of horses for the regular cavalry, it had become an infantry regiment once more. Only the officers rode.

At dawn they were with Grant approaching a ridge called Champion Hill.

CHAPTER VIII

CHAMPION HILL

Dick on that momentous morning did not appreciate the full magnitude of the event about to occur, nor did he until long afterward. He knew it was of high importance, and yet it might have ranked as one of the decisive battles of history. There were no such numbers as at Shiloh and Chancellorsville, but the results were infinitely greater.

Nor was it likely that such thoughts would float through the head of a lad who had ridden far, and who at dawn was looking for an enemy.

The scouts had already brought word that the Southerners were in strong force, and that they occupied Champion Hill, the crest of which was bare, but with sides dark with forests and thickets. They were riding at present through forests themselves, and they felt that their ignorance of the country might take them at any moment into an ambush.

"We know what army we're going against, don't we?" asked Pennington.

"Why, Pemberton's, of course," replied Dick.

"I'm glad of that. I'd rather fight him than Joe Johnston."

"They've been trying to unite, but we hear they haven't succeeded."

Pemberton, in truth, had been suffering from the most painful doubt. Having failed to do what Johnston had expected of him, he had got himself into a more dangerous position than ever. Then, after listening to a divided council of his generals, he had undertaken a movement which brought him within striking distance of Grant, while Johnston was yet too far away to help him.

Dick did not know how much fortune was favoring the daring that morning, but he and his comrades were sanguine. They felt all the time the strong hand over them. Like the soldiers, they had acquired the utmost confidence in Grant. He might make mistakes, but he would not doubt and hesitate and draw back. Where he led the enemy could not win anything without having to fight hard for it.

The early summer dawn had deepened, bright and hot, and the sun was now clear of the trees, turning the green of the forests to gold. Coffee and warm food were served to them during a momentary stop among the trees, and then the Winchester regiment moved forward again toward Champion Hill.

Rifle shots were now heard ahead of them. They were scattered, but the lads knew that the hostile skirmishers had come in contact. Presently the reports increased and through the woods they saw puffs of smoke. Trumpets to right and left were calling up the brigades.

"Open up for the guns!" cried an aide, and a battery lumbered through, the men swearing at their panting horses. But the Southern cannon were already at work. From the bare crest of Champion Hill they were sending shells which crashed in the ranks of the advancing foe. Two or three of the Winchesters were hit, and a wounded horse, losing its rider, ran screaming through the wood.

The forest and thickets now grew so dense that the officers dismounted, giving their horses to an orderly, and led on foot. The country before them was most difficult. Besides the trees and brush it was seared with ravines. A swarm of skirmishers in front whom they could not see now poured bullets among them, and the shells, curving over the heads of the ambushed sharpshooters, fell in the Union ranks. On either flank the battle opened and swelled rapidly.

"We may have got Pemberton trapped," said Pennington, "but he's got so many bristles that we can't reach in a hand and pull out our captive. My God, Dick, are you killed?"

He was pulling Dick to his feet and examining him anxiously.

"I'm all right," said Dick in a moment. "It was the wind of a big round shot that knocked me down. Just now I'm thanking God it was the wind and not the shot."

"I wish we could get through these thickets!" exclaimed Warner. "Our comrades must be engaged much more heavily than we are. What an uproar!"

The combat swelled to great proportions. The Southern army, being compelled to fight, fought now with all its might. The crest of the long hill blazed with fire. The men in gray used every advantage of position. Cannon and rifles raked the woods and thickets, and at many points the Union attack was driven back. The sun rose slowly and they still held the hill, fighting with all the fire and valor characteristic of the South. They were cheered at times by the expectation of victory, but the stubborn Grant brought up his remaining forces and continually pressed the battle.

The Winchester regiment crossed a ravine and knelt among the thickets. Its losses had not yet been heavy, as most of the cannon fire was passing over their heads. Grape and canister were whistling among the woods, and Dick was devoutly grateful that these deadly missiles were going so high. Yet if they did not hurt they made one shiver, and it was not worth while to recall that when he heard the sound the shot had passed already. One shivered anyhow.

As well as Dick could judge from the volume of sound the battle seemed to be concentrated directly upon the hill. He knew that Grant expected to make a general attack in full force, and he surmised that one of the commanders under him was not pushing forward with the expected zeal. His surmise was correct. A general with fifteen thousand men was standing almost passive in front of a much smaller force, but other generals were showing great fire and energy.

The Winchester regiment contained many excellent riflemen and they were so close now that they could use the weapons for which the Kentuckians were famous. Firing deliberately, they began to cut gaps in the first ranks of the defenders on the slope. Then they rose and with other regiments pushed forward again.

But they came to a road in the side of the hill defended powerfully by infantry and artillery, and a heavy fire, killing and wounding many, was poured upon them. They sought to cross the road and attack the defenders with the bayonet, but they were driven back and their losses were so heavy that they were compelled to take cover in the nearest thickets.

The men, gasping with heat and exhaustion, threw themselves down, a sleet of shells and bullets passing over their heads. Dick had a sense of failure, but it lasted only a moment or two. From both left and right came the fierce crash of battle, and he knew that, if they had been driven back before the road, their comrades were maintaining the combat elsewhere.

"It's merely a delay. We pause to make a stronger attack," said Colonel Winchester, as if he were apologizing to himself. "Are you all right, Dick?"

"Unhurt, sir, and so are Warner and Pennington, who are lying here beside me."

"Unhurt, but uneasy," said Warner. "I don't like the way twigs and leaves are raining down on me. It shows that if they were to depress their fire they would be shearing limbs off of us instead of boughs off the trees."

The sun was high and brilliant now, but it could not dispel the clouds of smoke gathering in the thickets. It floated everywhere, and Dick felt it stinging his mouth and throat. Murmurs began to run along the lines. They did not like being held there. They wanted to charge again. They were still confident of victory.

Dick was sent toward another part of the army for orders, and he saw that all along the hill the battle was raging fiercely. But Grant could not yet hear the roar of guns which should indicate the advance of McClernand and his fifteen thousand. The silent leader was filled with anger, but he reserved the expression of it for a later time.

Dick saw the fiery and impetuous Logan, noticeable for his long coal-black hair, lead a headlong and successful charge, which carried the Union troops higher up the hill. But another general was driven back, losing cannon, although he retook them in a second and desperate charge. Still no news from McClernand and his fifteen thousand! There was silence where his guns ought to have been thundering, and Grant burned with silent anger.

It was noon, and a half-hour past. The Union plans, made with so much care and judgment, and the movements begun with so much skill and daring seemed to be going awry. Yet Grant with the tenacity, rather than lightning intuition, that made him a great general, held on. His lieutenants clung to their ground and prepared anew for attack.

Dick hurried back to his own regiment, which was still lying in the thickets, bearing an order for its advance in full strength. Colonel Winchester, who was standing erect, walking among his men and encouraging them, received it with joy. Word was speedily passed to all that the time to win or lose had come. Above the cannon and rifles the music of the calling trumpets sounded. The fire of both sides suddenly doubled and tripled in volume.

"Now, boys," shouted Colonel Winchester, waving his sword, "up the hill and beat 'em!"

Uttering a deep-throated roar the Winchesters rushed forward, firing as they charged. Dick was carried on the top wave of enthusiasm. He discharged his pistol into the bank of fire and smoke in front of them and shouted incessantly. He heard the bullets and every form of missile from the cannon whining all about them. Leaves and twigs fell upon him. Many men went down under the deadly fire, but the rush of the regiment was not checked for an instant.

They passed out of the thicket, swept across the road, and drove the defenders up the hill. Along the whole line the Union army, fired with the prospect of success, rushed to the attack. Grant threw every man possible into the charge.

The Southern army was borne back by the weight of its enemy. All of the front lines were driven in and the divisions were cut apart. There was lack of coordination among the generals, who were often unable to communicate with one another, and Pemberton gave the order to retreat. The battle was lost to the South, and with it the chance to crush Grant between two forces.

The Union army uttered a great shout of victory, and Grant urged forward the pursuit. Bowen, one of the South's bravest generals, was the last to give way. The Winchester regiment was a part of the force that followed him, both fighting hard. Dick found himself with his comrades, wading a creek, and they plunged into the woods and thickets which blazed with the fire of South and North. A Confederate general was killed here, but the brave Bowen still kept his division in order, and made the pursuit pay a heavy cost for all its gain.

Dick saw besides the Confederate column many irregulars in the woods, skilled sharpshooters, who began to sting them on the flank and bring down many a good soldier. He caught a glimpse of a man who was urging on the riflemen and who seemed to be their leader. He recognized Slade, and, without a moment's hesitation, fired at him with his pistol. But the man was unhurt and Slade's return bullet clipped a lock of Dick's hair.

Then they lost each other in the smoke and turmoil of the battle, and, despite the energy of the pursuit by the Union leaders, they could not break up the command of Bowen. The valiant Southerner not only made good his retreat, but broke down behind him the bridge over a deep river, thus saving for a time the fragments of Pemberton's army.

The Winchester regiment marched back to the battlefield, and Dick saw that the victory had been overwhelming. Nearly a third of the Southern army had been lost and thirty cannon were the trophies of Grant. Yet the fighting had been desperate. The dead and wounded were so numerous that the veteran soldiers who had been at Shiloh and Stone River called it "The Hill of Death."

Dick saw Grant walking over the field and he wondered what his feelings were. Although its full result was beyond him he knew, nevertheless, that Champion Hill was a great victory. At one stroke of his sword Grant had cut apart the circle of his foes.

Dick came back from the pursuit with Colonel Winchester. He had lost sight of Warner and Pennington in the turmoil, but he believed that they would reappear unhurt. They had passed through so many battles now that it did not occur to him that any of the three would be killed. They might be wounded, of course, as they had been already, but fate would play them no such scurvy trick as to slay them.

"What will be the next step, Colonel?" asked Dick, as they stood together upon the victorious hill.

"Depends upon what Johnston and Pemberton do. Pemberton, I'm sure, will retreat to Vicksburg, but Johnston, if he can prevent it, won't let his army be shut up there. Still, they may not be able to communicate, and if they should Pemberton may disobey the far abler Johnston and stay in Vicksburg anyhow. At any rate, I think we're sure to march at once on Vicksburg."

A figure approaching in the dusk greeted Dick with a shout of delight. Another just behind repeated the shout with equal fervor. Warner and Pennington had come, unharmed as he had expected, and they were exultant over the victory.

"Come over here," said Warner to Dick. "Sergeant Whitley has cooked a glorious supper and we're waiting for you."

Dick joined them eagerly, and the sergeant received them with his benevolent smile. They were commissioned officers, and he gave them all the respect due to rank, but in his mind they were only his boys, whom he must watch and protect.

While the fires sprang up about them and they ate and talked of the victory, Washington was knowing its darkest moments. Lee had already been marching thirteen days toward Gettysburg, and he seemed unbeatable. Grant, who had won for the North about all the real success of which it could yet boast, was lost somewhere in the Southern wilderness. The messages seeking him ran to the end of the telegraph wires and no answer came back. The click of the key could not reach him. Many a spirit, bold at most times, despaired of the Union.

But the old and hackneyed saying about the darkest hour just before the dawn was never more true. The flame of success was already lighted in the far South, and Lincoln was soon to receive the message, telling him that Grant had not disappeared in the wilderness for nothing. Thereafter he was to trust the silent and tenacious general through everything.

They were up and away at dawn. Dick was glad enough to leave the hill, on which many of the dead yet lay unburied, and he was eager for the new field of conflict, which he was sure would be before Vicksburg. Warner and Pennington were as sanguine as he. Grant was now inspiring in them the confidence that Lee and Jackson inspired in their young officers.

"How big is this city of Vicksburg?" asked Pennington.

"Not big at all," replied Warner. "There are no big cities in the South except New Orleans, but it's big as a fortress. It's surrounded by earthworks, Frank, from which the Johnnies can pot you any time."

"Well, at any rate, I'll be glad to see it—from a safe distance. I wouldn't mind sitting down before a town. There's too much wet country around here to suit me."

"It's likely that you'll have a chance to sit for a long time. We won't take Vicksburg easily."

But the time for sitting down had not yet come. The confidence of the soldiers in their leader was justified continually. He advanced rapidly toward Vicksburg, and in pursuit of Pemberton's defeated men. The victory at Champion Hill had been so complete that the Southern army was broken into detached fragments, and the Southern generals were now having the greatest difficulty in getting them together again.

Grant, with his loyal subordinate, Sherman, continued to push upon the enemy with the greatest vigor. Sherman had not believed in the success of the campaign, had even filed his written protest, but when Grant insisted he had cooperated with skill and energy. He and Grant stood together on a hill looking toward the future field of conflict, and he told Grant now that he expected continued success.

It was the fortune of the young officers of the Winchester regiment sitting near on their horses to see the two generals who were in such earnest consultation, and who examined the whole circle of the country so long and so carefully through powerful glasses.

The effects of the victory deep in the South were growing hourly in Dick's mind, and the two figures standing there on the hill were full of significance to him. He had a premonition that they were the men more than any others who would achieve the success of the Union, if it were achieved at all. They had dismounted and stood side by side, the figure of Grant short, thick and sturdy, that of Sherman, taller and more slender. They spoke only at intervals, and few words then, but nothing in the country about them escaped their attention.

Dick had glasses of his own, and he, too, began to look. He saw a region much wooded and cut by deep streams. Before them lay the sluggish waters of Chickasaw Bayou, where Sherman had sustained a severe defeat at an earlier time, and farther away flowed the deep, muddy Yazoo.

"See the smoke, George, rising above that line of trees along the river?" said Dick.

"Yes, Dick," replied Warner, "and I notice that the smoke rises in puffs."

"It has a right to go up that way, because it's expelled violently from the smoke-stacks of steamers. And those steamers are ours, George, our warships. Our navy in this war hasn't much chance to do the spectacular, but we can never give it enough credit."

"That's right, Dick. It keeps the enemy surrounded and cuts off his supplies, while our army fights him on land. Whatever happens the waters are ours."

"And the Mississippi has become a Union river, splitting apart the Confederacy."

"Right you are, Dick, and we're already in touch with our fleet there. The boats do more than fight for us. They're unloading supplies in vast quantities from Chickasaw Bayou. We'll have good food, blankets, tents to shelter us from the rain, and unlimited ammunition to batter the enemy's works."

The investment of Vicksburg had been so rapid and complete that Johnston, the man whom Grant had the most cause to fear, could not unite with Pemberton, and he had retired toward Jackson, hoping to form a new army. Only three days after Champion Hill Grant had drawn his semicircle of steel around Vicksburg and its thirty thousand men, and the navy in the rivers completed the dead line.

Dick rode with Colonel Winchester and took the best view they could get of Vicksburg, the little city which had suddenly become of such vast military importance.

Now and then on the long, lower course of the Mississippi, bluffs rise, although at far intervals. Memphis stands on one group and hundreds of miles south Vicksburg stands on another. The Vicksburg plateau runs southward to the Big Bayou, which curves around them on the south and east, and the eastern slope of the uplift has been cut and gulleyed by many torrents. So strong has been the effect of the rushing water upon the soft soil that these cuts have become deep winding ravines, often with perpendicular banks. One of the ravines is ten miles long. Another cuts the plateau itself for six miles, and a permanent stream flows through it.

The colonel and Dick saw everywhere rivers, brooks, bayous, hills, marshes and thickets, the whole turned by the Southern engineers into a vast and most difficult line of intrenchments. Grant now had forty thousand men for the attack or siege, but he and his generals did not yet know that most of the scattered Confederate army had gathered together again, and was inside. They believed that Vicksburg was held by fifteen thousand men at the utmost.

"What do you think of it, Colonel?" asked Dick, as they sat horseback on one of the highest hills.

"It will be hard to take, despite the help of the navy. Did you ever see another country cut up so much by nature and offering such natural help to defenders?"

"I've heard a lot of Vicksburg. I remember, Colonel, that, despite its smallness, it is one of the great river towns of the South."

"So it is, Dick. I was here once, when I was a boy before the Mexican war. Down on the bar, the low place between the bluffs and the river, was the dueling ground, and it was also the place for sudden fights. It and Natchez, I suppose, were rivals for the wild and violent life of the great river."

"Well, sir, it has a bigger fight on its hands now than was ever dreamed of by any of those men."

"I think you're right, Dick, but the general means to attack at once. We may carry it by storm."

Dick looked again at the vast entanglement of creeks, bayous, ravines, forests and thickets. Like other young officers, he had his opinion, but he had the good sense to keep it to himself. He and the colonel rejoined the regiment, and presently the trumpets were calling again for battle. The men of Champion Hill, sanguine of success, marched straight upon Vicksburg. All the officers of the Winchester regiment were dismounted, as their portion of the line was too difficult for horses.

Their advance, as at Champion Hill, was over ground wooded heavily and they soon heard the reports of the rifles before them. Bullets began to cut the leaves and twigs, carrying away the bushes, scarring the trees and now and then taking human life. The Winchester men fired whenever they saw an enemy, and with them it was largely an affair of sharpshooters, but on both left and right the battle rolled more heavily. The Southerners, behind their powerful fortifications at the heads of the ravines and on the plateau, beat back every attack.

Before long the trumpets sounded the recall and the short battle ceased. Grant had discovered that he could not carry Vicksburg by a sudden rush and he recoiled for a greater effort. He discovered, too, from the resistance and the news brought later by his scouts that an army almost as numerous as his own was in the town.

The Winchester regiment made camp on a solid, dry piece of ground beyond the range of the Southern works, and the men, veterans now, prepared for their comfort. The comrades ate supper to the slow booming of great guns, where the advanced cannon of either side engaged in desultory duel.

The distant reports did not disturb Dick. They were rather soothing. He was glad enough to rest after so much exertion and so much danger and excitement.

"I feel as if I were an empty shell," he said, "and I've got to wait until nature comes along and fills up the shell again with a human being."

"In my school in Vermont," said Warner, "they'd call that a considerable abuse of metaphor, but all metaphors are fair in war. Besides, it's just the way I feel, too. Do you think, Dick, we'll settle down to a regular siege?"

"Knowing General Grant as we do, not from what he tells us, since he hasn't taken Pennington and you and me into his confidence as he ought to, but from our observation of his works, I should say that he would soon attack again in full force."

"I agree with you, Knight of the Penetrating Mind, but meanwhile I'm going to enjoy myself."

"What do you mean, George?"

"A mail has come through by means of the river, and my good father and mother—God bless 'em—have sent me what they knew I would value most, something which is at once an intellectual exercise, an entertainment, and a consolation in bereavement."

Dick and Pennington sat up. Warner's words were earnest and portentous. Besides, they were very long, which indicated that he was not jesting.

"Go ahead, George. Show us what it is!" said Dick eagerly.

Warner drew from the inside pocket of his waist coat a worn volume which he handled lovingly.

"This," he said, "is the algebra, with which I won the highest honors in our academy. I have missed it many and many a time since I came into this war. It is filled with the most beautiful problems, Dick, questions which will take many a good man a whole night to solve. When I think of the joyous hours I've spent over it some of the tenderest chords in my nature are touched."

Pennington uttered a deep groan and buried his face in the grass. Then he raised it again and said mournfully:

"Let's make a solemn agreement, Dick, to watch over our poor comrade. I always knew that something was wrong with his mind, although he means well, and his heart is in the right place. As for me, as soon as I finished my algebra I sold it, and took a solemn oath never to look inside one again. That I call the finest proof of sanity anybody could give. Oh, look at him, Dick! He's studying his blessed algebra and doesn't hear a word I say!"

Warner was buried deep in the pages of a plus b and x minus y, and Dick and Pennington, rising solemnly, walked noiselessly from the presence around to the other side of the little opening where they lay down again. The bit of nonsense relieved them, but it was far from being nonsense to Warner. His soul was alight. As he dived into the intricate problems memories came with them. Lying there in the Southern thickets in the close damp heat of summer he saw again his Vermont mountains with their slopes deep in green and their crests covered with snow. The sharp air of the northern winter blew down upon him, and he saw the clear waters of the little rivers, cold as ice, foaming over the stones. That air was sharp and vital, but, after a while, he came back to himself and closed his book with a sigh.

"Pardon me for inattention, boys," he said, "but while I was enjoying my algebra I was also thinking of old times back there in Vermont, when nobody was shooting at anybody else."

Dick and Pennington walked solemnly back and sat down beside him again.

"Returned to his right mind. Quite sane now," said Pennington. "But don't you think, Dick, we ought to take that exciting book away from him? The mind of youth in its tender formative state can be inflamed easily by light literature."

Warner smiled and put his beloved book in his pocket.

"No, boys," he said, "you won't take it away from me, but as soon as this war is over I shall advance from it to studies of a somewhat similar nature, but much higher in character, and so difficult that solving them will afford a pleasure keener and more penetrating than anything else I know."

"What is your greatest ambition, Warner?" asked Pennington. "Do you, like all the rest of us, want to be President of the United States?"

"Not for a moment. I've already been in training several years to be president of Harvard University. What higher place could mortal ask? None, because there is none to ask for."

"I can understand you, George," said Dick. "My great-grandfather became the finest scholar ever known in the West. There was something of the poet in him too. He had a wonderful feeling for nature and the forest. He had a remarkable chance for observation as he grew up on the border, and was the close comrade in the long years of Indian fighting of Henry Ware, who was the greatest governor of Kentucky. As I think I've told you fellows, Harry Kenton, Governor Ware's great-grandson and my comrade, is fighting on the other side."

"I knew of the great Dr. Cotter long before I met you, Dick," replied Warner. "I read his book on the Indians of the Northern Mississippi Valley. Not merely their history and habits, but their legends, their folk lore, and the wonderful poetic glow so rich and fine that he threw over everything. There was something almost Homeric in his description of the great young Wyandot chieftain Timmendiquas or White Lightning, whom he acclaimed as the finest type of savage man the age had known."

"He and Henry Ware fought Timmendiquas for years, and after the great peace they were friends throughout their long lives."

"And I've studied, too, his wonderful book on the Birds and Mammals of North America," continued Warner with growing enthusiasm. "What marvelous stores of observation and memory! Ah, Dick, those were exciting days, and a man had opportunities for real and vital experiences!"

Dick and Pennington laughed.

"What about Vicksburg, old praiser of past times?" asked Frank. "Don't you think we'll have some lively experiences trying to take it? And wasn't there something real and vital about Bull Run and Shiloh and Perryville and Stone River and all the rest? Don't you worry, George. You're living in exciting times yourself."

"That's so," said Warner calmly. "I had forgotten it for the moment. We've been readers of history and now we're makers of it. It's funny—and maybe it isn't funny—but the makers of history often know little about what they're making. The people who come along long afterward put them in their places and size up what they have done."

"They can give all the reasons they please why I won this war," said Pennington, "but even history-makers are entitled to a rest. Since there's no order to the contrary I mean to stretch out and go to sleep. Dick, you and George can discuss your problems all night."

But they went to sleep also.

CHAPTER IX

THE OPEN DOOR

"Dick," said Colonel Winchester the next morning, "I think you are the best scout and trailer among my young officers. Mr. Pennington, you are probably the best on the plains, and I've no doubt, Warner, that you would do well in the mountains, but for the hills, forests and rivers I'll have to choose Dick. I've another errand for you, my boy. You're to go on foot, and you're to take this dispatch to Admiral Porter, who commands the iron-clads in the river near the city. Conceal it carefully about you, but I anticipate no great danger for you, as Vicksburg is pretty well surrounded by our forces."

The dispatch was written on thin, oiled paper. Dick hid it away in the lining of his coat and departed upon another important mission, full of pride that he should be chosen for it. He had all the passwords and carried two good pistols in his belt. Rich in experience, he felt able to care for himself, even should the peril be greater than Colonel Winchester had expected.

The sun was not far above the horizon but it was warm and brilliant, and it lighted up the earth, throwing a golden glow over the plateau of Vicksburg, the great maze of ravines and thickets and the many waters.

He passed along the lines, walking rapidly southward, and saw more than one officer of his acquaintance. Hertford's cavalry were in a field, and the colonel himself sat on a portion of the rail fence that had enclosed it. He hailed the lad pleasantly.

"Into the forest again, Dick," he said.

"Not this time, sir," Dick replied. "It's just a little trip, down the river."

"Success to the trip and a speedy return."

Dick nodded and walked on. He was quite sure that his dispatch was an order from Grant for Porter to come up the stream and join in a general attack which everybody felt sure was planned for an early date.

As he passed through the regiments and brigades he received much good-humored chaff. The great war of America differed widely from the great wars of Europe. The officers and men were more nearly on a plane of equality. The vast majority of them had been volunteers in the beginning and perhaps this feeling of comradeship made them fight all the better. North and South were alike in it.

"Which way, sonny?" called a voice from a group. "You don't find the fighting down there. It's back toward Vicksburg."

Dick nodded and smiled.

"Maybe he's out walking for exercise. These officers ride too much."

Dick walked on with a steady swinging step. He regarded the sunbrowned, careless youths with the genuine affection of a brother. Many of them were as young as he or younger, but they were now veterans of battle and march. Napoleon's soldiers themselves could not have boasted of more experience than they.

He was coming to the last link in the steel chain, and the colonel of a regiment, an old man, warned him to be careful as he approached the river.

"Southern sharpshooters are among the ravines and thickets," he said. "They fired on our lads about dawn and then escaped easily in the thick cover."

"Thank you, sir," said Dick, "I'll be on my guard." Yet he did not feel the presence of danger. Youth perhaps becomes more easily hardened in war than middle age, or perhaps it thinks less of consequences. The Union cannon, many of great weight and power, had begun already to fire upon Vicksburg. Huge shells and shot were rained upon the city. Pemberton had two hundred guns facing the river and the army, but to spare his ammunition they made little reply.

Dick looked back now and then. He saw flakes of fire on the northern horizon, puffs of smoke and the curving shells. He felt that Vicksburg was no pleasant place to be in just now, and yet it must be full of civilians, many of them women and children. He was sorry for them. It was Dick's nature to see both sides of a quarrel. He could never hate the Southerners, because they saw one way and he another.

It was a passing emotion. It was too fine a morning for youth to grieve. At the distance the plumes of smoke made by the shells became decorative rather than deadly. From a crest he saw upon the plateau of Vicksburg and even discerned the dim outline of houses. Looking the other way, he saw the smoke of the iron-clads down the river, and he also caught glimpses of the Mississippi, gold in the morning sun over its vast breadth.

Then he entered the thickets, and, bearing in mind the kindly warning of the old colonel, proceeded slowly and with extreme caution. The Southerners knew every inch of the ground here and he knew none. He came to a ravine and to his dismay found that a considerable stream was flowing through it toward the bayou. It was yellow water, and he thought he might find a tree, fallen across the stream, which would serve him as a foot log, but a hunt of a few minutes disclosed none, and, hesitating no longer, he prepared to wade.

He put his belt with the pistols in it around his neck and stepped in boldly. His feet sank in the mud. The water rose to his knees and then to his waist. It was, in truth, deeper than he had expected—one could never tell about these yellow, opaque streams. He took another step and plunged into a hole up to his shoulders.

Angry that he should be wet through and through, and with such muddy water too, he crossed the stream.

He looked down with dismay at his uniform. The sun would soon dry it, but until he got a chance to clean it, it would remain discolored and yellow, like the jeans clothes which the poorer farmers of the South often wore. And yet the accident that he bemoaned, the bath in water thick with mud, was to prove his salvation.

Dick shook himself like a big dog, throwing off as much of the water as he could. He had kept his pistols dry and he rebuckled his belt around his waist. Then he returned to his errand. Among the thickets he saw but little. Vicksburg, the Mississippi, and the Union camp disappeared. He beheld only a soft soil, many bushes and scrub forest. After going a little distance he was compelled to stop again and consider. It was curious how one could lose direction in so small a space.

He paused and listened, intending to regain his course through the sense of hearing. From the north and east came the thunder of the siege guns. It had grown heavier and was continuous now. Once more he was sorry for Vicksburg, because the Union gunners were unsurpassed and he was sure that bombs and shells were raining upon the devoted town.

Now he knew that he must go west by south, and he made his way over difficult country, crossing ravines, climbing hills, and picking his path now and then through soft ground, the most exhausting labor of all. The sun poured down upon him and his uniform dried fast. He had just crossed one of the ravines and was climbing into the thicket beyond when a voice asked:

"See any of the Yanks in front?"

Dick's heart stood still, and then all his presence of mind came back. Not in vain had the kindly colonel warned him of the Southern sharpshooters in the bush.

"No," he replied. "They seem to be farther up. One of our

fellows told me he saw a whole regiment of them off there to the right."

He plunged deeper into the bush and walked on as if he were among his own comrades. He realized that his faded uniform with its dye of yellow mud had caused him to be mistaken for one of Pemberton's men. His accent, which was Kentuckian and therefore Southern, had helped him also. He passed three or four other men, bent over, rifle in hand and watching, and he nodded to them familiarly. In such a crisis he knew that boldness and ease were his best cards, and he said to one of the men, with a laugh:

"You'll have to tell us Tennesseeans about all your bayous and creeks. I've just fallen into one that had no right to be there."

"You Tennesseeans need a bath anyhow," replied the man, chuckling.

"We'd never choose a Mississippi stream for it," said Dick in the same vein, and passed on leaving the rifleman in high good humor. How wonderfully these Southerners were like the Northerners! He noticed presently a half-dozen other sharpshooters in the Confederate butternut, prowling among the bushes, and through an opening he saw his own people to the west, but too far away to be reached by anything but artillery. The slow, deep music of the Northern guns came steadily to his ear, but their fire was always turned toward Vicksburg.

Dick knew that his position was extremely critical. Perhaps it was growing more so all the while, but he was never cooler. A quiet lad, he always rose wonderfully to an emergency. He was quite sure that he was among Mississippi troops, and they could not possibly know all the soldiers from the other states gathered for the defense of Vicksburg. He did not differ from those around him in any respect, except that he did not carry a rifle.

He paused and looked back thoughtfully at the distant Union troops.

"Can you tell me how they're posted?" he said to a tall, thin middle-aged man who had a chew of tobacco in his cheek. "I carry dispatches to General Pemberton, and the more information I can give him the better."

"Yes, I kin tell you," replied the man, somewhat flattered. "They're posted everywhere. What, with their army and them boats of theirs in the river, they've got a high fence around us, all staked and ridered."

"It doesn't take any more work to tear a fence down than it does to build it up."

"I reckon you're right thar, stranger. But was you at Champion Hill?"

"No, I missed that."

"Then it was a good thing for you that you did. I didn't set much store by the Yanks when this war began. One good Southerner could whip five of 'em any time, our rip-roarin', fire-eatin' speech-makers said. I knowed then, too, that they was right, but I was up thar in Kentucky a while, an' after Donelson I reckoned that four was about as many as I wanted to tackle all to oncet. Then thar was Shiloh, an' I kinder had a thought that if three of 'em jumped on me at one time I'd hev my hands purty full to lick 'em. Then come Corinth, an,' reasonin' with myself, I said I wouldn't take on more'n two Yanks at the same time. An' now, since I've been at Champion Hill, I know that the Yank is a pow'ful good fighter, an' I reckon one to one jest about suits me, an' even then I'd like to have a leetle advantage in the draw."

"I feel that way about it, too. The Yankees are going to make a heap of trouble for us here. But I must be going. What's the best path into Vicksburg?"

"See that little openin' in the bushes. Follow it. Jest over the hill you'll run into a passel of our fellers, but pay no 'tention to 'em. If they ask you who you are an' whar you're boun' tell 'em to go straight to blazes, while you go to Vicksburg."

"Thank you," said Dick, "I like to meet an obliging and polite man like you. It helps even in war."

"Don't mention it. When I wuz a little shaver my ma told me always to mind my manners, an' when I didn't she whaled the life out of me. An', do you know, stranger, she's just a leetle, withered old woman, but if she could 'pear here right now I'd be willin' to set down right in these bushes an' say, 'Ma, take up that stick over thar an' beat me across the shoulders an' back with it as hard as you kin.' I'd feel good all over."

"I believe you," said Dick, who thought of his own mother.

He followed the indicated path until he was out of sight of everybody, and then he plunged into the bushes and marsh toward the river. When he was well hidden he stopped and considered.

It was quite evident that he had wandered from the right road, but it was no easy task to get back into it. There was an unconscious Confederate cordon about him and he must pass through it somewhere. He moved farther toward the river, but only went deeper into the swamp.

He turned to the south and soon reached firm ground, but he heard Confederate pickets talking in front of him. Then he caught glimpses of two or three men watching among the trees, and he lay down in a clump of bushes. He might pass them as he had passed the others, but he thought it wiser not to take the risk.

He was willing also to rest a little, as he had done a lot of hard walking. His clothing was now dry, and the mud had dried upon it.

He turned aside into one of the deep ravines and then into a smaller one leading from it. The bushes were dense there and he lay down among them, so completely hidden that he was invisible ten feet away. Here he still heard the mutter of the guns, which came in a long, droning sound, and occasionally a rifle cracked at some point closer by. The Union army was still busy and he felt a few moments of despondency. His dispatch undoubtedly was of great importance, and yet he was not able to deliver it. It was highly probable that for precaution's sake other messengers bore the same dispatch, but he was anxious to arrive with his nevertheless, and he wanted, too, to arrive first. The last now seemed impossible and the first improbable.

The crackling fire came nearer. Owing to the lack of percussion caps, Pemberton had ordered his men to use their rifles sparingly, but evidently a considerable body of sharpshooters near Dick were attempting a flanking movement of some kind, and meant to carry it out with bullets. He was impatient to see, but prudence kept him in his covert, a prudence that was soon justified, as presently he heard voices very near him and then the sound of footsteps.

He rose up a little and saw several hundred Confederate soldiers passing on the slopes not more than a hundred yards away. They went south of him, and he recognized with growing alarm that the wall across his way was growing higher. When they were gone and he could no longer hear their tread among the bushes he slipped from his hiding place and went directly toward Vicksburg. Being within an iron ring he thought that perhaps he would be safer somewhere near the center. He might make his way without much trouble through the vast confused crowd in Vicksburg, and then in the night go down the river's edge and to the fleet.

It was a daring idea, so very daring that it appealed to the strain of high adventure in the lad. He was encouraged, too, by his earlier and easy success in passing among the Confederate soldiers. But in order not to appear reckless and to satisfy his own conscience he tried once more for the way to the south. But the soldiers entirely barred the path there, and, being on some duty that required extreme vigilance, they were likely to prove exacting.

He advanced with a clear mind toward Vicksburg, picking his way among the forests and ravines, but, after long walking over most difficult ground, he saw before him extensive earthworks thronged with Southern troops. When he turned westward the result was the same, and then it became evident that there was no flaw in the iron ring. He could not go through to Porter, he could not go back to his own army, but Vicksburg invited him as a guest.

He would make the trial at night. It was a long wait, but he dared not risk it by day, and, going back into one of the ravines, he sought a secluded and sheltered place. Threshing the bushes to drive away possible snakes, he crawled into a clump and lay there. Resolved to be patient in spite of everything, he did not stir, but listened to the far throbbing of the cannon which poured an incessant storm of missiles upon unhappy Vicksburg.

The warmth and the heavy air in the ravine were relaxing. His brain grew so dull and heavy that he fell asleep, and when he awoke the twilight was coming. And yet he had lost nothing. He had gained rather. The time had passed. His body had been strengthened and his nerves steadied while he slept.

The distant booming of the guns still came. He had expected it. That was Grant. He had wrapped the coil of steel around Vicksburg and he would never relax. Dick felt that there was no hope for the town, unless Johnston outside could gather a powerful army and fight Grant on even terms. But he considered it impossible, and there, too, was the great artery of the river along which flowed men and supplies of every kind for the Union.

The Southern twilight turned swiftly into night and, coming from his lair, Dick walked boldly toward the town. He had eaten nothing since morning, but he had not noticed it, until this moment, when he began to feel a little faintness. He resolved that Vicksburg should supply him. It was curious how much help he expected of Vicksburg, a hostile town.

He saw lights soon both to right and to left and he strengthened his soul. He knew that he must be calm, but alert and quick with the right answer. With his singular capacity for meeting a crisis he advanced into the thick of danger with a smiling face, even as his great ancestor, Paul Cotter, had often done.

His calm was of short duration. There was a rushing sound, something struck violently, and a tremendous explosion followed. Fire flashed before Dick's eyes, pieces of red hot metal whistled past his head, earth spattered him and he was thrown to the ground.

He sprang up again, understanding all instantly. A shell from his own army had burst near him, and he had been thrown down by the concussion. But he had not been hurt, and in a few seconds his pulse beat steadily.

He heard a shout of laughter as he stood, brushing the fresh dirt from his clothing. He glanced up in some anger, but he saw at once that the arrival of the shell had been most fortunate for his plan. To come near annihilation by a Federal gun certainly invested him with a Confederate character.

It was a group of young soldiers who were laughing and their amusement was entirely good-natured. They would have laughed the same way had the harmless adventure befallen one of their own number. Dick judged that they were from the Southwest.

"Close call," he said, smiling that attractive smile, which was visible even in the twilight.

"It was a friendly shell," said one of the youths, "and it concluded not to come too close to you. These Yankee shells are so loving that sometimes they spray themselves in little pieces all over a fellow, like a shower of rice over a bride at a wedding."

"How long do you think the Yankees will keep it up?" asked Dick, putting indignation in his tone. "Haven't they any respect for the night?"

"Not a bit. That fellow Grant is a pounder. They say he'll blow away the whole plateau of Vicksburg if we don't drive him off."

"Well, we'll do it. You wait till old Joe Johnston comes up. Then we'll shut him between the jaws of a vise and squeeze the life out of him."

"Hope so. Where've you been?"

"Down below the town. I'm coming back with messages."

"So long. Good luck. Keep straight ahead, and you'll find all the generals you want."

The lights increased and he went into a small tavern, where he bought food and a cup of coffee, paying in gold. The tavern keeper asked no questions, but his eyes gleamed at sight of the yellow coin.

"Mighty little of this comes my way now," he said frankly, "and our own money is worth less and less every day. If things keep on the way they're headed it'll take a bale of it as big as a bale of cotton to pay for one good, square meal."

Dick laughed.

"Not so bad as that," he said. "You wait until we've given Grant a big thrashing and have cleared their boats out of the river. Then you'll see our money becoming real."

The man shook his head.

"Seein' will be believin'," he said, "an' as I ain't seein' I ain't believin'."

Dick with a friendly good night went out. Grant, the persistent, was still at work. His cannon flared on the dark horizon and the shells crashed in Vicksburg. Scarcely any portion of the town was safe. Now and then a house was smashed in and often the shells found victims.

The town was full of terror and confusion. Many of the rich

planters had come there with their families for refuge. Women and children hid from the terrible fire, and the civilians already had begun to burrow. Caves had been dug deep into the sides of the ravines and hundreds found in them a rude but safe shelter.

Dick now found that his plans were going wrong. He could wander about almost at will and to any one to whom he spoke he still claimed to be a Tennesseean, but he knew that it could not last forever. Sooner or later, some officer would question him closely, and then his tale would be too thin for truth.

Unable to make a way toward the river, he returned to the slopes and ravines, where they were digging the caves, and then fortune which had been smiling upon him turned its face the other way. A small man in butternut and an enormous felt hat passed near. He did not see Dick, but his very presence gave the lad a shiver. He believed afterward that before he saw him he had felt the proximity of Slade.

The man, carrying a rifle, was hurrying toward the center of the town, and Dick, after one long look, hurried at equal speed the other way. He knew that Slade, if he saw him, would recognize him at once. Dusk and a muddy uniform would not protect him.

It was his idea now to go down through the ravines and make another trial toward the South. He saw ahead of him a line of intrenchments, which he was resolved to pass in some fashion, but the face of fortune was still away from him. The unknown officers who at any time might ask too many questions appeared.

A captain, a sunbrowned, alert man, stopped him at the edge of the bushes which clothed the slopes of the ravine.

"Your regiment?" he asked sharply.

"Tennessee regiment, sir," replied Dick, afraid to mention any number, since this officer might be a Tennesseean himself, and would want further identification. But the man was not to be put off—Dick judged from his uniform that he was a colonel—and demanded sharply his regiment's number and his business.

The lad mumbled something under his breath, hopeful that he would pass on, but the officer stepped forward, looked at him closely and then suddenly turned back the collar of his army jacket, disclosing a bit of the under side yet blue.

"Thunderation, a Yankee spy!" he exclaimed.

Dick always believed that his life was due to a sudden and violent impulse, or rather a convulsive jerk, because he had no time to think. He threw off the officer's hand, dashed his fist into his face, and, without waiting to see the effect, ran headlong among the bushes down the side of the ravine. He heard a shouting behind him, the reports of several shots, the rapid tread of feet, and he knew that the man-hunt was on.

He had all the instincts of the hunted to seek cover, and the night was his friend. But few lights glimmered in that portion of Vicksburg, and in many parts of the ravine the bushes were thick. He darted down the slope at great speed, then turned and ran along its side, still keeping well under cover. Where the shadows were darkest and the bushes thickest he paused panting.

He heard his pursuers calling to one another, and he also heard the excited voices of people in the ravine. The civilians had been aroused by the shots so close by and he thought the confusion would help him. He stood in the deep shadow, his breath gradually growing easier, and then he started down the ravine, coming to a little path that led along the side of the slope. He noticed a dark opening, and as the voices of pursuers were now coming nearer, he popped into it, trusting to blind luck.

Dick had thought it was a mere wash-out or deep recess, but at the third step his foot struck upon a carpet and he saw ahead a dim light. He paused, amazed, and then he remembered that he had heard about the civilians digging caves for shelter from the shells and bombs. Evidently some forethoughtful man had prepared his cave early.

Uncertain what to do he did nothing, pressing his back against the earth and listening. No sound came, and the dim light still flickering ahead reassured him.

The opening through which he had come was large, and admitted plenty of fresh air. As he stood four or five feet from the entrance he saw several soldiers hurrying along the path, and he knew they were hunting for him. He realized then his fortune in finding this improvised cave-house. After the soldiers passed he walked gently toward the light. Apparently the regular occupants were gone away for the time, and he might find a hiding place there until it was safe to go out.

The passage was narrow, but the carpet was still under his feet, and further in, the sides and roof of the earthen walls had been covered with planks. The light grew brighter and he was quite sure that a room of some size was just ahead. His curiosity became so great that it smothered all apprehension, and he stepped boldly into the room, where the lamp burned on a table.

He would have stepped back as quickly, but a pair of great burning eyes caught his and held them. A bed was standing against the board wall of the cave, and in this bed lay an old man with a huge bald head, immense white eyebrows and eyes of extraordinary intensity.

Once more did Colonel Charles Woodville and Richard Mason stare into the eyes of each other, and for a long time neither spoke.

"I managed to escape from Jackson with my little family," said the colonel at length, "and I thought that in this, so to say, sylvan retreat I might drop all undesirable acquaintances that I made there."

The whole scene was grotesque and wild to Dick. It was like a passage out of the Arabian Nights, and an extraordinary spirit of recklessness seized him.

"I appreciate your words, sir," he said, "and I can understand your feelings. I have felt myself that it was never wise to go where one might not be welcome, and yet chance plays us such tricks that neither your wish nor mine is granted."

The old man then raised his head a little higher on the pillow. A spark leaped from the burning eyes.

"A lad of spirit," he said. "I would not withhold praise where praise is due. I recall meeting some one who resembled you very much. Perhaps a brother of yours, eh?"

"No, he was not my brother."

"Well, it does not matter and we will not pursue the subject. How does it happen that you have come into this hillside castle of mine?"

Young Mason saw a flicker of amusement in the eyes of the old man. He was aware that in his muddy uniform he made no imposing figure, but his spirit was as high as ever, and the touch of recklessness was still there.

"I saw some men coming down the path," he replied; "men with whom I do not care to associate, and I turned aside to avoid them. I beheld the open door and stepped within, but I did not know the chamber was occupied, and it was far from my purpose to intrude upon you or any one. I trust, sir, that you will believe me."

The lad took off his cap and bowed. His face was now revealed more clearly, and it was a fine one, splendidly molded, intellectual, and with noble blue eyes. After all, despite the mud and stains, he made a graceful figure as he stood there, so obviously confident of himself, but respectful.

The spark leaped again from the eyes of Colonel Woodville, and, remembering something, there was a slight warmth about the heart which lately had been so cold and bitter.

"I do not blame you," he said. "A lad, one in his formative years, cannot be too careful about his associates. Doubtless you were justified in taking advantage of the open door. But now that you are here may I ask you what you purpose next to do?"

"I admit, sir, that the question is natural," replied Dick,

suiting his tone and manner to those of the old man. "I have scarcely had time yet to form a purpose, but, since the danger of contamination of which we spoke still exists, it occurs to me that perhaps I might stay here a while. Is there some nook or a cover in which I might rest? I hope I do not trespass too much upon your hospitality."

Colonel Woodville pondered. His great white eyebrows were drawn together and, for a moment or two, he gazed down the beak of his nose.

"I confess," he said, "that the appeal to hospitality moves me. I am stirred somewhat, too, by pleasant recollections of the lad who looked like you. But wait, my daughter is coming. We will confer with her. Margaret is a most capable woman."

Dick heard a light step in the passage and he wheeled quickly. Miss Woodville was before him, a plain, elderly figure in a plain black dress, with a basket on her arm. The basket contained a fowl and some eggs which she had just bought at a great price. When she saw Dick her hand flew to her throat, but when the pulse ceased to beat so hard it came away and she looked at him fixedly. Then a slow smile like the dawn spread over the severe, worn face.

"Come in, Margaret, and put down your basket," said the colonel in a genial tone. "Meanwhile bid welcome to our unexpected guest, a young man of spirit and quality with whom I was holding converse before you came. He does not wish to go out to-night, because there are many violent men abroad, and he would avoid them."

Then he turned to Dick, and asked in a tone, sharp and commanding:

"I have your word, young sir, that your unexpected visit to our city was not of a secret nature; that is, it was not of a lawless character?"

"An accident, sir, an accident pure and simple. I answer you on my honor. I have seen nothing and I shall not seek to see anything which I should not see."

"Margaret," continued the colonel, and now his tone became deferential as behooved a gentleman speaking to a lady, "shall we ask him to share our simple quarters to-night?"

The lad slowly turned his gaze to the face of the woman. He felt with all the power of intuition that his fate rested on her decision. But she was a woman. And she was, too, a true daughter of her father. A kindred spark leaped up in her own soul, and she met Dick's gaze. She noted his fearless poise, and she saw the gallant spirit in his eye. Then she turned to her father.

"I think you wish him to stay, sir," she said, "and the wish seems right to me. Our narrow quarters limit our hospitality in quality, but not in intent. We can offer him nothing but the little alcove behind the blanket."

She inclined her head toward the blanket, which Dick had not noticed before. It hung near the bed and, wishing to cause this household little trouble, he said:

"Then I assume that you will shelter me for the night, and, if I may, I will go at once to my room."

Colonel Woodville lowered his head upon the pillow and laughed softly.

"A lad of spirit. A lad of spirit, I repeat," he said. "No, Margaret, you and I could not have turned him from our earthen roof."

Dick bowed to Miss Woodville, and that little ghost of a tender smile flitted about her thin lips. Then he lifted the blanket, stepped into the dark, and let the curtain fall behind him.

He stood for a space until his eyes, used to the dusk, could see dimly. It was a tiny room evidently used as a place of storage for clothing and bedding, but there was space enough for him to lie down, if he bent his knees a little.

The strain upon both muscle and nerve had been very great, and now came collapse. Removing his shoes and outer clothing he dropped upon a roll of bedding and closed his eyes. But he was grateful, deeply and lastingly grateful. The bread that he had cast upon the waters was returning to him fourfold.

He heard low voices beyond the blanket, and he did not doubt that they were those of Colonel Woodville and his daughter. The woman in plain black, with the basket on her arm, had seemed a pathetic figure to him. He could not blame them for feeling such intense bitterness. What were the causes of the war to people who had been driven from a luxurious home to a hole in the side of a ravine?

He slept, and when he woke it seemed to be only a moment later, but he knew from the slender edge of light appearing where the blanket just failed to touch the floor that morning had come. He moved gently lest he disturb his host in the larger room without, and then he heard the distant thunder, which he knew was the booming of Grant's great guns. And so the night had not stopped them! All through the hours that he slept the cannon had rained steel and death on Vicksburg. Then came a great explosion telling him that a shell had burst somewhere near. It was followed by the voice of Colonel Woodville raised in high, indignant tones:

"Can't they let a gentleman sleep? Must they wake him with one of their infernal shells?"

He heard a slight rustling sound and he knew that it was the great bald head moving impatiently on the pillows. Inferring that it was early, he would have gone back to sleep himself, but slumber would not come. He remained a while, thoughtful, for his future lay very heavy upon him, and then he heard the sound of several voices beyond the blanket.

He listened closely, trying to number and distinguish them. There were three and two belonged to Colonel Woodville and his daughter. The third repelled and puzzled him. It seemed to have in it a faint quality of the fox. It was not loud, and yet that light, snarling, sinister note was evident.

The sensitive, attuned mind can be easily affected by a voice, and the menace of the unknown beyond the blanket deepened. Dick felt a curious prickling at the roots of his hair. He listened intently, but he could not understand anything that was spoken, and then he drew himself forward with great caution.

They must be talking about something of importance, because the voices were earnest, and sometimes all three spoke at once. He reached a slow hand toward the blanket. The danger would be great, but he must see.

He drew back the blanket slightly, a quarter of an inch, maybe, and looked within the room. Then he saw the owner of the sinister voice, and he felt that he might have known from the first.

Slade, standing before Colonel Woodville's bed, his hat in his hand, was talking eagerly.

CHAPTER X

THE GREAT ASSAULT

The light from the door that was always open illumined the room. The rising sun must have struck full upon it, because it was almost as bright as day there. Slade was in his butternut uniform, and his rifle leaned against the wall. Now that he had made the slight opening Dick could understand their words.

"There are spies within Vicksburg, sir," said Slade. "Colonel Dustin detected one last night, but in the darkness he escaped down this ravine. The alarm was spread and he could not have got outside our lines. I must catch him. It will be a credit to me to do so. I was under your command, and, although not in active service owing to your wound, your word will go far. I want you to get me an order to search every house or place in which he could hide."

"Not too much zeal, my worthy Slade. Talleyrand said that, but you never heard of him. Excessive suspicion is not a good thing. It was your chief fault as an overseer, although I willingly pay tribute to your energy and attention to detail. This business of hunting spies is greatly overdone. The fate of Vicksburg will be settled by the cannon and the rifles."

"But, sir, they can do us great harm."

"Listen to that, my good Slade."

The deep booming note of the distant cannon entered the cave.

"That is the sound of Grant's guns. He can fight better with those weapons than with spies."

But Slade persisted, and Colonel Woodville, with an occasional word from his daughter, fenced with him, always using a light bantering tone, while the lad who lay so near listened, his pulses beating hard in his temples and throat.

"Your vigilance is to be commended, my good Slade," Dick heard Colonel Woodville say, "but to-day at least I cannot secure such a commission for you from General Pemberton. We hear that Grant is massing his troops for a grand attack, and there is little time to thresh up all our own quarters for spies. We must think more of our battle line. To-morrow we may have a plan. Come back to me then, and we will talk further on these matters."

"But think, sir, what a day may cost us!"

"You show impatience, not to say haste, Slade, and little is ever achieved by thoughtless haste. The enemy is closing in upon us, and it must be our chief effort to break his iron ring. Ah, here is my nephew! He may give us further news on these grave matters."

Dick saw the entrance darken for a moment, then lighten again, and that gallant youth, Victor Woodville, with whom he had fought so good a fight, stood in the room. He was still pale and he carried his left arm in a sling, but it was evident that his recovery from his wound had been rapid. Dick saw the stern face of the old colonel brighten a bit, while the tender smile curved again about the thin lips of the spinster.

Young Woodville gave a warm greeting to his uncle and elderly cousin, and nodded to Slade. Dick believed from his gesture that he did not like the guerilla leader, or at least he hoped so.

"Victor," said the colonel, "what word do you bring?"

"Grant is advancing his batteries, and they seem to be massing for attack. It will surely come in a day or two."

"As I thought. Then we shall need all our energies for immediate battle. And now, Mr. Slade, as I said before, I will see you again to-morrow about the matter of which we were speaking. I am old, wounded, and I grow weary. I would rest."

Slade rose to go. He was not a pleasant sight. His clothes were soiled and stained, and his face was covered with ragged beard. The eyes were full of venom and malice.

"Good day, Colonel Woodville," he said, "but I feel that I must bring the matter up again. As a scout and leader of irregulars for the Confederacy. I must be active in order to cope with the enemy's own scouts and spies. I shall return early to-morrow morning."

Colonel Woodville waved his hand and Slade, bowing, withdrew.

"Why was he so persistent, Uncle Charles?" asked Victor. "He seemed to have some underlying motive."

"He always has such a motive, Victor. He is a man who suspects everybody because he knows everybody has a right to suspect him. He may even have been suspecting me, his old, and, I fear, too generous employer. He has a mania about a spy hidden somewhere in Vicksburg."

Young Victor Woodville laughed gayly.

"What folly," he said, "for your old overseer, a man of Northern origin to boot, to suspect you, of all men, of helping a Yankee in any way. Why, Uncle Charles, everybody knows that you'd annihilate 'em if you could, and that you were making good progress with the task until you got that wound."

Colonel Woodville drew his great, white eyebrows together in his characteristic way.

"I admit, Victor, that I'm the prince of Yankee haters," he said.

"They've ruined me, and if they succeed they'll ruin our state and the whole South, too. We've fled for refuge to a hole in the ground, and yet they come thundering at the door of so poor an abode. Listen!"

They heard plainly the far rumble of the cannon. The intensity of the fire increased with the growing day. Shells and bombs were falling rapidly on Vicksburg. The face of Colonel Woodville darkened and the eyes under the white thatch burned.

"Nevertheless, Victor," he said, "hate the Yankees as I do, and I hate them with all my heart and soul, there are some things a gentleman cannot do."

"What for instance, Uncle?"

"He cannot break faith. He cannot do evil to those who have done good to him. He must repay benefits with benefits. He cannot permit the burden of obligation to remain upon him. Go to the door, Victor, and see if any one is lurking there."

Young Woodville went to the entrance and returned with word that no one was near.

"Victor," resumed Colonel Woodville, "this man Slade, who was so preposterously wrong, this common overseer from the hostile section which seeks with force to put us down, this miserable fellow who had the presumption to suspect me, lying here with a wound, received in the defense of the Confederacy, was nevertheless right."

Victor stared, not understanding, and Colonel Woodville raised himself a little higher on his pillows.

"Since when," he asked of all the world, "has a Woodville refused to pay his debts? Since when has a Woodville refused asylum to one who protected him and his in the hour of danger? Margaret, lift the blanket and invite our young friend in."

Dick was on his feet in an instant, and came into the chamber, uttering thanks to the man who, in spite of so much bitterness against his cause, could yet shelter him.

Young Woodville exclaimed in surprise.

"The Yankee with whom I fought at Bellevue!" he said.

"And the one who ignored your presence at Jackson," said Miss Woodville.

The two lads shook hands.

"And now," said Colonel Woodville, his old sharpness returning, "we shall be on even terms, young sir. Your uniform bears a faint resemblance to that of your own army, and Slade, cunning and cruel, may have had you shot as a spy. You would be taken within our lines and this is no time for long examinations."

"I know how much I owe you, sir," said Dick, "and I know how much danger my presence here brings upon you. I will leave as soon as the ravine is clear. The gathering of the troops for battle will give me a chance."

"You will do nothing of the kind. Having begun the task we will carry it through. Our cave home rambles. There is a little apartment belonging to Victor, in which you may put yourself in shape. I advise you to lie quiet here for a day or two, and then if I am still able to put my hand on you I may turn you over with full explanations to the authorities."

Dick noted the significance of the words, "if I am still able to put my hand on you," but he merely spoke of his gratitude and went with young Woodville into the little apartment. It was on the right side of the hall, and a round shutterless hole opened into the ravine, admitting light and air. The "window," which was not more than a foot in diameter faced toward the east and gave a view of earthworks, and the region beyond, where the Union army stood.

The room itself contained but little, a cot, some blankets, clothing, and articles of the toilet.

"Mason," said Woodville, "make yourself as comfortable as you can here. I did not know until I escaped from Jackson that it was you who ignored my presence there. You seem in some manner to have won the good opinion of my uncle, and, in any event, he could not bear to remain in debt to a Yankee. If you're careful you're safe here for the day, although you may be lonesome. I must go at once to our lines. Cousin Margaret will bring you something to eat."

They shook hands again.

"I can't do much fighting," said Woodville, "owing to this wounded arm of mine, but I can carry messages, and the line is so long many are to be taken."

He went out and Miss Woodville came soon with food on a tray. Dick suspected that they could ill spare it, but he must eat and he feared to offer pay. It embarrassed him, too, that she should wait upon him, but, in their situation, it was absolutely necessary that she do so, even were there a servant somewhere, which he doubted. But she left the tray, and when she returned for it an hour later she had only a few words to say.

Dick stood at the round hole that served as a window. There were bushes about it, and, at that point, the cliff seemed to be almost perpendicular. He was safe from observation and he looked over a vast expanse of country. The morning was dazzlingly clear, and he saw sections of the Confederate earthworks with their men and guns, and far beyond them other earthworks and other guns, which he knew were those of his own people.

While he stood there alone, free from the tension that had

lasted while Slade was present, he realized the great volume of fire that the Northern cannon were pouring without ceasing upon Vicksburg. The deep rumble was continually in his ears, and at times his imagination made the earth shake. He saw two shells burst in the air, and a shattering explosion told that a third struck near by. To the eastward smoke was always drifting. The Southern cannon seldom replied.

He resolved to attempt escape during the coming night. It hurt him to bring danger upon the Woodvilles and he wished, too, to fulfill his mission. Others, beyond question, would reach the fleet with the message, but he wished to reach it also.

Yet nothing new occurred during all the long day. Miss Woodville brought him more food at noon, but scarcely spoke. Then he returned to the hole in the cliff, and remained there until twilight. Young Woodville came, and he gathered from his manner that there had been no important movement of the armies, that all as yet was preparation. But he inferred that the storm was coming, and he told Victor that he meant to leave that night.

He was opposed vehemently. The line of Southern sentinels watched everywhere. Slade was most vigilant. He might come at any time into the ravine. No, he must wait. The next night, perhaps, but in any event he must remain a while.

Nor did he depart the next night either. Instead, two or three days passed, and he was still in the house dug in the hillside, a guest and yet a captive. The bombardment had gone on, his food was still brought to him by Miss Woodville, and once or twice Victor came, but Dick, as he was in honor bound, asked him no question about the armies.

The waiting, the loneliness and the suspense were terrible to one so young, and so ambitious. And yet he had fared better than he had a right to expect, a fact, however, that did not relieve his situation.

Another night came, and he went to sleep in his lonely cell in the wall, but he was awakened while it was yet intensely dark by a cannonade far surpassing in violence any that had gone before. He rushed to the hole, but he could see nothing in the ravine. Yet the whole plateau seemed to shake with the violence of the concussions and the crash of exploding shells.

The fire came from all sides, from the river as well as the land. The boom of the huge mortars on the boats there sounded above everything. Dick knew absolutely now that the message he was to carry had been delivered by somebody else.

He heard under the continued thunder of the guns sharp commands, and the tread of many troops moving. He knew that the

Southern forces were going into position, and he felt himself that the tremendous fire was the prelude to a great attack. His excitement grew. He strained his eyes, but he could see nothing in the dark ravine, or out there where the cannon roared, save the rapid, red flashes under the dim horizon. He had his watch and he had kept it running. Now he was able to make out that it was only three o'clock in the morning. A long time until day and he must wait until then to know what such a furious convulsion would achieve.

The slow time passed, and there was no decrease of the fire. Once or twice he came away from the window and listened at the entrance to his little room, but he could hear nothing stirring in the larger chamber. Yet it was incredible that Colonel Woodville and his daughter should not be awake. They would certainly be listening with an anxiety and suspense not less than his.

Dawn came after painful ages, and slowly the region out there where the Union army lay rose into the light. But it was a red dawn, a dawn in flame and smoke. Scores of guns crashed in front, and behind the heavy booming of the mortars on the boats formed the overnote of the storm.

The opening was not large, but it afforded the lad a good view, and he thrust his head out as far as he could, every nerve in him leaping at the deep roar of the cannonade. He had no doubt that the assault was about to be made. He was wild with eagerness to see it, and it was a cruel hurt to his spirit that he was held there, and could not take a part in it.

He thought of rushing from the place, and of seeking a way through the lines to his own army, but a little reflection showed him that it would be folly. He must merely be a witness, while Colonel Winchester, Warner, Pennington, the sergeant, Colonel Hertford, all whom he knew and the tens of thousands whom he did not know, fought the battle.

A tremendous sound, distant and steady, would not blot out much smaller sounds nearby, and now he heard noises in the larger chamber. The voice of Colonel Woodville was raised in sharp command.

"Lift me up!" he said, "I must see! Must I lie here, eating my soul out, when a great battle is going on! Help me up, I say! Wound or no wound, I will go to the door!"

Then the voice of Miss Woodville attempting to soothe was heard, but the colonel broke forth more furiously than ever, not at her, but at his unhappy fate.

Dick, spurred by impulse, left his alcove and entered the room.

"Sir," he said respectfully to Colonel Woodville, "you are eager to see, and so am I. May I help you?"

Colonel Woodville turned a red eye upon him.

"Young man," he said, "you have shown before a sense of fitness, and your appearance now is most welcome. You shall help me to the door, and I will lean upon you. Together we will see what is going to happen, although I wish for one result, and you for another. No, Margaret, it is not worth while to protest any further. My young Yankee and I will manage it very well between us."

Miss Woodville stepped aside and smiled wanly.

"I think it is best, Miss Woodville," Dick said in a low tone.

"Perhaps," she replied.

Colonel Woodville impatiently threw off the cover. He wore a long purple dressing gown, and his wound was in the leg, but it was partly healed. Dick helped him out of the bed and then supported him with his arm under his shoulder. Within that singular abode the roar of the guns was a steady and sinister mutter, but beneath it now appeared another note.

Colonel Woodville had begun to swear. It was not the torrent of loud imprecation that Dick had heard in Jackson, but subdued, and all the more fierce because it was so like the ferocious whine of a powerful and hurt wild animal. Swearing was common enough among the older men of the South, even among the educated, but Colonel Woodville now surpassed them all.

Dick heard oaths, ripe and rich, entirely new to him, and he heard the old ones in new arrangements and with new inflections. And yet there was no blasphemy about it. It seemed a part of time and place, and, what was more, it seemed natural coming from the lips of the old colonel.

They reached the door, the cut in the side of the ravine, and at once a wide portion of the battlefield sprang into the light, while the roar of the guns was redoubled. Dick would have stepped back now, but Colonel Woodville's hand rested on his shoulder and his support was needed.

"My glasses, Margaret!" said the colonel. "I must see! I will see! If I am but an old hound, lying here while the pack is in full cry, I will nevertheless see the chase! And even if I am an old hound I could run with the best of them if that infernal Yankee bullet had not taken me in the leg!"

Miss Woodville brought him the glasses, a powerful pair, and he glued them instantly to his eyes. Dick saw only the field of battle, dark lines and blurs, the red flare of cannon and rifle fire, and towers and banks of smoke, but the colonel saw individual human beings, and, with his trained military eye, he knew what the movements meant. Dick felt the hand upon his shoulder trembling with excitement. He was excited himself. Miss Woodville stood just behind them, and a faint tinge of color appeared in her pale face.

"The Yankees are getting ready to charge," said the colonel. "At the point we see they will not yet rush forward. They will, of course, wait for a preconcerted signal, and then their whole army will attack at once. But the woods and ravines are filled with their skirmishers, trying to clear the way. I can see them in hundreds and hundreds, and their rifles make sheets of flame. All the time the cannon are firing over their heads. Heavens, what a bombardment! I've never before listened to its like!"

"What are our troops doing, father?" asked Miss Woodville.

"Very little yet, and they should do little. Pemberton is showing more judgment than I expected of him. The defense should hold its fire until the enemy is well within range and that's what we're doing!"

The colonel leaned a little more heavily upon him, but Dick steadied himself. The old man still kept the glasses to his eyes, and swept them back and forth in as wide an arc as their position permitted. The hills shook with the thunder of the cannon, and the brilliant sun, piercing through the smoke, lighted up the vast battle line.

"The attack of the skirmishers grows hotter," said the old man. "The thickets blaze with the fire of their rifles. Heavy masses of infantry are moving forward. Now they stop and lie on their arms. They are awaiting the word from other parts of the field, and it shows with certainty that a grand attack is coming. Two batteries of eight guns each have come nearer. I did not think it possible for the fire of their cannon to increase, but it has done so. Young sir, would you care to look through the glasses?"

"I believe not, Colonel. I will trust to the naked eye and your report."

It was an odd feeling that made Dick decline the glasses. If he looked he must tell to the others what he saw, and he wished to show neither exultation nor depression. The colonel, the duty of courtesy discharged, resumed his own position of witness and herald.

"The columns of infantry are getting up again," he said. "I see a man in what I take to be a general's uniform riding along their front. He must be making a speech. No doubt he knows the desperate nature of the attack, and would inspire them. Now he is gone and other officers, colonels and majors are moving about."

"What are the skirmishers doing, Colonel?"

"Their fire is not so hot. They must be drawing back. They

have made the prelude, and the importance of their role has passed. The masses of infantry are drawing together again. Now I see men on horseback with trumpets to their lips. Yes, the charge is coming. Ah-h! That burnt them!"

There was a terrific crash much nearer, and Dick knew that it was the Southern batteries opening fire. The shoulder upon which the colonel's hand rested shook a little, but it was from excitement. He said nothing and Colonel Woodville continued:

"The smoke is so heavy I can't see what damage was done! Now it has cleared away! There are gaps in the Yankee lines, but the men have closed up, and they come on at the double quick with their cannon still firing over their heads!"

In his excitement he took his hand off Dick's shoulder and leaned forward a little farther, supporting himself now against the earthen wall. Dick stood just behind him, shielded from the sight of any one who might be passing in the ravine, although there was little danger now from searchers with a great battle going on. Meanwhile he watched the combat with an eagerness fully equal to that of the old colonel.

The mighty crash of cannon and rifles together continued, but for a little while the smoke banked up in front so densely that the whole combat was hidden from them. Then a wind slowly rolled the smoke away. The figures of the men began to appear like shadowy tracery, and then emerged, distinct and separate from the haze.

"They are nearer now," said the Colonel. "I can plainly see their long lines moving and their light guns coming with them. But our batteries are raking them horribly. Their men are falling by the scores and hundreds."

Miss Woodville uttered a deep sigh and turned her face away. But she looked again in a few moments. The terrible spell was upon her, too.

Dick's nerves were quivering. His heart was with the assailants and theirs with the assailed, but he would not speak aloud against the hopes of Colonel Woodville and his daughter, since he was in their house, such as it was, and, in a measure, under their protection.

"Their charge is splendid," continued the colonel, "and I hope Pemberton has made full use of the ground for defense! He will need all the help he can get! Oh, to be out of the battle on such a day! The smoke is in the way again and I can see nothing. Now it has passed and the enemy is still advancing, but our fire grows hotter and hotter! The shells and the grape and the canister and the bullets are smashing through them. They cannot live under it! They must go back!"

Nevertheless the blue lines came steadily toward the Southern earthworks. Dick saw officers, some ahorse, and some afoot, rushing about and encouraging the men, and he saw many fall and lie still while the regiments passed on.

"They are in the nearer thickets," cried the colonel, "and now they're climbing the slopes! Ah, you riflemen, your target is there!"

The Northern army was so near now that the Southern rifle fire was beating upon it like a storm. Never flinching, the men of the west and northwest hurled themselves upon the powerful fortified positions. Some reached shelves of the plateau almost at the mouths of the guns and hung there, their comrades falling dead or dying around them, but now the rebel yell began to swell along the vast line, and reached the ears of those in the ravine.

"The omen of victory!" exclaimed the colonel exultantly. "Our brave lads feel that they're about to triumph! Grant can't break through our line! Why doesn't he call off his men? It's slaughter!"

Dick's heart sank. He knew that the colonel's words were true. The Southern army, posted in its defenses, was breaking the ring of steel that sought to crush it to death. Groups of men in blue who had seized ground in the very front of the defenses either died there or were gradually driven back. The inner ring along its front of miles thundered incessantly on the outer ring, and repelled every attempt to crush it.

"They yield," said the colonel, after a long time. "The Northern fire has sunk at many points, and there! and there! they're retreating! The attack has failed and the South has won a victory!"

"But Grant will come again," said Dick, speaking his opinion for the first time.

"No doubt of it," said Colonel Woodville, "but likely he will come to the same fate."

He spoke wholly without animosity. The battle now died fast. The men in gray had been invincible. Their cannon and rifles had made an impenetrable barrier of fire, and Grant, despite the valor of his troops, had been forced to draw off. Many thousands had fallen and the Southern generals were exultant. Johnston would come up, and Grant, having such heavy losses, would be unable to withstand the united Confederate armies.

But Grant, as Colonel Woodville foresaw, had no idea of retreating. Fresh troops were pouring down the great river for him, and while he would not again attempt to storm Vicksburg, the ring of steel around it would be made so broad and strong that Pemberton could not get out nor could Johnston get in.

When the last cannon shot echoed over the far hills Colonel Woodville turned away from the door of his hillside home.

"I must ask your shoulder again, young sir," he said to Dick. "What I have seen rejoices me greatly, but I do not say it to taunt you. In war if one wins the other must lose, and bear in mind that you are the invader."

"May I help you back to your bed, sir?" asked Dick.

"You may. You are a good young man. I'm glad I saved you from that scoundrel, Slade. As the score between us is even I wish that you were out of Vicksburg and with your own people."

"I was thinking, too, sir, that I ought to go. I may take a quick departure."

"Then if you do go I wish you a speedy and safe journey, but I tell you to beware of one, Slade, who has a malicious heart and a long memory."

Dick withdrew to his own cell, as he called it, and he passed bitter hours there. The repulse had struck him a hard blow. Was it possible that Grant could not win? And if he could not win what terrible risks he would run in the heart of the Confederacy, with perhaps two armies to fight! He felt that only the Mississippi, that life-line connecting him with the North, could save him.

But as dusk came gradually in the ravine he resolved that he would go. His supper, as usual, was brought to him by Miss Woodville. She was as taciturn as ever, speaking scarcely a half-dozen words. When he asked her if Victor had gone through the battle unharmed she merely nodded, and presently he was alone again, with the dusk deepening in the great gully.

Dick was confident that nobody but Colonel Woodville, his daughter, and himself were in the cave-home. It was but a small place, and new callous places on her hands indicated that she was doing the cooking and all other work. His resolve to risk everything and go was strengthened.

He waited patiently until the full night had come and only the usual sounds of an army in camp arose. Then he made ready. He had surrendered his holster and pistols to Colonel Woodville, and so he must issue forth unarmed, but it could not be helped. He had several ten dollar gold pieces in his pocket, and he put one of them on the tiny table in his cell. He knew that it would be most welcome, and he could not calculate how many hundreds in Confederacy currency it was worth. He was glad that he could repay a little at least.

Then he stepped lightly toward the larger chamber in which Colonel Woodville lay. The usual candle was burning on the table near his bed, but the great bald head lay motionless on the pillow, and the heavy white eyebrows drooped over closed lids. Sound asleep! Dick was glad of it. The colonel, with his strong loyalty to the

South, might seek to hold him, at least as his personal prisoner, and now the trouble was avoided.

He moved gently across the floor, and then passed toward the open door. How good that puff of fresh air and freedom felt on his face! He did not know that Colonel Woodville raised his head on the pillow, glanced after him, and then let his head sink back and his eyes close again. A low sigh came between the colonel's lips, and it would have been difficult to say whether it was relief or regret.

Dick stepped into the narrow path cut in the side of the ravine and inhaled more draughts of the fresh air. How sweet and strong it was! How it filled one's lungs and brought with it life, courage and confidence! One had to live in a hole in a hill before he could appreciate fully the blessed winds that blew about the world. He knew that the path ran in front of other hollows dug in the earth, and he felt sorry for the people who were compelled to burrow in them. He felt sorry, in truth, for all Vicksburg, because now that he was outside his fears for Grant disappeared, and he knew that he must win.

While he remained in the path a deep boom came from the direction of the Union army and a huge shell burst over the town. It was followed in a moment by another and then by many others. While the besieged rejoiced in victory the besiegers had begun anew the terrible bombardment, sending a warning that the iron ring still held.

Dick paused no longer, but ran rapidly along the path until he emerged upon the open plateau and proceeded toward the center of the town. He judged that in the hours following a great battle, while there was yet much confusion, he would find his best chance.

He had reckoned rightly. There was a great passing to and fro in Vicksburg, but its lights were dim. Oil and candles alike were scarce, and there was little but the moon's rays to disclose a town to the eye. The rejoicings over the victory had brought more people than usual into the streets, but the same exultation made them unsuspicious, and Dick glided among them in the dusk, almost without fear.

He had concluded that "the longest way around was the shortest way through," and he directed his steps toward the river. He had formed a clear plan at last, and he believed that it would succeed. Twisting and turning, always keeping in the shadows, he made good progress, descended the bluff, and at last stood behind the ruins of an old warehouse near the stream.

Southern batteries were not far away from him and he heard the men talking. Then, strengthening his resolution, he came from behind the ruins, flung himself almost flat on the ground, and crawled toward the river, pushing in front of him a board, which some Northern gun had shot from the warehouse.

He knew that his task was difficult and dangerous, though in the last resort he could rush to the water and spring in. But he was almost at the edge before any sentinel saw the black shadow passing over the ground.

A hail came, and Dick flattened himself against the ground and lay perfectly still. Evidently the sentinel was satisfied that his fancy had been making merry with him, as he did not look further at the shadow, and Dick, after waiting two or three minutes, resumed his slow creeping.

He reached the edge, shoved the board into it, and dropped gently into the water beside it, submerged to the head. Then, pushing his support before him, he struck out for the middle of the stream.

CHAPTER XI

THE TAKING OF VICKSBURG

Dick was a fine swimmer, he had a good stout plank, and the waters of the river were warm. He felt that the chief dangers were passed, and that the muddy Mississippi would now bear him safely to the blockading fleet below. He gave the plank another shove, sending it farther out into the stream, and then raised himself up until his elbows rested upon it. He could thus float gently with a little propulsion from his legs to the place where he wanted to go.

He saw lights along the bluff and the bar below, and then, with a sudden shoot of alarm he noticed a dim shadow move slowly from the shore. It was a long boat, holding a dozen rowers, and several men armed with rifles, and it was coming toward him. He did not know whether it was merely an ordinary patrol, or whether they had seen the darker blot on the stream that he and the plank made, but in any event the result would be the same.

He slipped his arm off the plank and sank in the stream to the chin. Then, propelling it gently and without any splashing of the water, he continued to move down the stream. He was hopeful that the riflemen would mistake him and his plank for one of those stumps or logs which the Mississippi carries so often on its bosom.

The head of the boat turned from him a little, and he felt sure now that he would drift away unnoticed, but one of the soldiers suddenly raised his rifle and fired. Dick heard the bullet clip the water close beside him, and he swam as hard as he could for a few moments. Then he settled again into quiet, as he saw the boat was not coming toward him. Doubtless the man had merely fired the shot to satisfy himself that it was really a log, and if Dick allowed it to float naturally he would be convinced.

It was a tremendous trial of nerves to run the gantlet in this way, but as it was that or nothing he exerted all his will upon his body, and let himself float slowly, sunk again to the mouth and with his head thrown back, so it would present only a few inches above the surface.

The boat turned, and seemed once upon the point of coming toward him. He could hear the creaking of the oars and the men talking, but they turned again suddenly and rowed up the stream. Again, his fate had hung on a chance impulse. He drifted slowly on until the town and the bluffs sank in the darkness. Then he drew himself upon his plank and swam, doubling his speed. He knew that some of the Union gunboats lay not far below, and, when he rounded a curve, he saw a light in the stream, but near the shore.

He approached cautiously, knowing that the men on the vessel would be on guard against secret attack, and presently he discerned the outlines of a sidewheel steamer, converted into a warship and bearing guns. He dropped down by the side of his plank until he was quite close, and then, raising himself upon it again, he shouted with all his voice: "Ship ahoy!"

He did not know whether that was the customary method of hailing on the Mississippi, but it was a memory from his nautical reading, and so he shouted a second and yet a third time at the top of his voice: "Ship ahoy!" Figures bearing rifles appeared at the side, and a rough voice demanded in language highly unparliamentary who was there and what he, she or it wanted.

Dick was in a genial mood. He had escaped with an ease that surprised him, and the warmth of the water in which he was immersed had saved him from cramp or chill. The spirit of recklessness seized him again. He threw himself astride his plank, and called out:

"A detachment of the army of the United States escaped from captivity in Vicksburg, and wishing to rejoin it. It's infantry, not marines, and it needs land."

"Then advance infantry and give the countersign."

"Grant and Victory," replied Dick in a loud, clear voice.

A laugh came from the steamer, and the rough voice said again:

"Let the detachment advance again, and holding up its hands, show itself."

Dick paddled closer and, steadying himself as well as he could, threw up his hands. The light of a ship's lantern was thrown directly on his face, and the same voice ordered men to take a small boat and get him.

When Dick stepped upon the deck of the steamer, water streaming from his clothes, several men looked at him curiously. One in a dingy blue uniform he believed to be the owner of the rough voice. But his face was not rough.

"Who are you?" asked the man.

"Lieutenant Richard Mason of Colonel Winchester's regiment in the army of General Grant, sent several days ago with a message to the fleet, but driven by Confederate scouts and skirmishers into Vicksburg, where he lay hidden, seeking a chance of escape."

"And he found it to-night, coming down the river like a big catfish."

"He did, sir. He could find no other way, and he arrived on the useful board which is now floating away on the current."

"What proof have you that you are what you say."

"That I saw you before you saw me and hailed you."

"It's not enough."

"Then here is the message that I was to have delivered to the commander of the fleet. It's pretty wet, but I think you can make it out."

He drew the dispatch from the inside pocket of his waistcoat. It was soaked through, but when they turned the ship's lantern upon it the captain could make out its tenor and the names. Doubt could exist no longer and he clapped his hands heartily upon the lad's shoulder.

"Come into the cabin and have something to eat and dry clothes," he said. "This is the converted steamer Union, and I'm its commander, Captain William Hays. I judge that you've had an extraordinary time."

"I have, captain, and the hardest of it all was when I saw our army repulsed to-day."

"It was bad and the wounded are still lying on the field, but it doesn't mean that Vicksburg will have a single moment of rest. Listen to that, will you, lieutenant?"

The far boom of a cannon came, and Dick knew that its shell would break over the unhappy town. But he had grown so used to the cannonade that it made little impression upon him, and, shrugging his shoulders, he descended the gangway with the captain.

Clothing that would fit him well enough was found, and once more he was dry and warm. Hot coffee and good food were brought him, and while he ate and drank Captain Hays asked him many questions. What was the rebel strength in Vicksburg? Were they exultant over their victory of the day? Did they think they could hold out? What food supply did they have?

Dick answered all the questions openly and frankly as far as he could. He really knew little or nothing about those of importance, and, as for himself, he merely said that he had hid in a cave, many of which had been dug in Vicksburg. He did not mention Colonel Woodville or his daughter.

"Now," said Captain Hays, when he finished his supper, "you can have a bunk. Yes, lieutenant, you must take it. I could put you ashore to-night, but it's not worth while. Get a good night's sleep, and we'll see to-morrow."

Dick knew that he was right, and, quelling his impatience, he lay down in one of the bunks and slept until morning.

Then, after a solid breakfast, he went ashore with the good wishes of Captain Hays, and, a few hours later, he was with the Union army and his own regiment. Again he was welcomed as one dead and his own heart was full of rejoicing because all of his friends were alive. Warner alone had been wounded, a bullet cutting into his shoulder, but not hurting him much. He wore a bandage, his face had a becoming pallor, and Pennington charged that he was making the most of it.

"But it was an awful day," said Warner, "and there's a lot of gloom in the camp. Still, we're not moving away and the reinforcements are coming."

Dick explained to Colonel Winchester why he had failed in his mission, and the colonel promised to report in turn to the commander that the hand of God had intervened. Dick's conscience was now at rest, and he resumed at once his duties with the regiment.

Many days passed. While Grant did not make any other attack upon Vicksburg his circle of steel grew tighter, and the rain of shells and bombs upon the devoted town never ceased. Reinforcements poured forward. His army rose to nearly eighty thousand men, and Johnston, hovering near, gathering together what men he could, did not dare to strike. Dick was reminded more than once of Caesar's famous siege of Alesia, about which he had read not so long ago in Dr. Russell's academy at Pendleton.

There were long, long days of intrenching, skirmishing and idleness. May turned into June, and still the steel coil enclosed Vicksburg. Here the Union men were hopeful, but the news from the East was bad. Not much filtered through, and none of it struck a happy note. Lee, with his invincible legions, was still sweeping northward. Doubtless the Confederate hosts now trod the soil of a free State, and Dick and his comrades feared in their very souls that Lee was marching to another great victory.

"I wish I could hear from Harry Kenton," said Dick to Warner. "I'd like to know whether he passed through Chancellorsville safely."

"Don't you worry about him," said Warner. "That rebel cousin of yours has luck. He also has skill. Let x equal luck and y skill. Now x plus y equals the combination of luck and skill, which is safety. That proves to me mathematically that he is unharmed and that he is riding northward—to defeat, I hope."

"We've got to win here," said Dick. "If we don't, I'm thinking the cause of the Union will be more than doubtful. We don't seem to have the generals in the East that we have in the West. Our leaders hang on here and they don't overestimate the enemy."

"That's so," said Pennington. "Now, I wonder what 'Pap' Thomas is doing."

"He's somewhere in Tennessee, I suppose, watching Bragg," said Dick. "That's a man I like, and, I think, after this affair here is over, we may go back to his command. If we do succeed in taking Vicksburg, it seems likely to me that the heavy fighting will be up there in Tennessee, where Bragg's army is."

"Do you know if your uncle, Colonel Kenton, is in Vicksburg?"

"I don't think so. In fact, I'm sure he isn't. His regiment is with Bragg. Well, George, what does your algebra tell us?"

Warner had taken out his little volume again and was studying it intently. But he raised his head long enough to reply.

"I have just achieved the solution of a very important mathematical problem," he answered in precise tones. "An army of about thirty-five thousand men occupies a town located on a river. It is besieged by another army of about seventy-five thousand men flushed with victory. The besiegers occupy the river with a strong fleet. They are also led by a general who has shown skill and extraordinary tenacity, while the commander of the besieged has not shown much of either quality and must feel great discouragement."

"But you're only stating the side of the besieged."

"Don't interrupt. It's impolite. I mean to be thoroughly fair. Now come the factors favoring the besieged. The assailing army, despite its superior numbers, is far in the enemy's country. It may be attacked at any time by another army outside, small, but led by a very able general. Now, you have both sides presented to you, but I have already arrived at the determining factor. What would you say it is, Dick?"

"I don't know."

"You haven't used your reasoning powers. Remember that the man who not merely thinks, but who thinks hard and continuously always wins. It's very simple. The answer is in four letters, f-o-o-d, food. As we know positively, Pemberton was able to provision Vicksburg for five or six weeks. We can't break in and he can't break out. When his food is exhausted, as it soon will be, he'll have to give up. The siege of Vicksburg is over. I know everything, except the exact date."

Dick was inclined to believe that Warner was right, but he forgot about his prediction, because a mail came down the river that afternoon, and he received a letter from his mother, his beautiful young mother, who often seemed just like an elder sister.

She was in Pendleton, she wrote, staying comfortably in their home. The town was occupied by three companies of veteran Union troops who behaved well. They were always glad to have a garrison of good soldiers whether Federal or Confederate—sometimes it was one and sometimes the other. But she thought the present Union force would remain quite a while, as she did not look for the reappearance of the Southern army in Kentucky. But if the town were left without troops she would go back to her relatives in the Bluegrass, as Bill Skelly's band to the eastward in the mountains was raiding and plundering and had become a great menace. Guerillas were increasing in numbers in those doubtful regions.

"The regular troops will have to deal with those fellows later on," said Dick.

"Dr. Russell has had a letter from Harry Kenton," continued Mrs. Mason. "It was written from some point near the Pennsylvania line, and, while Harry did not say so in his letter, I know that General Lee is expecting a great victory in the North. Harry was not hurt at Chancellorsville, but he says he does not see how he escaped, the fire of the cannon and rifles being more awful than any that he had ever seen before. He was present when General Jackson was mortally wounded, and he seems to have been deeply affected by it. He writes that the Confederacy could better have lost a hundred thousand men."

There was more in the letter, but it was strictly personal to Dick, and it closed with her heartfelt prayer that God, who had led him safely so far, would lead him safely through all.

After reading it several times he put it in a hidden pocket. Soldiers did not receive many letters and they always treasured them. Ah, his dear, beautiful young mother! How could any one ever harm her! Yet the thought of Skelly and his outlaws made him uneasy. He hoped that the Union garrison would remain in Pendleton permanently.

His mind was soon compelled to turn back to the siege. They were digging trenches and creeping closer and closer. Warner had made no mistake in his mathematics. The army and the people in Vicksburg had begun to suffer from a lack of food. They were down to half rations. They had neither tea nor coffee, and medicines were exhausted. Many and many a time they looked forth from their hills and prayed for Johnston, but he could not come. Always the Union flag floated before them, and the ring of steel so strong and broad was contracting inch by inch.

The Northern engineers ran mines under the Confederate works. They used every device of ingenious minds to push the siege. Spies brought word that all food would soon be gone in Vicksburg, and Grant, grim of purpose, took another hitch in the steel belt about the hopeless town. The hostile earthworks and trenches were now so near that the men could hear one another talking. Sometimes in a lull of the firing they would come out and exchange tobacco or news. It was impossible for the officers to prevent it, and they really did not seek to do so, as the men fought just as well when they returned to their works.

June now drew to a close and the great heats of July were at hand. Dick was convinced that the defense of Vicksburg was drawing to a like close. They had proof that some of the irregulars in Vicksburg had escaped through the lines and he was convinced that Slade would be among them. They were the rats and Vicksburg was the sinking ship.

They heard that Johnston had gathered together twenty-five thousand men and was at last marching to the relief of the town. Dick believed that Grant must have laughed one of his grimmest laughs. They knew that Johnston's men were worn and half-starved, and had been harassed by other Union troops. Johnston was skillful, but he would only be a lean and hungry wolf attacking a grizzly bear. He was sure that all danger from him had passed.

Now, as they closed in the Northern guns increased their fire. It seemed to Dick that they could have blown away the whole plateau of Vicksburg by this time. The storm of shells raked the town, and he was glad that the people had been able to dig caves for refuge. Colonel Woodville must be doing some of his greatest swearing now. Dick thought of him with sympathy and friendliness.

"I don't think it can last much longer, Mr. Mason," said Sergeant Daniel Whitley on the morning of the second of July. "Their guns don't answer ours often and it means that they're out of ammunition, or almost. Besides, you can stand shells and bullets easier than lack of food. 'Pears to me I can nearly feel 'em crumpling up before us."

Trumpets blew the next morning. All the firing ceased suddenly and the three lads saw a Southern general with several officers of lower rank, riding forward under a white flag. It was Bowen, who came out to meet Grant.

Dick drew a deep, long breath. He knew that this was the end. So did his comrades. A cheer started and swept part of the way along the lines, but the officers quickly stopped it.

"Vicksburg is ours," said Dick.

"Looks like it," said Warner.

But Grant told Bowen that he would treat only with Pemberton, and after delays General Pemberton came out. General Grant went forward to meet him. The two stood alone under a tree within seventy yards of the Confederate lines and talked.

Chance or fortune presented a startling coincidence. Almost at the very moment that Grant and Pemberton met under the tree Pickett's men were rising to their feet and preparing for the immortal but fatal charge at Gettysburg. While the cannon had ceased suddenly at Vicksburg they were thundering from many score mouths at Gettysburg. Fortune was launching two thunderbolts upon the Confederacy at the same moment. They were to strike upon fields a thousand miles apart, and the double blow was to be mortal.

But Dick knew nothing of Gettysburg then, nor was he to know anything until days afterward. He certainly had no thought of the East while he watched the two generals under the tree. Dick's comrades were with him, but so intense was their curiosity that none of them spoke. Thousands of men were gazing with the same eagerness, and the Southern earthworks were covered with the defenders.

It was one of the most dramatic scenes in Dick's life, the two men under the tree, and the tens of thousands who watched. Nobody moved. It seemed that they scarcely breathed. After the continuous roar of firing the sudden silence was oppressive, and Dick felt the blood pounding in his ears.

The heat was close and heavy. Black clouds were floating up in the west, and lightning glimmered now and then on the horizon. Although the storm threatened no one noticed. All eyes were still for Grant and Pemberton. After a while each returned to his own command, and there was an armistice until the next day, when the full surrender was made, and Grant and his officers rode into Vicksburg. At the same time Lee was gathering his men for the retreat into the South from the stricken field of Gettysburg. It was the Fourth of July, the eighty-seventh anniversary of the Declaration of Independence, and no one could have possibly conceived a more striking celebration.

As soon as Dick was free for a little space he hurried to the ravine, and, as before, found there the open door. He passed in without hesitation.

The light as of old filtered into the room, and Colonel Woodville lay just as before in bed with his great bald head upon the pillow. Miss Woodville sat beside the bed, reading aloud from Addison. Dick's step was light, but the colonel heard him and held up a finger. The lad paused until Miss Woodville, finishing a long sentence, closed the book. Then the colonel, raising a little the great white thatch of his eyebrows, said:

"Young sir, you have returned again, and, personally, you are welcome, but I do not conceive how you can stand the company you keep. My daughter informs me that the Yankees are in Vicksburg, and I have no reason to doubt the statement."

He paused, and Dick said:

"Yes, Colonel, it's true."

"I suppose we must endure it. I should have gone myself and have offered my sword to General Grant, but this confounded leg of mine is still weak."

"At least, sir, we come with something besides arms. May I bring you rations?"

"You are generous, young man, and my daughter and I appreciate the obvious nature of your errand here. Speaking for both of us, a little food will not be unwelcome."

"Tell me first, what has become of your nephew. Has he escaped from the city?"

"He slipped out nearly a week ago, and will join his father's regiment in Bragg's command. That scoundrel, Slade, is gone too. Since the city had to be surrendered I would gladly have made you a present of Slade, but it's out of my power now."

Dick soon returned with ample food for them and helped them later, when they moved to quarters outside in the shell-torn city. Dick saw that they were comfortable, and then his mind turned toward Tennessee. Detachments from Grant's army were to be sent to that of Rosecrans, who was now heavily threatened by Bragg, and the Winchester regiment, which really belonged with him, was sure to go.

The order to march soon came, and it was welcome. The regiment, or rather what was left of it, promptly embarked upon one of the river steamers and started northward.

As they stood on the deck and looked down at the yellow waters in which Dick had swum on his trusty plank Warner said:

"I've news of importance. It arrived in a telegram to General Grant, and I heard it just as we were coming on board."

"What is it?" asked Dick.

"General Lee was defeated in a great battle at a little place called Gettysburg in Pennsylvania, and has retreated into Virginia."

"Gettysburg and Vicksburg!" exclaimed Dick. "The wheel has turned nearly 'round. The Confederacy is doomed now."

"I think so, too," said Warner.

CHAPTER XII

AN AFFAIR OF THE MOUNTAINS

Although they were on board one of the fastest steamers in the Union service, Dick and his comrades had a long journey by river. But it was not unpleasant. They enjoyed the rest and ease after the weeks of fighting and service in the trenches before Vicksburg. The absence of war and the roar of cannon and rifles was like a happy dream between days of fighting. As they went northward on the great river it almost seemed as if peace had returned.

Warner studied his algebra and two other books of mathematics which he was lucky enough to find on board. Pennington slept a great deal of the time.

"I learned it on the plains from the Indians," he said. "When they don't have anything to do they sleep and gather strength for the hour of need. I think the time is coming soon when they won't let me sleep at all, and then I can draw on the great supply I have in stock."

"Likely enough it's near," said Dick dreamily. "They say Bragg has a great army now, and you know that, while Rosecrans is slow he's pretty sure. Thomas and McCook and the others are with him, too. I expect to see 'Pap' Thomas again. He's a general to my liking."

"And to mine, too," said Pennington, "but we can talk about him later on, because I'm going to sleep again inside of a minute."

Dick was not averse to silence, as he, too, was half asleep; that is, he was in a dreamy stage, and he was at peace with the world and his fellow men. From under drooping eyelids he was vaguely watching the low shores of the Mississippi, and the great mass of yellow waters moving onward from the far vague forests of the North in their journey of four thousand miles to the gulf.

Like all boys of the great valley, Dick always felt the romance and spell of the Mississippi. It was to him and them one of the greatest facts in the natural world, the grave of De Soto, the stream on which their fathers and forefathers had explored and traded and fought since their beginnings. Now it was fulfilling its titanic role again, and the Union fleets upon its bosom were splitting the Confederacy asunder.

He, too, fell asleep before long. Warner glanced at his comrades who slept so well on a hard bench, and his look was rather envious. He returned his beloved algebra to his pocket, leaned back on the bench also, and, although he had not believed it possible, slept also inside of five minutes. Colonel Winchester passing smiled sympathetically, but his glance lingered longest on Dick.

After days on the water the regiment disembarked, marched more days across the country, joining other regiments on the way, and reached the rear guard of the army of Rosecrans, which was already marching southward in the direction of Chattanooga to meet that of Bragg. They advanced now over the Cumberland mountains through a country wild and thinly inhabited. The summer was waning, but it was cool on the mountains and in the passes, nor was it so dry as the year before, when they fought that terrible battle at Perryville in Kentucky.

Dick was glad to be again in the high country, the land of firm soil and of many clear, rushing streams. Heart and lungs expanded, when he looked upon the long ridges, clothed in deep forest, and breathed the pure air that blew down from their summits. Yet his dream of peace was over. As they advanced through the forests and passes they were harassed incessantly by sharpshooters on the slopes, who melted away before them, but who returned on the very heels of the vain pursuit to vex them again with bullets.

They heard soon that the most daring of these bands was led by a man named Slade, and Dick's pulse took a jump. He felt in a curious sort of way that this man Slade was still following him. It seemed more than a decree of chance that their fates should be intertwined. He hoped that Slade would never hear how he had been hidden in that hole in the ravine with the Woodvilles. Trouble could come of it for gallant young Victor Woodville, and even for his uncle. He was sure that Victor was now with Bragg and they might meet face to face again.

As they rode through a defile and came into a wide valley they saw before them an extensive Union camp, and they were overjoyed to learn that it was the division of Thomas, the general to whom they were to report. Dick had once received the personal thanks of Thomas, and the grave, able man inspired him with immense respect, mingled with affection.

He stood before Thomas in his tent that evening, Colonel Winchester having yielded to his request to take him with him when he reported the arrival of his regiment. Thomas, usually so taciturn, delighted the soul of the lad by remembering him at once.

"It was you, Lieutenant Mason, who came to me there in the Kentucky mountains with the dispatches," he said, "and you were also with us at Perryville and Stone River."

"I was, sir," said Dick, flushing with pride.

"And you were with General Grant at the taking of Vicksburg!

It was a great exploit, and it has lifted us up mightily. But I'm glad to have you back along with Colonel Winchester and the rest of his brave lads. I think you'll see action before long, action perhaps on a greater scale than any witnessed hitherto in the West."

Dick saluted and withdrew. He knew that a young lieutenant must not stay too long in the presence of a commanding general and he quickly rejoined Warner and Pennington.

"How's the old man?" asked Pennington, with the familiarity of youth, which was not disrespectful in the absence of the "old man."

"'Pap' Thomas is looking well," replied Dick. "I fancy that his digestion was never better. He did not act in a belligerent way, but I think he's hunting for a fight."

"Since you and Warner and I have arrived he can begin it."

"I think it's coming," said Dick earnestly. "Often you can feel when things are moving to some end, and I'm sure that we'll measure strength again with Bragg before the autumn has gone far."

The valley in which the camp lay was green and beautiful, and a deep, clear little river from the mountains, ran rushing, through it. The three lads lay on their blankets near the bank and listened to the musical sweep of the stream. Pennington suddenly sprang up and hailed:

"Hey, Ohio, is that you? Come here!"

A tall youth emerged from the dusk and looked at them inquiringly.

"Ohio," said Pennington, "don't you remember your friends?"

The long, lean lad looked again, and then he was enthusiastically shaking hands with each in turn.

"Remember you!" he exclaimed. "Of course I do. If it hadn't been so dark I'd have seen you and called to you first. I'm glad you're alive. It's a lot to live in these times. I tried to find out about you fellows but couldn't. We came in a detachment ahead of you. But if you'll invite me, I'll stay awhile with you and talk."

They offered him a blanket and he stretched out upon it, turning his eyes up to the sky, in which the stars were now coming.

"What are you thinking about, Ohio?" asked Dick.

"I'm thinking how fast I'm growing old. Two years and a half in the war, but it's twenty-five years in fact. I hadn't finished school when I left home and here I am, a veteran of more battles than any soldiers have fought since the days of old Bonaparte. If I happen to live through this war, which I mean to do, I wonder how I'll ever settle down at home again. Father will say to me: 'Get the plough and break up the five-acre field for corn,' and me, maybe a veteran of a dozen pitched battles in every one of which anywhere from one hundred thousand to two hundred thousand men have been engaged, not to mention fifty or a hundred smaller battles and four or five hundred skirmishes.

"When the flies begin to buzz around me I'll think they make a mighty poor noise compared with the roar of three or four hundred big cannon and a hundred thousand rifles that I've listened to so often. If a yellow jacket should sting me, I'd say what a little thing it is, compared with the piece of shrapnel that hit me at some battle not yet fought. Maybe I'd find things so quiet I just couldn't stand it. Wars are mighty unsettling."

"I'm thinking," said Dick, "that before this war is over all of us will get enough of it to last a lifetime. We've got the edge on 'em now, since Vicksburg and Gettysburg, but the Graybacks are not yet beaten by a long shot. We've heard how Lee drew off from Gettysburg carrying all his guns and supplies, and even with Gettysburg we haven't been doing so well in the East as we have in the West. You know that, Ohio?"

"Of course, I do. But I think the Johnnies have made their high-water mark. Great work our army did down there at Vicksburg, and we'll have the chance to do just as well against Bragg. We'll defeat him, of course. Now, Mason, notice that light flickering on the mountain up there!"

He pointed to the crest of a ridge two or three miles away, where Dick saw a point of flame appearing and reappearing, and answered by another point farther down, which flickered in the same manner.

"Signals of some kind, I suppose," replied Dick, "but I don't know who makes them or what they mean."

"I don't know what they mean, either," said Ohio; "but I can guess pretty well who's making them. That's Slade."

"Slade!" said Dick.

"Yes, you seem to have heard of him?"

"So I have, and I've seen him, also. I heard, too, that he was up here making things unhappy for our side. He was in Vicksburg, although you may not have heard of him there, but he got out before the surrender. A cunning fellow. A sort of land pirate."

"He's all of that. Since we've been coming through the mountains he and his band have picked off a lot of our men. Those signals must mean that they're preparing for another raid. I shouldn't like to be a half-mile from our lines to-night."

"Why can't we smoke him out, Ohio?"

"Because when we're half way up the slope he and his men are gone on the other side. Besides, they can rake us with bullets from ambush, while we're climbing up the ridge. And when we get there, they're gone. It's these mountains that give the irregulars their chance. See, two lights are winking at each other now!"

"How far apart would you say they are, Ohio?"

"A mile, maybe, but one is much higher than the other up the mountain. The lower light, doubtless, is signaling information about us to the higher. I see your colonel and our colonel talking together. Maybe we're going to set a trap. It would be a good thing if we could clean out those fellows."

"I'm thinking that your guess is a good one," said Dick, as he rose to his feet, "because Colonel Winchester is beckoning to me now."

"And there's a call for me, too," said Ohio, rising. "Talk of a thing and it happens. We're surely going for those lights."

They had reckoned right. General Thomas, when he saw the signals, had summoned some of his best officers and they had talked together earnestly. The general had not said much before, but the incessant sharpshooting from the bushes and slopes as they marched southward had caused him intense annoyance, and, if continued, he knew that it would hurt the spirit of the troops.

"We shall try to trap Slade's band to-night," said Colonel Winchester to Dick and the other young officers who gathered around him. "We think he has three or four hundred men and my regiment can deal with that number. We will defile to the right without noise and make our way up the mountain. An Ohio regiment, which can also deal with Slade if it catches him, will defile to the left. Maybe we can trap these irregulars between us. Sergeant Whitley will guide my force."

The sergeant stepped forward, proud of the honor and trust. Dick, looking at him in the moonlight, said to himself for the hundredth time that he was a magnificent specimen of American manhood, thick, powerful, intelligent, respectful to his superior officers, who often knew less than he did, a veteran from whom woods, hills, and plains hid few secrets. He thought it a good thing that the sergeant was to be their guide, because he would lead them into no ambush.

As Dick turned away for departure Ohio said to him:

"We'll meet on the mountain side, and I hope we'll catch our game, but don't you fellows fire into us in the dark."

Dick promised and his regiment marched away toward the slope. All were on foot, of course, and they had received strict instructions to make no noise. They turned northward, left the camp behind them, and were soon hidden in the dark.

Dick was at the head of the column with Colonel Winchester and the sergeant. Warner and Pennington were further back. The darkness was heavy in the shadow of the slope and among the bushes, but, looking backward, Dick clearly saw the camp of General Thomas with its thousands of men and dozens of fires. Figures passed and repassed before the flames, and the fused noises of a great camp came from the valley.

Dick took only a glance or two. His whole attention now was for the sergeant, who was looking here and there and sniffing the air, like a great hound seeking the trail. The soldier had melted into the scout, and Colonel Winchester, knowing him so well, had, in effect, turned the regiment over to him.

Dick and other young officers were sent back through the column to see that they marched without noise. It was not difficult to enforce the orders, as the men were filled with the ardor of the hunt, and would do everything to insure its success. When Dick came back to the head of the column he merely heard the tread of feet and the rustling of uniforms against the bushes behind them.

The sergeant led on with unerring skill and instinct. They were rising fast on the slope, and the great forest received and hid them as if they were its wild children returned to their home. The foliage was so dense that Dick caught only flitting glimpses of the camp below, although many fires were yet burning there.

The wisdom of putting the regiment into the hands of the sergeant was now shown. Rising to the trust, he called up all his reserves of wilderness lore. He listened attentively to the voice of every night bird, because it might not be real, but instead the imitation call of man to man. He searched in every opening under the moonlight for traces of footsteps, which he alone could have seen, and, when at last he found them, Dick, despite the dusk, saw his figure expand and his eyes flash. He had been kneeling down examining the imprints and when he arose the colonel asked:

"What is it, Whitley?"

"Men have passed here, sir, and, as they couldn't have been ours, they were the enemy. The tracks lead south on the slope, and they must have been going that way to join Slade's command."

"Then you think, Sergeant, we should follow this trail?"

"Undoubtedly, sir, but we must look out for an ambush. These men know the mountains thoroughly, and if we were to walk into their trap they might cut us to pieces."

"Then we won't walk into it. Lead on, Sergeant. If the enemy is near, I know that you will find him in time."

The sergeant's brown face flushed with pride, but he followed on the trail without a word and behind him came the whole regiment, implicit in its trust, and winding without noise like a great coiling serpent through the forest.

Dick was a woodsman himself, and he kept close to the sergeant, watching his methods, and seeking also what he could find. While they lost the trail now and then, he saw the sergeant recover it in the openings. He noted, too, that it was increasing in size. Little trails were flowing into the big one like brooks into a river, and the main course was uniformly south, but bearing slightly upward on the slope.

The sergeant stopped at the melancholy cry of an owl, apparently three or four hundred yards ahead. Both he and Dick raised their heads and listened for the answer, which they felt sure was ready. The long, sinister hoot in reply came from a point considerably farther away, but at about the same height on the slope.

"They have two forces, sir," said the sergeant to Colonel Winchester, "and I think they're about to unite."

"As a wilderness fighter, what would you suggest, Sergeant?"

"To wait here a little and lie hidden in the brush. We're rightly afraid of an ambush if we go on, then why not make the same danger theirs? I think it likely that the other force is coming this way. Anyway, we can tell in a minute or two, 'cause them owls are sure to hoot again. If I'm right, we can catch 'em napping."

"An excellent idea, Sergeant. Ah! there are the signals you predicted!"

The owl hooted again from the same point directly in front, and then came the reply of the other, now nearer. The sergeant drew a deep breath of satisfaction.

"Yes, sir, I was right," he said. "Their meeting place is straight in front. Will you let me slip forward a little through the brush and see?"

"Go ahead, Sergeant. We need all the information we can get, but don't walk into any trap yourself, leaving us here without eyes or ears."

"Never fear, sir. I won't be caught."

Then he disappeared with a suddenness that made the colonel and Dick gasp. He was with them, and then he was not. But he returned in ten minutes, and, although Dick could not see it in his face, he was triumphant.

"There's a glade not more'n four hundred yards ahead," he whispered to the colonel, "and about a hundred and fifty men, armed with long rifles, are lying down in it waiting for a second force, which I judge from the cry of the owl will be there inside of five minutes."

"Then," said Colonel Winchester, breathing fast, "we'll wait ten minutes and attack. It would be a great stroke to wipe out

Slade's band. I'm sorry for those Ohio fellows, but the luck's ours tonight, or I should say that the sergeant's skill as a trailer has given us the chance."

It was soon known along the black, winding line that the enemy was at hand, and the men were eager to attack, but they were ordered to have patience for a little while. Their leader wished to destroy Slade's whole force at one stroke.

Colonel Winchester took out his watch and held it before him in the faint moonlight. He would not move until the ten minutes exactly had passed. Then he closed the watch and gave the signal, but stationed officers along the line to see that the men made as little noise as possible. The long black column moved again through the forest and Dick, full of excitement was at its head with the colonel and the sergeant.

They reached a slope, crept up it, and then spread out, as they knew that the valley and the enemy were within rifle shot. Dick, glancing through the bushes, saw the glitter of steel and caught the murmur of voices. He knew that their presence was not yet suspected, and he did not like the idea of firing from ambush upon anybody, but there was no occasion for testing his scruples, as the advance of so many men created noise sufficient to reach the alert ears in the glade.

"Up, men! The enemy!" he heard a voice shout. Colonel Winchester at the same moment ordered his men to fire and charge with the bayonet.

A terrible volley was poured into the valley, and it seemed to Dick that half of Slade's force went down, but as they rushed forward to finish the task they met a fire that caused many of the Union soldiers to drop. Slade was evidently a man of ability. Dick saw him springing about and blowing a little silver whistle, which he knew was a call to rally.

But the surprise was too sudden and great. The irregulars, fighting hard, were driven out of the valley and into the woods on the upper side of the glade. Sheltered in the underbrush, they might have made a good defense there, but a sudden tremendous cheer arose, and they were charged in the flank by the Ohio regiment, coming up on the run.

Spurred by emulation the Winchester men also rushed into the underbrush, and those of Slade's men who had not fallen quickly threw down their arms. But they did not catch the leader, nor did they know what had become of him, until Dick caught sight of a little, weazened figure under an enormous wide-brimmed hat running with three or four others along the mountain-side.

"Slade! Slade!" he cried, pointing, and instantly a score, Dick and the sergeant among them, were hotfoot after the fugitives. Several shots were fired, but none hit, and the chase lengthened out.

Sergeant Whitley exclaimed to Dick:

"We catch the pack, but if we don't catch the leader there'll be another pack soon."

"Right you are! We must have that little man under the big hat!"

Dick heard panting breaths, and Warner and Pennington drew up by his side.

"Slade's about to escape!" exclaimed Dick. "We must get him!"

"I'm running my best," said Warner. "Look out!" Slade suddenly faced about and fired a heavy pistol. Dick had dropped down at Warner's warning cry and the bullet sang over his head. The sergeant fired in return, but the light was too faint, and Slade and the three who were with him ran on unharmed.

The pursuit, conducted with such vigor, soon led to the top of the mountain, and they began the descent of the far side. Several more shots were fired, but they did no damage, and neither side was able to gain. Two of the fugitives turned aside into the woods, but the pursuit kept straight after Slade, and his remaining companion, a slender, youthful figure.

"I think we'll get 'em," panted the sergeant. As he spoke one of the little mountain rivers so numerous in that region came into view. It was narrow, but deep, and without hesitating an instant the fugitives sprang into it and shot down the stream, swimming with all their strength, and helped by the powerful current.

Slade was in advance, and he was already disappearing in the shadows on the far bank, but his comrade, he of the slender figure, was still in the moonlight, which fell across his face for a moment. A soldier raised his rifle to fire, but Dick stumbled and fell against him and the bullet went high in the air.

The moment had been long enough for Dick to recognize Victor Woodville. He did not know how he happened to be with Slade, but he did not intend that he should be shot there in the water, and his impulse was quick enough to save Victor's life. In another moment the young Mississippian was gone also in the shadows, and although several of the Union men swam the river they could discover no trace of either.

"I'm sorry," said the sergeant as they walked back to the other side of the mountain, "that they got away."

"Yes," said Dick, "it was too bad that Slade escaped."

CHAPTER XIII

THE RIVER OF DEATH

Dick knew that he had saved young Woodville's life, but his conscience was quite clear. If he had the same chance he would do it over again, but he was sorry they had not caught Slade. He felt no hostility toward the regular soldiers of the Confederacy, but he knew there were guerillas on their side, as well as his own, who would stop at nothing. He remembered Skelly, who, claiming to be a Union partisan, nevertheless robbed and even killed those of either party whenever he felt it safe to do so. Slade was his Southern complement, and he would surely get together a new force as venomous as the old.

But Colonel Winchester and the commander of the Ohio regiment were full of pride in their exploit, as they had a right to be. They had destroyed a swarm of wasps which had been buzzing and stinging almost beyond endurance, and they were still prouder when they received the thanks of General Thomas.

The corps moved forward the next day, and soon the whole army was united under Rosecrans. It was a powerful force, about ninety thousand men, the staunch fighters of the West, veterans of great battles and victories, and to the young officers it appeared invincible. Their feeling that it was marching to another triumph was confirmed by the news that Bragg was retreating.

Yet the two armies were so close to each other that the Northern vanguard skirmished with the Southern rearguard as they passed through the mountains. At one point in a gap of the Cumberland Mountains the Southerners made a sharp resistance, but they were quickly driven from their position and the Union mass rolled slowly on. Exultation among the troops increased.

"We'll drive Bragg away down into the South against Grant," said Ohio to Dick, "and we'll crush him between the two arms of the vise. That will finish everything in the West."

While Dick was exultant, too, he had certain reservations. He had seen a like confidence carried to disaster in the East, although it did not seem possible that the result here could be similar.

"I don't think they'll keep on retreating forever, Ohio," he said. "All our supplies are coming from Nashville, and we are getting farther away from our base every day."

But Ohio laughed.

"Our chief task is to catch Bragg," he said. "They said he was going to occupy Chattanooga and wait for us. He's been in Chattanooga, but he didn't wait for us there. He's left it already and gone on, anxious to reach the Gulf before winter, I suppose."

The Union army in its turn entered Chattanooga, a little town of which Dick had seldom heard before, although he greatly admired its situation. The country about it was bold and romantic. It stood in a sharp curve of the great river, the Tennessee. Not far away was the lofty uplift of Lookout Mountain, a half-mile high, and there were long ridges between which creeks or little rivers flowed down to the Tennessee.

One of these streams was the Chickamauga, which in the language of the Cherokee Indians who had once owned this region means "the river of death." Why they called it so no one knew, but the name was soon to have a terrible fitness. Chattanooga itself meant in the Cherokee tongue "the hawk's nest," and anybody could see the aptness of the term.

While Lookout Mountain was the loftiest summit, some of the other ridges rose almost as high, through the gaps of which the Northern army must pass if it continued the pursuit of Bragg.

September had now come and the winds were growing crisper in the high country. The feel of autumn was in the air, and the coolness made the marching brisker. The division to which Dick belonged was advancing slowly. He often saw Thomas, and his admiration for the grave, silent man grew. It was said that Thomas was slow, but that he never made mistakes. Now the rumor was spreading that he had warned Rosecrans to be cautious, that Bragg had a powerful army and when he reached favorable positions, would certainly turn and fight.

Not many were impressed by these reports. They merely said it was "Pap" Thomas' way of looking at the dark side of things first. Hadn't they driven Bragg through the Cumberland Mountains and out of Chattanooga, and now they would soon be on his heels deep down in Georgia. But Dick, noticing Colonel Winchester's serious face, surmised that he at least shared the opinion of his chief. And when the lad looked up at the great coils and ridges he felt that, in truth, they might go too far. If the Northern men were veterans, so were the Southern, and neither had taken much change of the other at Shiloh, Perryville and Stone River.

The Winchester regiment was thrown forward as the vanguard of the infantry, and the face of the colonel grew more serious than ever, when the best scouts rode in with reports that the Southern retreat was now very slow. There was news, too, that Slade had a new band much larger than before, and they formed a rear guard of skirmishers which made every moment of a Northern scout's life a moment of danger. The Winchester regiment itself was often fired upon from ambush, and there were vacant places in the ranks.

Dick did not know whether it was his own intuition or the influence that flowed from the opinions of Thomas and Winchester, but much of his high exultation was abated. He regarded the lofty ridges and the deep gaps with apprehension. It was a difficult country and the Southern leaders must know that the Northern army was extended over a long line, with Thomas holding the left.

His premonitions had ample cause. Bragg as he fell back slowly had gathered new forces. Rosecrans did not yet know it, but the army before him was the most powerful that the South ever assembled in the West. Polk and Cleburne and Breckinridge and Forrest and Fighting Joe Wheeler and a whole long roll of famous Southern generals were there. Nor had the vigilant eyes of the Confederacy in the East failed to note the situation.

Just as the armies were coming into touch a division of the Army of Northern Virginia was passing by train over the mountains. It was led by a thick-bearded, powerful man, no less a general than the renowned Longstreet, sent to help Bragg. The veterans of the Army of Northern Virginia would swell Bragg's ranks, and the great army, turning a sanguine face northward, was eager for Rosecrans to come on. The Southern force would number more than ninety thousand men, more numerous than ever before or afterward in the West.

It was now late in September, the eve of the eighteenth, and Dick and his comrades lay near the little creek with the rhythmical name, Chickamauga. It was the very night that a portion of the Army of Northern Virginia had arrived in Bragg's camp. The preceding days had been full of detached fighting, and the night had come heavy with omens and presages. The least intelligent knew now that Bragg had stopped, but they did not know that Longstreet was to be with him.

Dick and his comrades sat by a smothered fire, and the vast tangle of mountains and passes, of valleys and streams looked sinister to them. There had been skirmishing throughout the day, and as the darkness closed down they still heard occasional rifle shots on the slopes and ridges.

"Don't these mountains make you think of your native Vermont, George?" asked Dick.

"In a way, yes," replied Warner, "but my hills are not bristling with steel as these are."

"No, you New Englanders are fortunate. The war will never be carried on on your soil. You shed your blood, but, after all, the states that are trodden under foot by the armies suffer most."

"There are lights winking on the mountains again," said Pennington.

"Let 'em wink," said Dick. "Their signals can't amount to much now. We know that Bragg is before us, and a great battle can't be delayed long. Fellows, I'm not so sure about the result."

"Come! Come, Dick!" said Warner. "It's not often you're downhearted. What's struck you?"

"Nothing, George, but, between you and me and the gate post, I wish that our old 'Pap' Thomas commanded all the army, instead of the left merely. I've learned a few things to-day. The enemy is spreading out, trying to enfold us on both wings."

"What of it?"

"It means that they are sanguine of victory, and they want to stand between us and Chattanooga, so they can cut off our retreat, after we're beaten, as they think we surely will be. But their main force is not far from us now, so a scout told me. It's massed heavily along the right bank of the Chickamauga."

"And if there's a battle to-morrow we're likely to receive the first attack?"

"Could it come any better than at the place where Thomas stands?"

They sat long by the fire and Dick could not rest. Shiloh, his capture, and his knowledge of the secret Southern advance, of which he could give no warning, came back to him with uncommon vividness. He knew that no such surprise could occur here, but they seemed to be lost in the wilderness. The mountains and forests oppressed him.

"Well, Dick," said Warner, "we're posted strongly. We've rows of sentinels as thick as hedges, and I've the colonel's permission to go to sleep. I'll be slumbering in ten minutes, and I'd advise you to do the same."

He lay on a blanket and soon slept. Pennington followed him to slumberland, but Dick lingered. He saw lights still flashing on the mountains, and he heard now and then reports from the rifles of the skirmishers, who yet sought each other despite the darkness. But he yielded at last and he, too, slept until the dawn, which should bring nearly two hundred thousand men face to face in mortal combat.

Dick was awake early. The September morning came, crisp and clear, the sun showing red gleams over the mountains. He heard already the sound of distant rifle shots in front, and, through his glasses, he saw far away faint puffs of smoke. But it was a familiar sound in this mighty war, and he found himself singularly calm. He never knew how he was going to feel on the eve of battle. Sometimes the constriction at his heart was painful, and sometimes its beat was smooth and regular.

All the officers of the Winchester regiment were dismounted owing to the rough nature of the country in which they were stationed. They held the most uneven part of the center, where thickets and ravines were many. Hot food and coffee were served to them, and new warmth and courage flowed through their bodies.

The distant fire increased, and, standing on a hillock, Dick looked long through his glasses. A faint haze which had hung in the south was clearing away. The rays of the sun were intensely bright. The brown of autumn glowed like gold, and the red splashes here and there burned scarlet. He saw pink dots appearing on a long line and he knew that the skirmishers were active and wary.

"There can be no doubt of the advance!" he said to Warner. "A strong body of our cavalry disclosed their forward movement, and there are the skirmishers signaling that Bragg is near. Wonderful fellows, those sharpshooters! They're the eyes of the army. We stand in mass and fight together, but every one of them individually takes his life in his own hands. The firing is coming nearer. I think we'll be attacked first."

After a little pause Warner said:

"I'm sorry our line is extended so much. What if they should cut through and get behind us?"

"They'll never do it while General Thomas is here. I believe they called him 'Old Slow Top' at West Point, but if he's slow in advance he's still slower in retreat. I'd rather have him commanding us just now than any other general in the world."

"I think you're right, and here he comes! Listen to the cheering!"

General Thomas rode slowly along his line, inspecting the position of every regiment and making some changes. He showed no trace of excitement. The face was calm and the heavy jaw was set firmly. If Grant was a bulldog Thomas was another. The men knew him. They had seen him stand like a rock before, and the thrill of confidence and courage which help so much to win ran through them all.

Dick saw the general speak to Colonel Winchester and then ride on and out of sight. All the men in the regiment were lying down, but the officers walked back and forth in front of the line. It was the especial pride of the younger ones to appear unconcerned, and some were able to make a brave pretense.

But all the while the battle was rolling nearer. It was no longer an affair of scouting parties. The skirmishers were driven in on either side and the mighty Southern advance was coming forward in full battle array. Shells began to shriek and fall among the Northern masses, and the fire of cannon and rifles mingled in a sinister crash. But the Union regiments, although not yet replying, remained steady, although the shower of steel that was beginning to beat upon them found many a mark. Vast columns of smoke pierced by fire rose in front.

It seemed to Dick's vivid fancy that the earth was shaking with the tread of the advancing brigades and the thunder of their artillery. But he was still able to preserve his air of indifference, although his heart was now beating hard and fast. Now and then when the smoke eddied or the banks of it broke apart he raised his glasses and with their powerful vision saw the long and deep Southern columns advancing, the field batteries in the intervals pouring a storm of death.

It was a sinister and terrible sight. The South presented here an army outnumbering its force at Shiloh two to one, and they were veterans now, led by veteran commanders. Moreover, they had Longstreet and his matchless fighters from Lee's army to bear them up.

"What do you see, Dick?" asked Pennington, his voice distinctly audible through the steady roar.

"Johnnies! Johnnies! Johnnies! Thousands and thousands of them and then many thousands more. They're going to strike full upon us here!"

"Let 'em come. We're taking root, growing deep into the ground and old 'Pap' Thomas has grown deepest of us all! It'll be impossible to move us!"

"I hope so. There go our own cannon, too, and it's a welcome sound! I can see the gaps smashed in their ranks by our fire, and ah, I see, too—"

He stopped short in amazed surprise, and Pennington in wonder asked:

"What is it you see, Dick?"

"There's a heavy cavalry force on their flank, and I caught a glimpse of a man on a great horse leading it. I know him. He's Colonel George Kenton, father of Harry Kenton, that cousin of mine, of whom I've spoken to you so often."

"And here he comes charging you! But it's happened hundreds and hundreds of times in this war that relatives have come face to face in battle, and it'll happen hundreds of times more. Are they within rifle shot, Dick?"

"Not yet, but they soon will be."

He slung the glasses back over his shoulder. The eye alone

was sufficient now to watch the charging columns. All the artillery on both sides was coming into action, and the ripping crash of so many cannon became so great that the officers could no longer hear one another unless they shouted. The gorges and hills caught up the sound and gave it back in increased volume.

Dick heard a new note in the thunder. It was made by the swift beat of hoofs, thousands of them, and the hair on his neck prickled at the roots. Forrest and the wild cavalry of the South were charging on their flanks. He felt a sudden horror lest he be trampled under the hoofs of horses. By some curious twist of the mind his dread of such a fate was far more acute at that moment than his fear of shells and bullets.

Colonel Winchester, shouting imperiously, ordered him and all the other young officers to step back now and lie down. Dick obeyed, and he crouched by the side of Warner and Pennington. The great bank of fire and smoke was rolling nearer and yet nearer, and the cannon were fighting one another with all the speed and power of the gunners. Off on the flank the ominous tread of Southern horsemen was coming fast.

Bullets began now to rain among them. The regiment would have been swept away bodily had the men not been lying down. But their time to wait and hold their fire was at an end. The colonel gave the word, and a sheet of light leaped from the mouths of their rifles. A vast gap appeared in the Southern line before them, but in a minute or two it closed up, and the Southern masses came on again, as menacing as ever. Again Dick's regiment poured its shattering fire upon the Southern columns and their front lines were blown away. Colonel Winchester at once wheeled his men into a new position to meet the mass of Forrest's cavalry rushing down upon their flank. He was just in time to help other troops, not in numbers enough to withstand the shock.

There were few moments in the lives of these lads as terrifying as those when they turned to face the fierce Forrest, the uneducated mountaineer who had intuitively mastered Napoleon's chief maxim of war, to pour the greatest force upon the enemy's weakest point.

The hurricane sweeping down upon them sent a chill to their hearts. Dick saw a long line of foaming mouths, the lips drawn back from the cruel white teeth, and manes flying wildly. Above them rose the faces of the riders, their own eyes bloodshot, their sabers held aloft for the deadly sweep. And the thunder of galloping hoofs was more menacing than that of the cannon.

Dick looked around him and saw faces turning pale. His own might be whiter than any of theirs for all he knew, but he shouted with the other officers:

"Steady! Steady! Now pour it into 'em!"

It was well that most of the men in the regiment had become sharpshooters, and that despite the thumping of their hearts, they were able to stand firm. Their sleet of bullets emptied a hundred saddles, and slipping in the cartridges they fired again at close range. The cavalry charge seemed to stop dead in its tracks, and in an instant a scene of terrible confusion occurred. Wounded horses screaming in pain rushed wildly back upon their own comrades or through the ranks of the foe. Injured men, shot from their saddles, were seeking to crawl out of the way. Whirling eddies of smoke alternately hid and disclosed enemies, and from both left and right came the continuous and deafening crash of infantry in battle.

But Forrest's men paused only a moment or two. A great mass of them galloped out of the smoke, over the bodies of their dead comrades and directly into the Winchester regiment, shouting and slashing with their great sabers. It was well for the men that their leader had so wisely chosen ground rough and covered with bushes. Using every inch of protection, they fired at horses and riders and thrust at them with their bayonets.

The battle became wild and confused, a turmoil of mingled horse and foot, of firing and shouting and of glittering swords and bayonets. A man on a huge horse made a great sweep at Dick's head with a red saber. The boy dropped to his knees, and felt the broad blade whistle where his head had been.

The swordsman was borne on by the impetus of his horse, and Dick caught one horrified glimpse of his face. It was Colonel Kenton, but Dick knew that he did not know, nor did he ever know. It was never in the lad's heart to tell his uncle how near he had come unwittingly to shearing off the head of his own nephew.

The charge of the cavalrymen carried them clear through the Winchester regiment, but a regiment coming up to the relief drove them back, and the great mass turning aside a little attacked anew and elsewhere. A few moments of rest were permitted Dick and his comrades, although the mighty battle wheeled and thundered all about them.

But their regiment was a melancholy sight. A third of its numbers were killed or wounded. The ground was torn and trampled, as if it had been swept by a hurricane of wind and red rain. Dick had one slight wound on his shoulder and another on his arm, but he did not feel them. Pennington and Warner both had scratches, but the colonel was unharmed.

"My God," exclaimed Warner, "how did we happen to survive it!"

"I live to boast that I've been ridden over by old Forrest himself," said Pennington.

"How do you know it was Forrest?"

"Because his horse was eight feet high and his sword was ten feet long. He slashed at me with it a hundred times. I counted the strokes."

Then Pennington stopped and laughed hysterically, Dick seized him by the arm and shook him roughly.

"Stop it, Frank! Stop it!" he cried. "You're yourself, and you're all right!"

Pennington shook his body, brushed his hands over his eyes and said:

"Thanks, Dick, old man; you've brought me back to myself."

"Get ready!" exclaimed Warner. "The cavalry have sheered off, but the infantry are coming, a million strong! I can hear their tread shaking the earth!"

The broken regiment reloaded, drew its lines together and faced the enemy anew. It seemed to their bloodshot eyes that the whole Southern army was bearing down upon them. The Southern generals, skillful and daring, were resolved to break through the Northern left, and the attack attained all the violence of a convulsion.

The great Southern line, blazing with fire and steel, advanced, never stopping for a moment, while the fire of their cannon beat incessantly upon the devoted brigades. It was well for the Northern army, well for the Union that here was the Rock of Chickamauga. Amid all the terrible uproar and the yet more terrible danger, Thomas never lost his courage and presence of mind for a moment. Dick saw him more than once, and he knew how he doubly and triply earned the famous name which that day and the next were to give him.

But the weight was so tremendous that they began to give ground. They went back slowly, but they went back. Dick felt as if the whole weight were pressing upon his own chest, and when he tried to shout no words would come.

Back they went, inch by inch, leaving the ground covered with their dead. Dick was conscious only of a vast roar and shouting and the continuous blaze of cannon and rifles in his very face. But he understood the immensity of the crisis. By a huge victory in the West the Confederacy would redress the loss of Gettysburg in the East. And now it seemed that they were gaining it. For the first and only time in the war they had the larger numbers in a great battle, and the ground was of their own choosing.

Elated over success gained and greater success hoped, the

Southern leaders poured their troops continually upon Thomas. If they could break that wing, cut it off in fact, and rush in at the gap, they would be between Rosecrans and Chattanooga and the Northern army would be doomed. They made gigantic efforts. The cavalry charged again and again. Huge masses of infantry hurled themselves upon the brigades of Thomas, and every gun that could be brought into action poured shot and shell into his lines.

Many of the young as well as the old officers in Thomas' corps felt the terrible nature of the crisis. Dick knew despite the hideous turmoil that Thomas was the chief target of the Southern army. He divined that the fortunes of the Union were swinging in the balance there among those Tennessee hills and valleys. If Thomas were shattered the turn of Grant farther south would come next. Vicksburg would have been won in vain and the Union would be broken in the West.

Order and cohesion were lost among many of the regiments, but the men stood firm. The superb, democratic soldier fought for himself and he, too, understood the crisis. They re-formed without orders and fought continuously against overwhelming might. Ground and guns were lost, but they made their enemy pay high for everything, and the slow retreat never became a panic.

"We're going back," shouted Warner in Dick's ear. "Yes, we're going back, but we'll come forward again. They'll never crush the old man."

Yet the pressure upon them never ceased. Bragg and his staff had the right idea. Had any one but Thomas stood before them they would have shattered the Union left long since, but his slow, calm mind rose to its greatest heights in the greatest danger. He understood everything and he was resolved that his wing should not be broken. Wherever the line seemed weakest he thrust in a veteran regiment, and he went quickly back and forth, observing with a measuring eye every shift and change of the battle.

The Winchester regiment in its new position was still among the gullies and bushes, and they were thankful for such shelter. Although veterans now, most were lads, and they did not scorn to take cover whenever they could. For a little while they did not reply to the enemy's fire, but lay waiting and seeking to get back the breath which seemed to be driven from their bodies by the very violence of the concussion. Shrapnel, grape and canister whistled incessantly over their heads, and on either flank the thunder of the battle swelled rapidly.

The Southern attack was spreading along the whole front, and it was made with unexampled vigor. It even excelled the fiery rush at Stone River, and the generals on both sides were largely the same that had fought the earlier great battle. Polk, the bishop-general, still led one wing for the South, Buckner massed Kentuckians who faced Kentuckians on the other side, and Longstreet and Hill were to play their great part for the South. Resolved to win a victory, the veteran generals spared nothing, and the little Chickamauga, so singularly named by the Indians "the river of death," was running red.

Dick crouched lower as the storm of shells swept over him. Despite all his experience impulse made him bow his head while the whistling death passed by. He felt a little shame that he, an officer, should seek protection, but when he stole a look he saw that all the others, Colonel Winchester included, were doing the same. Sergeant Whitley had sunk down the lowest of them all, and, catching Dick's glance, he said in clear, low tones audible under the storm:

"Pardon me for saying it to you, an officer, Mr. Mason, but it's our business not to get killed when it's not needed, so we can save ourselves to be killed when it is needed."

"I suppose you're right, Sergeant. At any rate I'm glad enough to keep under cover, but do you see anything in those woods over there? We're on the extreme left flank here, and maybe they're trying to overlap us."

"I think I do. Men with rifles are in there. I'll speak to the colonel."

He crawled to Colonel Winchester, who was crouched a dozen feet away, and pointed to the wood, or rather thicket of scrub. But Dick meanwhile saw increasing numbers of men there. They were beyond the line of battle and were not obscured by the clouds of smoke. As he stared he saw a weazened figure under an enormous, broad-brimmed hat, and, although he could not discern the face at the distance, he knew that it was Slade, come with a new and perhaps larger body of riflemen to burn away the extreme left flank of the Union force.

As the colonel and the sergeant crawled back Dick told them what he had seen, and they recognized at once the imminence of the danger. Colonel Winchester looked at the great columns of fire and smoke in front of him. He did not know when the main attack would sweep down upon them again, but he took his resolution at once.

He ordered his men to wheel about, and, using Slade's own tactics, to creep forward with their rifles. Most of his men were sharpshooters and he felt that they would be a match for those whom the guerrilla led. Sergeant Whitley kept by his side, and out of a vast experience in border warfare advised him.

Dick, Warner and Pennington armed themselves with rifles of the fallen, and they felt fierce thrills of joy as they crept forward.

Burning with the battle fever, and enraged against this man Slade, Dick put all his soul in the man-hunt. He merely hoped that Victor Woodville was not there. He would fire willingly at any of the rest.

Before they had gone far Slade and his riflemen began to fire. Bullets pattered all about them, clipping twigs and leaves and striking sparks from stones.

Had the fire been unexpected it would have done deadly damage, but all of the Winchesters, as they liked to call themselves, had kept under cover, and were advancing Indian fashion. And now a consuming rage seized them all. They felt as if an advantage had been taken of them. While they were fighting a great battle in front a sly foe sought to ambush them. They did not hate the Southern army which charged directly upon them, but they did hate this band of sharpshooters which had come creeping through the woods to pick them off, and they hated them collectively and individually.

It was Dick's single and fierce desire at that moment to catch sight of Slade, whom he would shoot without hesitation if the chance came. He looked for him continually as he crept from bush to bush, and he withheld his fire until fortune might bring into his view the flaps of that enormous hat. The whole vast battle of Chickamauga passed from his mind. He was concentrated, heart and soul, upon this affair of outposts in the thickets.

Men around him were firing, and the bullets in return were knocking up the leaves about him, but Dick's finger did not yet press the trigger. The great hat was still hidden from view, but he heard Slade's whistle calling to his men. Sergeant Whitley was by the lad's side, and he glanced at him now and then. The wise sergeant read the youth's face, and he knew that he was upon a quest, a deadly one.

"Is it Slade you're looking for, Mr. Mason?" he asked.

"Yes, I want him!"

"Well, if we see him, and you miss him, I think I'll take a shot at him myself."

But Slade, crafty and cunning, kept himself well hidden. The two bands fighting this Indian combat, while the great battle raged so near them, were now very near to each other, but as they had both thickets and a rocky outcrop for refuge, they fought from hiding. Nevertheless many fell. Dick, the ferocity of the man-hunt continuing to burn his brain, sought everywhere for Slade. Often he heard his silver whistle directing his troop, but the man himself remained invisible. In his eagerness the lad rose too high, but the sergeant pulled him down in time, a bullet whistling a second later through the air where his head had been.

"Careful, Mr. Mason! Careful!" said Sergeant Whitley. "It

won't do you much good for one of his men to get you while you are trying to get him!"

Dick became more cautious. At last he caught a glimpse of the great hat that he could not mistake, and, aiming very carefully, he fired. Then he uttered an angry cry. He had missed, and when the sergeant was ready to pull the trigger also Slade was gone.

Now, the colonel called to his men, and rising they charged into the wood. It was evidently no part of Slade's plan to risk destruction as he blew a long high call on his whistle, and then he and all his men save the dead melted away like shadows. The Winchesters stood among the trees, gasping and staunching their wounds, but victorious.

Now they had only a few moments for rest. Bugles called and they rushed back to their old position just as the Southern cavalry, sabers circling aloft swept down upon them again. They went once more through that terrible turmoil of fire and flashing steel, and a second time the Winchesters were victorious. But they could have stood no more, and Thomas watching everything hurried to their relief a regiment, which formed up before them to give them breathing time.

The young soldiers threw themselves panting upon the ground, and were assailed by a burning thirst. The canteens were soon emptied, and still their lips and throats were parched. Exhausted by their tremendous exertions, many of them sank into a stupor, although the battle was at its zenith and the earth shook with the crash of the heavy batteries.

"General Thomas has had news that we're driven in elsewhere," said Dick.

"And we've yielded ground here, too," said Warner.

"But so slowly that it's been only a glacial movement. We've made 'em pay such a high price that I think old 'Pap' can boast he has held his ground."

Dick did not know it then nor did the general himself, but 'Pap' Thomas could boast of far more than having held his ground. His long and stubborn resistance, his skill in moving his troops from point to point at the right time, his coolness and judgment in weighing and measuring everything right, in all the vast turmoil, confusion and uncertainty of a great battle, had saved the Northern army from destruction.

Now, as the Winchester men lay gasping behind the fresh regiment, Thomas, who continually passed along the line of battle, came among them. He was a soldier's soldier, a soldier's general, and he spoke encouraging words, most of which they could not hear amid the roar of the battle, but his calm face told their import, and fresh courage came into their hearts.

The news spread gradually that Thomas only was holding fast, but now his men instead of being discouraged were filled with pride. It was they and they alone whom the Southerners could not overwhelm, and Thomas and his generals inspired them with the belief that they were invincible. Charge after charge broke against them. More ground was yielded, but at the same immense price, and the corps, sullen, indomitable, maintained its order, always presenting a front to the foe, blazing with death.

Thomas stood all day, while the Southern masses, flushed by victory everywhere else, pressed harder. Terrible reports of defeat and destruction came to him continually, but he did not flinch. He turned the same calm face to everything, and said to the generals that whatever happened they would keep their own front unbroken.

The day closed with the men of Thomas still grim and defiant. The dead lay in heaps along their front, but as the darkness settled down on the unfinished battle they meant to fight with equal valor and tenacity on the morrow. The first day had favored the South, had favored it largely, but on the Union left hope still flamed high.

Darkness swept over the sanguinary field. A cold wind of autumn blew off the hills and mountains, and the men shivered as they lay on the ground, but Thomas allowed no fires to be lighted. Food was brought in the darkness, and those who could find them wrapped themselves in blankets. Between the two armies lay the hecatombs of dead and the thousands of wounded.

Dick, his comrades and the rest of the regiment sat together in a little open space behind a thicket. It was to be their position for the fighting next day. Thomas, passing by, had merely given them an approving look, and then had gone on to re-form his lines elsewhere. Dick knew that all through the night he would be conferring with his commander, Rosecrans, McCook and the others, and he knew, too, that many of the Union soldiers would be at work, fortifying, throwing up earthworks, and cutting down trees for abattis. He heard already the ring of the axes.

But the Winchester men rested for the present. Nature had made their own position strong with a low hill, and a thicket in front. They lay upon the ground, sheltering themselves from the cold wind, which cut through bodies relaxed and almost bloodless after such vast physical exertions and excitement so tremendous.

CHAPTER XIV

THE ROCK OF CHICKAMAUGA

Dick, after eating the cold food which was served to him, sank into a state which was neither sleep nor stupor. It was a mystic region between the conscious and the unconscious, in which all things were out of proportion, and some abnormal.

He saw before him a vast stretch of dead blackness which he knew nevertheless was peopled by armed hosts ready to spring upon them at dawn. The darkness and silence were more oppressive than sound and light, even made by foes, would have been. It numbed him to think there was so little of stirring life, where nearly two hundred thousand men had fought.

Then a voice arose that made him shiver. But it was only the cold wind from the mountains whistling a dirge. Nevertheless it seemed human to Dick. It was at once a lament and a rebuke. He edged over a little and touched Warner.

"Is that you, Dick?" asked the Vermonter.

"What's left of me. I've one or two wounds, mere scratches, George, but I feel all pumped out. I'm like one of those empty wineskins that you read about, empty, all dried up, and ready to be thrown away."

"Something of the same feeling myself, Dick. I'm empty and dried up, too, but I'm not ready to be thrown away. Nor are you. We'll fill up in the night. Our hearts will pump all our veins full of blood again, and we'll be ready to go out in the morning, and try once more to get killed."

"I don't see how you and Pennington and I, all three of us, came out of it alive to-day."

"That question is bothering me, too, Dick. A million bullets were fired at each of us, not to count thousands of pieces of shell, shrapnel, canister, grape, and slashes of swords. Take any ratio of percentage you please and something should have got us. According to every rule of algebra, not more than one of us three should be alive now. Yet here we are."

"Maybe your algebra is wrong?"

"Impossible. Algebra is the most exact of all sciences. It does not admit of error. Both by algebra and by the immutable law of averages at least two of us are dead."

"But we don't know which two."

"That's true. Nevertheless it's certain that those two, whoever they may be, are here on borrowed time. What do your wounds amount to, Dick?"

"Nothing, I had forgotten 'em. I've lost a little blood, but what does it amount to on a day like this, when blood is shed in rivers?"

"That's true. My own skin has been broken, but just barely, four times by bullets. I've a notion that those bullets were coming straight for some vital part of me, but seeing who it was, and knowing that such a noble character ought not to be slain, they turned aside as quickly as possible, but not so quickly that they could avoid grazing my skin."

Dick and Pennington laughed. Warner's fooling amused them and relieved the painful tension of their minds.

"But, George," said Pennington, "suppose one of the bullets failed to turn aside and killed you. What could we say then for you?"

"That it was a silly, ignorant bullet not knowing whence it came, or where it was going. Ah, there's light in the darkness! Look across the hill and see that shining flame!"

Dick rose and then the three walked to the brow of the hill, where Colonel Winchester stood, using his glasses as well as he could in the dusk.

"It's the pine forest on fire in places," he said. "The shells did it, and it's been burning for some time, spreading until it has now come into our own sight."

But they were detached fires, and they did not fuse into a general mass at any time. Clumps of trees burnt steadily like vast torches and sent up high flames. Bands of men from either side worked silently, removing as many of the wounded as they could. It was a spontaneous movement, as happened so often in this war, and Dick and his comrades took a part in it.

North and South met in friendliness in the darkness or by the light of the burning pines, and talked freely as they lifted up their wounded. Dick asked often about Colonel Kenton, meeting at last some Kentuckians, who told him that the colonel had gone through the day without a wound, and was with Buckner. Then Dick asked if any Mississippians were along the line.

"What do you want with 'em?" asked a long, lank man with a bilious yellow face.

"I've got a friend among 'em. Woodville is his name, and he's about my own age."

"I've heard of the Woodvilles. Big an' rich family in Missip. 'Roun' Vicksburg and Jackson mostly. I'm from the Yazoo valley myself, an' if I hear of the young fellow I'll send him down this way. But I can't stay out long, 'cause it'll soon be time for me to have my chill. Comes every other night reg'lar. But I'll be all right for battle to-morrow, when we lick you Yankees out of the other boot, having licked you out of one to-day."

"All right, old Yazoo," laughed Dick. "Go on and have your chill, but if you see Woodville tell him Mason is waiting down here by the wood."

"I'll shorely do it, if the chill don't git me fust," said the yellow Mississippian as he strolled away, and Dick knew that he would keep his word.

The lad lingered at the spot where he had met the man, hoping that by some lucky chance Woodville might come, and fortune gave him his wish. A slender figure emerged from the dark, and a voice called softly:

"Is that you, Mason?"

"Nobody else," replied Dick gladly, stepping forward and offering his hand, which young Woodville shook warmly. "I was hoping that I might meet you, and I see, too, that you can't be hurt much, if at all."

"I haven't been touched. It's my lucky day, I suppose."

"Where's your uncle? I hope he's in some safe place, recovering from his wound."

Victor Woodville laughed softly.

"Uncle Charles is recovering from his wound perhaps faster than you hope," he said, "but he's not in a safe place. Far from it."

"I don't understand."

"His wound is so much better that he can walk, though with a hop, and he's right here in the thick of this battle, leading his own Mississippi regiment. His horse was killed under him early this morning, and he's fought all day on foot, swearing in the strange and melodious fashion that you know. It's hop! swear! hop! swear! in beautiful alternation!"

"Good old colonel!"

"That's what he is, and he's also one of the bravest men that ever lived, if he is my uncle. His regiment did prodigies to-day and they'll do greater prodigies to-morrow. The Woodvilles are well represented here. My father is present, leading his regiment, and there are a dozen Woodville cousins of mine whom you've never met."

"And I hope I won't meet 'em on this field. What about your aunt?"

"She's well, and in a safe place."

"I'm glad of that. Now, tell me, Victor, how did you happen to be with Slade on that raid? Of course it's no business of mine, but I was surprised."

"I don't mind answering. I suppose it was a taste for

adventure, and a desire to serve our cause. After I got up the bank and climbed into the bushes, I looked back, and I think, Mason, that you may have saved me from a bullet. I don't know, but I think so."

Dick said nothing, but despite the dusk Woodville read the truth in his eyes.

"I shan't forget," said the young Mississippian as he moved away.

Dick turned back to his own group. They had noticed him talking to the lad in gray, but they paid no attention, nor thought it anything unusual. It was common enough in the great battles of the American civil war, most of which lasted more than one day, for the opposing soldiers to become friendly in the nights between.

"I think, sir," said Sergeant Whitley, "that we won't be able to get any more of our wounded to-night. Now, pardon me for saying it, Lieutenant, but we ought to have some rest, because when day comes there's going to be the most awful attack you ever saw. Some of our spies say that Longstreet and the last of the Virginians did not come until night or nearly night and that Longstreet himself will lead the attack on us."

"Do you think, Sergeant, that it will be made first on our own corps?"

"I don't know, Mr. Mason. We've stood firmest, and them rebel generals are no fools. They'll crash in where we've shown the most weakness."

The sergeant walked on, carrying the corner of a litter. Warner, who had stood by, whispered to Dick:

"There goes a general, but he'll never have the title. He's got a general's head on his shoulders, and he thinks and talks like a general, but he hasn't any education, and men with much poorer brains go past him. Let it be a lesson to you, Dick, my son. After this war, go to school, and learn something."

"Good advice, George, and I'll take it," laughed Dick. "But he isn't so badly off. I wonder if those fires in the pine forest are going to burn all night?"

"Several of 'em will. The big one on our left will be blazing when day comes, and I'm glad of it since no wounded are now in its way. The night's cold. That's a sharp and searching wind, and the sight of flames makes one feel warm even if they are far away."

It would not be long until day now, and the axes ceased to ring in the forest. A long and formidable line of abattis had been made, but the men were compelled to seek some rest. Despite the cold they suffered from a burning thirst, and they could reach no water, not even the red stream of the Chickamauga. Dick suffered like the rest, but he was philosophical.

"I fancy that after sunrise we won't have time to think about water," he said.

But Dick was not destined to sleep. He lay down for a while, and he saw hundreds of others around him lying motionless as if dead. Warner and Pennington were among them, but he could not close his own eyes. His brain was still hot and excited, and to calm himself if possible he walked along the slope until he saw a faint light in the valley behind it. A tall figure, which he recognized as that of Colonel Winchester, was going toward the light.

Dick, being on such good terms with his colonel, would have followed him, but when he came to the edge of the glade he drew back. General Thomas was sitting on the huge, upthrust root of an oak, and he was writing dispatches by the light of a flickering candle held by an aide. Officers of high rank, one of whom Dick recognized as the young general, Garfield, stood around him. Colonel Winchester joined the group, and stood waiting in silence to receive orders, too, Dick supposed.

The lad withdrew hastily, but driven by an overmastering curiosity, and knowing that he was doing no harm, he turned back and watched for a little space beside a bush.

The flame of the candle wavered under the wind, and sometimes the light shone full upon the face of Thomas. It was the same face that Dick had first beheld when he carried the dispatches to him in Kentucky. He was calm, inscrutable at this, the most desperate crisis the Union cause ever knew in the west. Dick could not see that his hand trembled a particle as he wrote, although lieutenant and general alike knew that they would soon be attacked by a superior force, flushed with all the high enthusiasm of victory. And lieutenant and general alike also knew that their supreme commander, Rosecrans, was no genius like Lee or Jackson, who could set numbers at naught, and choose time and place to suit themselves. Only stubborn courage to fight and die could avail.

But Dick drew courage from the strong, thick figure sitting there so impassively and apparently impervious to alarm. When he quit writing and began to give verbal orders, he spoke in even tones, in which no one could detect a trace of excitement. When the name, "The Rock of Chickamauga," became general, Dick remembered that night and knew how well it was deserved.

Thomas gave his last order and his generals went to their commands. Dick slipped back to his regiment, and lay down, but again could not sleep.

He waited in painful anxiety for the day. He had never before been in such a highly nervous state, not at Shiloh, nor Stone River, nor anywhere else. In those battles the chances were with the

Union, but here they were against it. He recognized that once more, save for Thomas, the North had been outgeneraled. The army of Rosecrans had marched from Chattanooga directly upon the positions chosen by Bragg, where he was awaiting them with superior numbers. And the Confederate government in the East had been quick enough to seize the opportunity and quick enough to send the stalwart fighter, Longstreet, and his corps to help close down the trap.

He wondered with many a painful throbbing of the heart what the dawn would bring, and, unable to keep still any longer, he rose and went to the brow of the low hill, behind which they lay. Colonel Winchester was there walking through the scrub and trying to pick out something in the opposing forest with his glasses. The cold wind still blew from the mountains, and there were three high but distant torches, where the clumps of pines still burned.

"Restless, Dick?" said the Colonel. "Well, so am I."

"We have cause to be so, sir."

"So we have, my lad. We thought the danger to the Union had passed with Vicksburg and Gettysburg, but the day so soon to come may shatter all our hopes. They must have a hundred thousand men out there, and they've chosen time and place. What's more, they've succeeded so far. I don't hesitate to talk to you in this way, Dick, but you mustn't repeat what I say."

"I shouldn't dream of doing so, sir."

"I know you would not, but General Thomas apprehends a tremendous and terrible attack. Whatever happens, we have not long to wait for it. I think I feel the touch of the dawn in the wind."

"It's coming, sir. I can see a faint tinge of gray in that cleft between the hills toward the east."

"You have a good eye, Dick. I see it now, too. It's growing and turning to the color of silver. But I think we'll have time to get our breakfasts. General Thomas does not believe the first attack will be made upon our wing."

The wind was freshening, as if it brought the dawn upon its edge. The night had been uncommonly cold for the time of the year in that latitude, and there was no sun yet to give warmth. But the men of Thomas were being awakened, and, as no fires were allowed, cold food was served to them.

"What's happened, Dick, while I was asleep?" asked Pennington.

"Nothing. The two armies are ready, and I think to-day will decide it."

"I hope so. Two days are enough for any battle."

Pennington's tone was jocular, but his words were not. His

face was grave as he regarded the opposing forest. He had the feeling of youth that others might be killed, but not he. Nevertheless he was already mourning many a good comrade who would be lost before the night came again.

"There are the wasps!" said Warner, bending a listening ear. "You can always hear them as they begin to sting. I wonder if skirmishers ever sleep?"

The shots were on the right, but they came from points far away. In front of them the forest and hills were silent.

"It's just as General Thomas thought," said Dick. "The main volume of their attack will be on our right and center. They know that Thomas stands here and that he's a mighty rock, hard to move. They expect to shatter all the rest of the line, and then whirl and annihilate us."

"Let 'em come!" exclaimed Warner, with heightening color. "Who's afraid?"

The dawn was spreading. The heavy mists that hung over the Chickamauga floated away. All the east was silver, and the darkness rolled back like a blanket. The west became silver in its turn, and the sun burned red fire in the east. The wind still blew fresh and cool off the mountains. The faint sound of trumpets came from far points on the Southern line. The crackling fire of the skirmishers increased.

"It's a wait for us," said Colonel Winchester, standing amid his youthful staff. "I can see them advancing in great columns against our right and center. Now their artillery opens!"

Dick put up his glasses and he, too, saw the mighty Southern army advancing. Their guns were already clearing the way for the advance, and the valleys echoed with the great concussion. Longstreet and Hill, anxious to show what the veterans of the East could do, were pouring them forward alive with all the fire and courage that had distinguished them in the Army of Northern Virginia.

The battle swelled fast. It seemed to the waiting veterans of Thomas that it had burst forth suddenly like a volcano. They saw the vast clouds of smoke gather again off there where their comrades stood, and, knowing the immense weight about to be hurled upon them, they feared for those men who had fought so often by their side.

Yet Thomas had been confident that the first attack would be made upon his own part of the line, that Bragg with an overwhelming force would seek to roll up his left. Nor had he reckoned wrong. The lingering of the bishop-general, Polk, over a late breakfast saved him from the first shock, and upset the plans of the Southern commander, who had given him strict orders to advance.

Dawn was long past, and to Bragg's great astonishment Polk had not moved. It seems incredible that the fate of great events can turn upon such trifles, and yet one wonders what would have happened had not Polk eaten breakfast so late the morning of the second day of Chickamauga. But when he did advance he attacked with the energy and vigor of those great churchmen of the Middle Ages, who were at once princes and warriors, leading their hosts to battle.

Portions of the men of Thomas were now coming into the combat, but the Winchesters were not yet engaged. They were lying down just behind the crest of their low hill and many murmurs were running through the ranks. It was the hardest of all things to wait, while shells now and then struck among them. They saw to their right the vast volume of fire and smoke, while the roaring of the cannon and rifles was like the continued sweep of a storm.

The youthful soldier may be nervous and excited, or he may be calm. This was one of Dick's calm moments, and, while he watched and listened and tried to measure all that he saw and heard, he noted that the crash of the battle was moving slowly backward. He knew then that the Southern advance was succeeding, succeeding so far at least. He was quite sure now that the attack upon Thomas would be made soon and that it would come with the greatest violence.

He rose and rejoined Colonel Winchester again, and the two looked with awe at the gigantic combat, raging in a vast canopy of smoke, rent continuously by flashes of fire. Dick observed that the colonel was depressed and he knew the reason.

"Our men are being driven back," he said.

"So they are," said the colonel, "and I fear that there is confusion among them, too."

"But we'll hold fast here as we did yesterday!"

"I hope so. Yes, I know so, Dick. I've seen General Thomas twice this morning, and I know that this corps will never be routed. He's made up his mind to hold on or die. He's the Rock of Chickamauga."

It was a name that Dick was to hear often afterward, and he repeated under his breath: "The Rock of Chickamauga! The Rock of Chickamauga!" It rolled resoundingly off the tongue, and he liked it.

Then came a beat of hoofs and a cavalry regiment galloped into open ground beside them. It was Colonel Hertford's, numbering about three hundred men, some of whom were wounded. Their leader was excited, and, springing to the ground, he ran to Colonel Winchester. The two talked in quick, short sentences.

"Colonel," exclaimed Hertford, "we've just had a sharp brush with that demon, Forrest, and we've left some good men back there. But I've come both to help and to warn you. We're being driven back everywhere else, and now they're gathering an immense mass of troops for a gigantic attack on Thomas!"

Dick heard and his breath came fast. Colonel Hertford would bring no false news, and he could see with his own eyes that the storm was curving toward them. The two men hurried to Thomas, but in a few minutes returned. Colonel Hertford sprang into the saddle and formed his cavalry on the flank as a screen against the dreaded sweep of Forrest.

There was a lull for a moment in the tremendous uproar, and, Colonel Winchester walking back and forth before his men, spoke to them briefly. He was erect, pale and handsome, and his words came without a quiver. Dick had never admired him more.

"Men," he said, "you have never been beaten in battle, but your greatest test is now at hand. Within a few minutes you will be attacked by a force outnumbering you more than two to one. But these are the odds we love. We would not have them less. I tell you, speaking as a man to men who understand and fear not, that the fate of the day may rest with you. Many gallant comrades of ours have gone already to the far shore, and if we must go, too, to-day, let our journey be not less gallant than theirs. We can die but once, and if we must die, let us die here where we can serve our country most."

His manner was quiet, but his words were thrilling, and the men of the regiment, springing to their feet, uttered a deep, full-throated cheer. Then sinking down again at the motion of his hand, they turned their faces to the enemy. The time had come.

The vast Southern front rushed from the wood, and the gray horsemen of Forrest, careless of death, swept down. It was a terrifying sight, that army coming on amid the thunder and lightning of battle, tens of thousands of rifle muzzles, tens of thousands of fierce brown faces showing through the smoke, and the tremendous battle yell of the South swelling over everything.

Dick felt a quiver, and then his body stiffened, as if it were about to receive a physical shock. The whole regiment fired as one man, and a gap appeared in the charging Southern column. Hertford and his horse charged upon the hostile cavalry, and all the brigades of Thomas met the Southern attack with a fire so heavy and deadly that the army of Bragg reeled back.

Then ensued the most tremendous scene through which Dick had yet passed. The Southern army came again. Bragg,

Breckinridge, Buckner, Longstreet, Hill, Cleburne and the others urged on the attacks. They had been victors everywhere else and they knew that they must drive back Thomas or the triumph would not be complete. They struck and spared not, least of all their own men. They poured them, Kentuckians, Tennesseeans, Georgians, Mississippians and all the rest upon Thomas without regard to life.

Kentuckians on the opposing sides met once again face to face. Dick did not know it then, but a regiment drawn from neighboring counties charged the Winchesters thrice and left their dead almost at his feet. He had little time to notice or measure anything amid the awful din and the continued shock of battle in which thousands of men were falling.

The clouds of smoke enveloped them at times, and at other times floated away. New clumps of pines, set on fire by the shells, burned brightly like torches, lighting the way to death. Smoke, thick with the odors of burned gunpowder clogged eye, nose and throat. Dick and the lads around him gasped for breath, but they fired so fast into the dense Southern masses that their rifle barrels grew hot to the touch.

The South was making her supreme effort. Her western sons were performing prodigies of valor, and Longstreet and the Virginians were fighting with all the courage that had distinguished them in the East.

But however violent the charge, and however tremendous the fire of cannon and rifles, the Rock of Chickamauga merely sank deeper in the soil, and nothing could drive him from his base. The Union dead heaped up, regiments were shattered by the Southern fire, but Thomas, calm, and, inspiring courage as on the day before, passed here and there, strengthening the weak points, and sending many great guns to the crest of Missionary Ridge, whence they swept the front of the enemy with a devastating fire.

The hail of death from the heights enabled the infantry and cavalry below to gather breath and strength for the new attacks of the enemy. They knew, too, that their cannon were now giving them more help than before, and defiant cheers swept along the line in answer to the mighty battle cry of the South. The Rock of Chickamauga had not moved a foot.

Dick caught gleams of the sun through the smoky canopy, but he did not know how far the day had advanced. He seemed to have been in battle many hours, but in such moments one had little knowledge of time. He was aware that the battle had been lost in the center and on the right, but he had sublime faith in Thomas. The left would stand, and while it stood the South could win but a barren triumph.

The peril was imminent and deadly. A strong Southern force, having cut through another portion of the line, was endeavoring to take Thomas on the flank. Rosecrans, seeing the danger and almost in despair, sent Thomas orders which his stern lieutenant fortunately could not obey. The rock did not move.

Bragg, an able leader, increased the attack upon Thomas. His generals gathered around him, and seconded his efforts. Their view was better than that of the Union commanders, and they knew it was vital to them to move the rock from their path. Brigades, already victorious on other parts of the field, came up, and were hurled, shouting their triumphant battle cry against Thomas, only to be hurled back again.

The resolution of the defenders increased with their success. A sort of fever seized upon them all. Death had become a little thing, or it was forgotten. The blood in their veins was fire, and, transported out of themselves, they rained shells and bullets upon men whom in their calm moments they did not hate at all.

Dick's regiment had suffered with the rest, but Pennington and Warner and the colonel were alive, and he caught a few glimpses of Hertford with his gallant horsemen beating back every attack upon their flank. But nothing stood out with sharp precision. The whole was a huge turmoil of fire, smoke, confusion and death. The weight upon them seemed at last to become overwhelming. In spite of courage the most heroic, and dreadful losses, the right of Thomas was driven back, his center was compelled to wheel about, but his left where the Winchester regiment stood with others held on. Thomas himself was there among them, still cool and impassive in face of threatened ruin.

About twenty thousand men were around Thomas, and they alone stood between the Union army and destruction. At all other points it had been not only defeated, but routed. Vast masses of fugitives were fleeing toward Chattanooga. Rosecrans himself withdrew, and, now wholly in despair, telegraphed at four o'clock in the afternoon to Washington: "My army has been whipped and routed."

But Thomas was neither routed nor whipped. Many of the brave generals elsewhere refused to flee with the troops, but gathering as many soldiers as possible joined Thomas. Among them was young Sheridan, destined to so great a fame, who brought almost all his own division and stood beside the Rock of Chickamauga, refusing to yield any further to the terrible pressure.

The line of Thomas' army was now almost a semicircle. Polk was leading violent attacks upon his left and center. Longstreet, used to victory, was upon his right and behind him, and the veterans from the Army of Northern Virginia had never fought better.

Dick saw the enemy all around him, and he began to lose hope. How could they stand against such numbers? And if they tried to retreat there was Longstreet to cut off the way. He bumped against Sergeant Whitley in the smoke and gasped out:

"We're done for, Sergeant! We're done for!"

"No, we're not!" shouted the sergeant, firing into the advancing mass. "We'll beat 'em back. They can't run over us!"

The sergeant, usually so cool, was a little mad. He was wounded in the head, and the blood had run down over his face, dyeing it scarlet. His brain was hot as with fire, and he hurled epithets at the enemy. His life on the plains came back to him, and, for the time, he was like a hurt Sioux chief who defies his foes. He called them names. He dared them to come on. He mocked them. He told them how they had attacked in vain all day long. He counted the number of their repulses and then exaggerated them. He reminded them it was yet a long time until dark, and asked them why they hesitated, why they did not come forward and meet the death that was ready for them.

Dick gazed at him in astonishment. He heard many of his words through the roar of the guns, and he saw his ensanguined face, through which his eyes burned like two red-hot coals. Was this the quiet and kindly Sergeant Whitley whom he had known so long? No, it was a raging tiger. Still waters run deep, and, enveloped, at last, with the fury of battle the sergeant welcomed wounds, death or anything else it might bring.

He shouted and fired his rifle again. Then he fell like a log. Dick rushed to him at once, but he saw that he had only fainted from loss of blood. He bound up the sergeant's head as best he could, and, easing him against a bank, returned to the battle front.

A shout suddenly arose. Officers had seen through their glasses a column of dust rising far behind them. It was so vast that it could only be made by a great body of marching troops. But who were the men that were making it? In all the frightful din and excitement of the battle the question ran through the army of Thomas. If fresh enemies were coming upon their rear they were lost! If friends there was yet hope!

But they could not watch the tower of dust long. The enemy in front gave them no chance. Polk was still beating upon them, and Longstreet, having seized a ridge, was pouring an increased fire from his advanced position.

"If that cloud of dust encloses gray uniforms we're lost!" shouted Warner in Dick's ear.

"But it mustn't enclose 'em," Dick shouted back. "Fate wouldn't play us such an awful trick! We can't lose, after having done and suffered so much!"

Fate would not say which. They could not send men to see, but as they fought they watched the cloud coming nearer and nearer, and Dick, whose lips had been moving for some time, realized suddenly that he was praying. "O God, save us! save us!" he was saying over and over. "Send the help to us who need it so sorely. Make us strong, O God, to meet our enemies!"

He and all his comrades wore masks of dust and burned gunpowder, often stained with scarlet. Their clothing was torn by bullets and reddened by dripping wounds. When they shouted to one another their voices came strained and husky from painful throats. Half the time they were blinded by the smoke and blaze of the firing. The crash did not seem so loud to them now, because they were partly deafened for the time by a cannonade of such violence and length.

Dick looked back once more at the great cloud of dust which was now much nearer, but there was nothing yet to indicate what it bore within, the bayonets of the North or those of the South. His anxiety became almost intolerable.

Thomas himself stood at that moment entirely alone in a clump of trees on the elevation called Horseshoe Ridge, watching the battle, seeing the enemy in overpowering numbers on both his flanks and even in his rear. Apparently everything was lost. Taciturn, he never described his feelings then, but in his soul he must have admired the magnificent courage with which his troops stood around him, and repelled the desperate assaults of a foe resolved to win. Although his face grew grimmer and his teeth set hard, he, too, must have watched the approaching cloud of dust with the most terrible anxiety. If it bore enemies in its bosom, then in very truth everything would be lost.

Down a road some miles from the battlefield a force of eight thousand men had been left as a reserve for one of the armies. They had long heard the terrific cannonade which was sending shattering echoes through the mountains, and both their chief and his second in command were eager to rush to the titanic combat. They could not obtain orders from their commander, but, at last, they marched swiftly to the field, all the eight thousand on fire with zeal to do their part.

It was the eight thousand who were making the great cloud of dust, and, as they came nearer and nearer, the suspense of Thomas' shattered brigades grew more terrible. Dick, reckless of shell and bullets, tried to pierce the cloud with his eyes. He caught a glimpse of a flag and uttered a wild shout of joy. It was the stars and stripes. The eight thousand were eight thousand of the North! He danced up and down on the stump, and shouted at the top of his voice:

"They're our own men! Help is here! Help is here!"

A vast shout of relief rose from Thomas' army as the eight thousand still coming swiftly joined them. Granger was their leader, but Steedman, his lieutenant, galloped at once to Thomas, who still stood in the clump of trees, and asked him what he wanted him to do. The general, calm and taciturn as ever, pointed toward a long hill that flamed with the enemy's guns, and said three words:

"Take that ridge!"

Steedman galloped back and the eight thousand charged at once. The battle in front sank a little, as if the others wished to watch the new combat. Dick had been dragged down from the stump by Warner, but the two stood erect with Pennington, their eyes turned toward the ridge. Colonel Winchester was near them, his attention fixed upon the same place.

The eight thousand firing their rifles and supported by artillery charged at a great pace. The whole ridge blazed with fire, and the dead and wounded went down in sheaves. But Dick could not see that they faltered. Hoarse shouts came again from his dry and blackened lips:

"They will take it! they will take it! Look how they face the guns!" he was crying.

"So they will!" said Warner. "See what a splendid charge! Now they're hidden! What a column of smoke! It floats aside, and, look, our men are still going on! Nothing can stop them! They must have lost thousands, but they reach the slope, and as sure as there's a sun in the heavens they're going up it!"

That tremendous cheer burst again from the beleaguered Union army. Granger and Steedman, with their fresh troops, were rushing up the slopes of the formidable ridge, and though three thousand of the eight thousand fell, they took it, hurling back the advancing columns of the South, and securing the rear of Thomas.

Then the Winchester men and others about them went wild with joy. They leaped, they danced, they sang, until they were commanded to make ready for a new attack. Rosecrans in Chattanooga, with the most of his army there also in wild confusion, had sent word to Thomas to retire, to which Thomas had replied tersely: "It will ruin the army to withdraw it now; this position must be held till night."

And he made good his resolve. The Southern masses attacked once more with frightful violence, and once more Thomas withstood them. The field was now darkening in the twilight, and, having saved the Union army from rout and wreck, Thomas, impervious to attack, fell back slowly to Chattanooga.

The greatest battle of the West, one of the most desperate ever fought, came to a close. Thirty-five thousand men, killed or wounded, had fallen upon the field. The South had won a great but barren victory. She had not been able to reap the fruits of so much skill and courage, because Thomas and his men, like the Spartans at Thermopylae, had stood in the way. Never had a man more thoroughly earned the title of honor that he bore throughout the rest of his life, "The Rock of Chickamauga."

Chickamauga, though, was a sinister word to the North. Gettysburg and Vicksburg had stemmed the high tide of the Confederacy, and many had thought the end in sight. But the news from "The River of Death" told them that the road to crowning success was still long and terrible.

CHAPTER XV

BESIDE THE BROOK

When the slow retreat began Dick looked for the sergeant. But a stalwart figure, a red bandage around the head, rose up and confronted him. It was Sergeant Whitley himself, a little unsteady yet on his feet, but soon to be as good as ever.

"Thank you for looking for me, Mr. Mason," he said, "but I came to, some time ago. I guess the bullet found my skull too hard, 'cause it just ran 'roun' it, and came out on the other side. I won't even be scarred, as my hair covers up the place."

"Can you walk all right?" asked Dick, overjoyed to find the sergeant was not hurt badly.

"Of course I can, Mr. Mason, an' I'm proud to have been with General Thomas in such a battle. I didn't think human bein's could do what our men have done."

"Nor did I. It was impossible, but we've done it all the same."

Colonel Winchester rejoiced no less than the lads over the sergeant's escape. All the officers of the regiment liked him, and they had an infinite respect for his wisdom, particularly when danger was running high. They were glad for his own sake that he was alive, and they were glad to have him with them as they retreated into Chattanooga, because the night still had its perils.

The moon, though clouded, was out as they withdrew slowly. On their flanks there was still firing, as strong detachments skirmished with one another, but the Winchester men as yet paid little attention to it. They said grimly to one another that two days in the infernal regions were enough for one time. They looked back at the vast battlefield and the clumps of pines burning now like funeral torches, and shuddered.

The retreat of Thomas was harried incessantly. Longstreet and Forrest were eager to push the attack that night and the next day and make the victory complete. They and men of less rank dreamed of a triumph which should restore the fortunes of the Confederacy to the full, but Bragg was cautious. He did not wish to incur the uttermost risk, and the roll of his vast losses might well give him pause also.

Nevertheless Southern infantry and cavalry hung on the flanks and rear of the withdrawing Union force. The cloudy moon gave sufficient light for the sharpshooters, whose rifles flashed continuously. The lighter field guns moved from the forests and bushes, and the troops of Thomas were compelled to turn again and again to fight them off.

The Winchester regiment was on the extreme flank, where the men were exposed to the fiercest attacks, but fortunately the thickets and hills gave them much shelter. At times they lay down and returned the fire of the enemy until they beat him off. Then they would rise and march on again.

All the officers had lost their horses, and Colonel Winchester strode at the head of his men. Just behind were Dick, Pennington and some other members of his staff. The rest had fallen. Further back was Sergeant Whitley, his head in a red bandage, but all his faculties returned. In this dire emergency he was taking upon himself the duties of a commissioned officer, and there was none to disobey him. Once more was the wise veteran showing himself a very bulwark of strength.

Despite the coolness of the night, they had all suffered on the second day of the battle from a burning thirst. And now after their immense exertions it grew fiercer than ever. Dick's throat and mouth were parched, and he felt as if he were breathing fire. He felt that he must have water or die. All the men around him were panting, and he knew they were suffering the same torture.

"This country ought to be full of brooks and creeks," he said to Pennington. "If I see water I mean to make a dash for it, Johnnies or no Johnnies. I'm perfectly willing to risk my life for a drink."

"So am I," said Warner, who overheard him, "and so are all who are left in this regiment. If they see the flash of water nothing can hold them back, not even Bragg's whole army. How those skirmishers hang on to us! Whizz-z! there went their bullets right over our head!"

The Winchesters turned, delivered a heavy volley into a thicket, whence the bullets had come, and marched on, looking eagerly now for water. They began to talk about it. They spoke of the cool brooks, "branches" they called them, that they had known at home, and they told how, when they found one, they would first drink of it, and then lie down in its bed and let its water flow over them.

But Dick's thirst could not wholly take his mind from the tremendous scenes accompanying that sullen and defiant retreat. Hills and mountains were in deepest gloom, save when the signal lights of the Southern armies flashed back and forth. The clouded moon touched everything nearer by with somber gray. The fire of cannon rolled through the forest and gorges with redoubled echoes.

A shout suddenly came from the head of the Winchester column.

"Water! Water!" they cried. A young boy had caught a glimpse of silver through some bushes, and he knew that it was made by the swift current of a brook. In an instant the regiment broke into a run for the water. Colonel Winchester could not have stopped them if he had tried, and he did not try. He knew how great was their need.

"We're off!" cried Pennington.

"I see it! The water!" shouted Dick.

"I do, too!" exclaimed Warner, "and it's the most beautiful water that ever flowed!"

But they stopped in their rush and dropped down in the thickets. Sergeant Whitley had given the warning shout, and fortunately most of a volley from a point about a hundred yards beyond the stream swept over their heads. A few men were wounded, and they not badly.

Dick crawled to the head of the column. The sergeant was already there, whispering to Colonel Winchester.

"They've taken to cover, too, sir," said the sergeant.

"How many do you suppose they are?" asked the colonel.

"Not more than we are, sir."

"They run a great risk when they attack us in this manner."

"Maybe, sir," said Dick, "they, too, were coming for the water."

Colonel Winchester looked at Sergeant Whitley.

"I'm of the opinion, sir," said the sergeant, "that Mr. Mason is right."

"I think so, too," said Colonel Winchester. "It's a pity that men should kill each other over a drink of water when there's enough for all. Has any man a handkerchief?"

"Here, sir," said Warner; "it's ragged and not very clean, but I hope it will do."

The Colonel raised the handkerchief on the point of his sword and gave a hail. The bulk of the two armies had passed on, and now there was silence in the woods as the two little forces confronted each other across the stream.

Dick saw a tall form in Confederate gray rise up from the bushes on the other side of the brook.

"Are you wanting to surrender?" the man called in a long, soft drawl.

"Not by any means. We want a drink of water, and we're just bound to have it."

"You don't want it any more than we do, and you're not any more bound to have it than we are."

The colonel hesitated a moment, and then, influenced by a generous impulse, said:

"If you won't fire, we won't."

The tall, elderly Southerner, evidently a colonel, also said:

"It's a fair proposition, sir. My men have been working so hard the last two days licking you Yanks that they're plum' burnt up with thirst."

"I don't admit the licking, although it's obvious that you've gained the advantage so far, but is it agreed that we shall have a truce for a quarter of an hour?"

"It is, sir; the truce of the water, and may we drink well! Come on, boys!"

Colonel Winchester gave a similar order to his men, and each side rose from the thickets, and made a rush for the brook. It was a beautiful little stream, the most beautiful in the world just then to Dick and his friends. Clear and cold, the color of silver in the moonlight, it rushed down from the mountains. On one side knelt the men in blue, and on the other the men in gray, and the pure water was like the elixir of heaven to their parched and burning throats.

Dick drank long, and then as he raised his face from the stream he saw opposite him a tall, lean youth, evidently from the far South, Louisiana perhaps, a lad with a tanned face and a wide mouth stretched in a friendly grin.

"Tastes good, doesn't it, Yank?" he said.

"Yes, it does, Reb," replied Dick. "I felt that I was drying up and just crumbling away like old dead wood. As soon as the gallon that I've drunk has percolated thoroughly through my system I intend to hoist aboard another gallon."

"I don't know what percolate means, but I reckon it has something to do with travelin' about through your system. I think I need a couple of gallons myself. Say, will you give a fair answer to a fair question?"

"Yes, go ahead."

"Don't you Yanks feel powerful bad over the thrashing we've given you?"

"Not so bad. Besides I wouldn't call it a thrashing. It's just a temporary advantage. And you wait. We'll take it away from you."

"I don't know about that, but I can't argue with you now. I'm due for my second gallon."

"So am I."

Each bent down and drank again a long, life-giving draught from the rushing stream. For a distance of a hundred yards or more heads black, brown and sometimes yellow were bent over the brook. Far off, both to east and west, the cannon thundered in the darkness, but with the drinkers it was a peaceful interlude of a quarter of an hour. Such moments often occurred in this war when the men on both sides were blood brethren.

Colonel Winchester stood up, and the grizzled Confederate colonel stood up on the other side of the stream, facing him. Their hands rose in a simultaneous salute of respect.

"Sir," said Colonel Winchester, "I'm happy to have met you in this manner."

"Sir," said the Southern colonel ornately, "we are happy to have drunk from the same stream with such brave foes, and now, sir, I propose as we retire that neither regiment shall fire a shot within the next five minutes."

"Agreed," said Colonel Winchester, and then as the colonels gave the signals the two regiments withdrew beyond their respective thickets. The truce of the water was over, but these foes did not meet again that night.

The regiment had left a great proportion of its numbers dead upon the field. Half the others were wounded more or less, but the slightly wounded marched on with the unhurt. Many of them were now barely conscious. They were either asleep upon their feet or in a daze. Nevertheless they soon rejoined the main command.

Dick, having his pride as an officer, sought to keep himself active and alert. He passed among the lads of his own age, and encouraged them. He told them how the older men were already speaking of the wonders they had done, and presently he saw Thomas himself riding along with the young general, Garfield, who had been with him throughout the afternoon. All the Winchester men saw their commander, and, worn as they were, they stopped and gave a mighty cheer. Thomas was moved. Under the cloudy moon Dick saw him show emotion for the first time. He took off his hat.

"Gentlemen, comrades," he said, "we have lost the battle of Chickamauga, but if all our regiments fight as you fought to-day the war is won."

Another cheer, enthusiastic and spontaneous, burst from the regiment, and Thomas rode on. Dick had never heard him make another speech so long.

When they reached the little town of Chattanooga within its mountains they began to realize the full grandeur of their exploit. The remainder of the army of Rosecrans was almost a mob, and brave as he undoubtedly was he was soon removed to another field, leaving Thomas in supreme command until Grant should come.

Dick had no rest until the next night, when tents were set for the battered remains of the Winchester regiment. He, Warner, Pennington and three others were assigned to one of the larger tents. He had been without sleep for two days and two nights, and the tremendous tension that had kept him up so long was relaxing fast. He felt that he must sleep or die. Yet they talked together a little before they stretched themselves upon their blankets.

"Do you think Bragg will attack us in Chattanooga, Dick?" asked Pennington.

"I don't. Our position here is too strong, and, as he was the assailant, his losses must be something awful. Moreover, the rivers are always ours and reinforcements will soon pour in to us. I think that General Thomas saved the Union. What have you to say, George?"

"Just about what you are saying, Dick. We've been beaten, but not enough to suit the Johnnies. They have on their side present victory. We have on ours present but not total defeat. You might say they have x, while we have $x + y$. Wait until I look into my algebra, and I can find further mathematical and beautiful propositions proving my contention beyond the shadow of a doubt."

He took out his algebra and opened it. A bullet fell from the leaves into his lap. Warner picked it up and examined it carefully. Then he looked at the book.

"It went half way through," he said in tones of genuine solemnity. "If it had gone all the way it would have pierced my heart and I could never have known how this war is going to end. It has saved my life, and I shall always keep it over my heart until we go back home."

Dick was asleep the next minute, and they did not wake him for twelve hours. When he came from the tent he stood blinking in the sun, and a tall lean youth hailed him with a joyous shout:

"Why, it's Mason—Mason of Kentucky!" exclaimed the lad, extending a hardened hand. "I'm glad you're alive. How are those friends of yours, Warner and Pennington?"

"Well, save for scratches, Ohio. They're about somewhere."

They shook hands again, hunted up the others, and celebrated their escape from death.

Dick learned later that all the Woodvilles were still alive and that Colonel Kenton, although wounded, was recovering fast. Slade, with troublesome raids, soon gave evidence of his own continued existence.

Then, as they expected, reinforcements poured in. Grant came, and Dick and his comrades took part in the fight at Missionary Ridge and the battle "above the clouds" on Lookout Mountain. He witnessed great triumphs and he had a share in them.

He saw Bragg's army broken up, and he rejoiced with the others when the news came that Grant for his brilliant successes had been made commander of all the armies of the Union, and would go east to match himself against the mighty Lee. The Winchester regiment would go with him and Dick, Warner, Pennington and Sergeant Whitley, who was entirely recovered, talked of it gravely:

"We've been in the East before," said Pennington, "but we won't be under any doubting general now."

"I fancy it will be the death grapple," said Warner.

"And the continent will shake with it," said Dick.

The three, as if by the same impulse, turned and faced the distant East, where the shades were already gathering over the Wilderness.

CPSIA information can be obtained
at www.ICGtesting.com
Printed in the USA
LVHW090235071219
639763LV00003B/125/P

9 781618 957412